SAFE HARBOUR

Also by Mike Martin in the Sgt. Windflower Mystery Series

The Walker on the Cape
The Body on the T
Beneath the Surface
A Twist of Fortune
A Long Ways from Home
A Tangled Web
Darkest Before the Dawn
Fire, Fog and Water
A Perfect Storm

Christmas in Newfoundland: Mysteries and Memories

SAFE HARBOUR

MIKE MARTIN

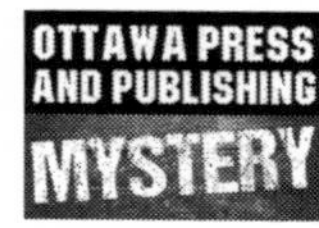

ottawapressandpublishing.com

ISBN 978-1-988437-73-6 (Pbk.)
ISBN 978-1-988437-74-3 (EPUB)
ISBN 978-1-988437-75-0 (MOBI)

Published in Canada

Design and composition: Magdalene Carson RGD, New Leaf Publication Design
Cover based on a photograph by Larry Mahoney.

Library and Archives Canada Cataloguing in Publication

Title: Safe harbour / Mike Martin.
Names: Martin, Mike, 1954- author.
Description: Series statement: A Sgt. Windflower mystery
Identifiers: Canadiana (print) 20210218916 | Canadiana (ebook) 20210218959 | ISBN 9781988437736 (softcover) | ISBN 9781988437743 (EPUB) | ISBN 9781988437750 (Kindle)
Classification: LCC PS8626.A77255 S24 2021 | DDC C813/.6—dc23

To Joan.
Thank you for being
my muse, my light in the darkness.
The adventure continues.

ACKNOWLEDGEMENTS

I would like to thank a number of people for their help in getting this book out of my head and onto these pages. That includes beta readers and advisers: Mike MacDonald, Barb Stewart, Robert Way, Lynne Tyler, Denise Zendel and Karen Nortman. Bernadette Cox for her excellent support and copy editing and Alex Zych for final proofreading.

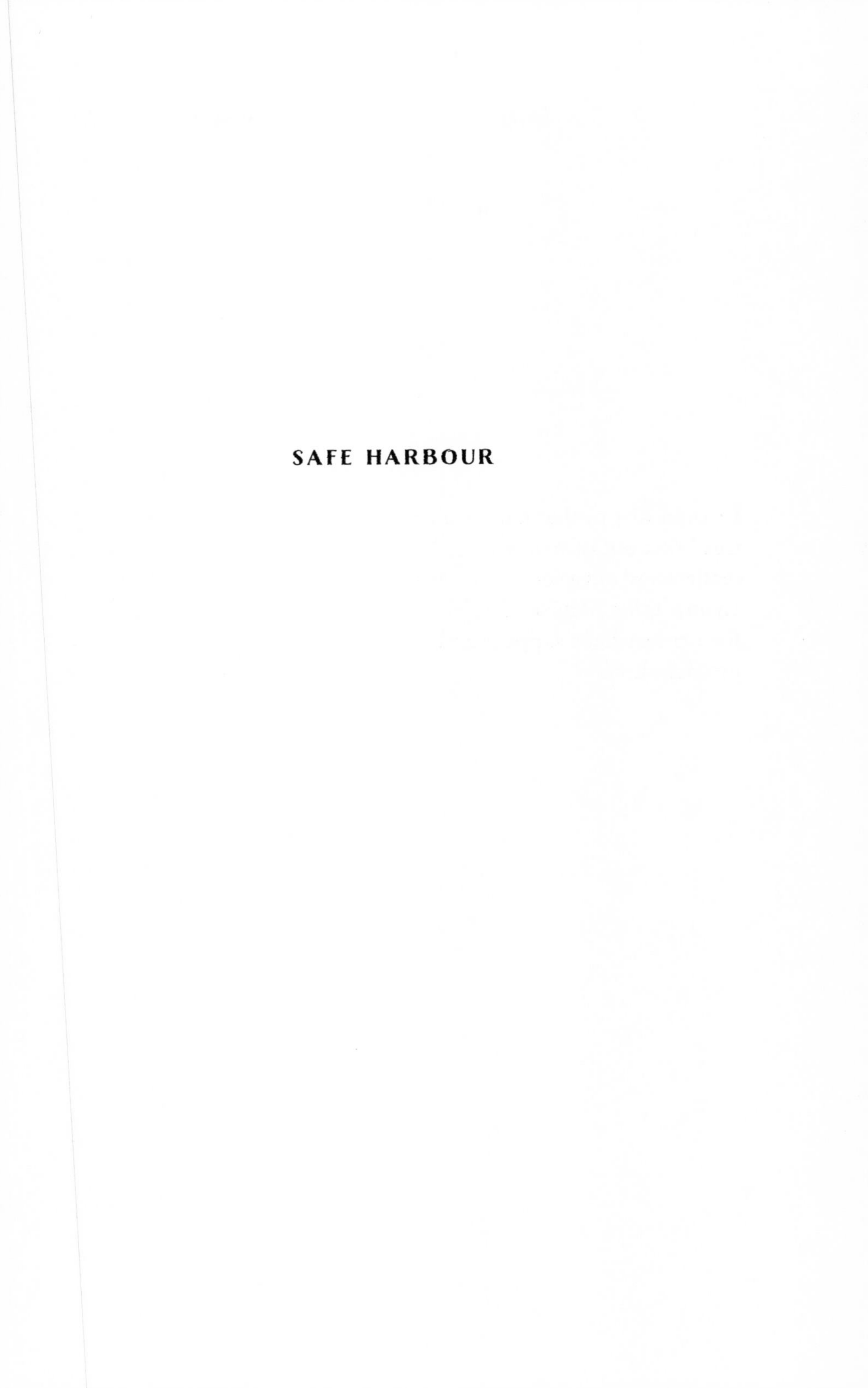

SAFE HARBOUR

1

Windflower looked across the lake. Well, he would have if he could have seen anything through the thick blanket of fog that had been sitting on Quidi Vidi Lake for the past seven days. One whole week, he thought. Every day since they had arrived in the port city of St. John's, it had been the same. Windflower knew the lake was out there because he remembered running around it as his daily exercise when he was temporarily stationed here a few years back.

Sheila Hillier, his wife, knew the lake was out there as well. She'd spent a couple of months doing rehab at the nearby Miller Centre when she was recovering from a serious car accident. If there wasn't any fog, she could look out her window in May and see the rowers getting their practice in as part of their training for the Royal St. John's Regatta, an annual event that took place down there in August.

But it was a long way from spring as Windflower gazed out his window at the typical scenery for a January morning. He was the first one up, except for Lady, his collie, and Molly, the cat who never seemed to sleep anyway. She would close her eyes sometimes, but Windflower had never come into a room with her in it when she wasn't awake and watching him. Windflower liked this time of day when his two children got up. They were Amelia Louise, his soon-to-be two-year-old daughter, and his almost-daughter, Stella, who he and Sheila were fostering.

He liked this house on Forest Road, too. It wasn't similar to his and Sheila's in Grand Bank on the southeast coast of Newfoundland, but for a rental it suited them perfectly. It had four bedrooms, two and a half baths and a large backyard for the kids to play in and, if the weather held, for Windflower to barbeque. But the likelihood of the weather staying just simply foggy and damp was not good. There was snow in the forecast and more snow coming after that.

Windflower had been in snowstorms in St. John's before. It was hard to miss one if you travelled here regularly in the fall, winter or spring. And they didn't come with a few flakes or a few inches of accumulation. No, snowstorms here often meant feet of snow, sometimes in the double digits, and he had come out some mornings to look for his car, only to find it buried under a virtual mountain of snow. The worst storms came in double or even triple waves. That's when a storm system would blow through and dump one load of snow and then drift out to the nearby Atlantic Ocean. Unfortunately for the good people of St. John's, it would blow back in and repeat the damage—sometimes more than once.

Windflower grabbed his anorak and hat and took Lady out to the backyard. He also brought his smudging kit. Inside were small packets of his four sacred medicines: cedar, sage, sweetgrass and tobacco. There was also an abalone shell, a small box of wooden matches and an eagle feather fan that had been gifted to him by his grandfather many years ago.

He placed small amounts of each medicine in his abalone shell and lit them with a wooden match. Smudging was a way to cleanse his body, mind and spirit, and how he smudged was to use a fan or the feather to pass the smoke from the burning herbs over his head and body. He even sent the smoke under his feet.

He had been taught to pass the smoke over his head to give him clear thoughts and wisdom, over his heart to keep it pure and lead him to wisdom, and under his feet to let him walk a straightforward path in his daily life. He would also allow the smoke to linger around him as long as he could to remember that he was not alone in the world. Then, when he was finished, he would lay the ashes on bare ground so that all negative thoughts and feelings would be absorbed by Mother Earth. Lastly, he would pray. Today his prayers were all about gratitude.

This was a good morning to be grateful, thought Windflower. Amelia Louise was a happy, healthy child. Sheila was happy to be back in school full-time as she pursued her dreams of an MBA. And little Stella, their four-and-a-half-year-old who'd been through a lot in her life, including the recent loss of her mother, was starting to settle into their household. Windflower himself had just started a new assignment as public outreach coordinator with the regional Royal Canadian Mounted Police office in St. John's.

Sergeant Winston Windflower had been a Mountie for all his working life. After training in Regina, he was posted to British Columbia for two years on highway patrol and another couple of years in Halifax before arriving to the province nine years ago for a posting in Grand Bank. Wow, he thought. That was a long time. Most of his career had been spent in the field and on the ground, so he was a bit apprehensive about this job in St. John's. It was only for a year, but it was his first desk job. He wondered if he'd become stir-crazy sitting in the office so much. But that was something else he could pray about.

His last prayer was for himself. He didn't pray for patience. His uncle told him never to pray for patience because Creator would only send more opportunities to practice it. Instead, he prayed for calmness and guidance, and for the wisdom and courage to ask for help. That was something he wasn't very good at, and something he surely needed.

His prayers and rituals complete, he and Lady went back inside to start the rest of their day. Things happened quickly in his house once everyone was up in the morning. Windflower put on the coffee to get himself ready. Soon, he could hear Amelia Louise calling out and Sheila moving to get her. He went upstairs and saw that Stella was also awake but shy and uncertain about what to do.

Windflower went through her clothes for the day with her. Stella was going to school for the first time, junior kindergarten, and Windflower could tell she was both excited and afraid. He and Sheila had talked to her about it again last night to try to reassure her, and this morning Stella was trying to put on her brave little girl face. But she started to cry as Windflower was leaving, so he went back and held her. Once she stopped crying, he left her to get dressed and went downstairs.

It was Sheila's first day back at school, and she was looking a little anxious too. Windflower went to her and gave her a hug.

"I guess it's a big day for everybody," said Sheila. "New job for you, Stella and I both going to school and Amelia Louise to daycare. Are we out of our minds?"

Windflower laughed. "It will be different, but once we all get our routines down, it'll be fine," he said. He poured both of them a cup of coffee. "I'll make some oatmeal if you check on Stella. She looked like she might be having second thoughts about this school thing."

"Like the rest of us," said Sheila. "I'll leave Amelia Louise to help you."

That was one way to describe Amelia Louise's activities while Windflower got breakfast ready. From teasing the cat, to trying to pull Lady's tail off, to upsetting Sheila's craft basket in the living room, Amelia Louise kept her father busy and alert. But somehow he managed to slice up some fruit and get everyone a bowl of oatmeal with nuts and maple syrup. An even bigger miracle was getting everyone out the door on time.

Windflower helped Sheila put Amelia Louise in the car so she could drop her off at daycare first and then take Stella to her kindergarten class. She would go into Memorial University later for her first morning class. He was fine. He could take his time and walk over to the RCMP offices across the lake, the one he couldn't see for the fog. He cleaned up, got the pets all organized and started his first morning walk to work.

2

It was damp and foggy but not totally unpleasant, and Windflower managed to keep up a brisk pace all the way around the side of the lake. He only had to pause when he crossed over the boulevard at the stop lights. That's where he started seeing the signs on the telephone poles. "Missing: Larissa Murphy, 15-year-old girl. Last seen Downtown St. John's." It had a date on it that had been smeared in the rain and fog along with a number to call at the Royal Newfoundland Constabulary, the provincial police force. They were responsible for monitoring all criminal activity in this region, while the Mounties were the national police.

That can't be good, thought Windflower. He said a silent prayer that she be found safely and hurried towards work. The RCMP offices, which were located in the neighbourhood of what was called the White Hills, finally came into view as he rounded the corner past the Legion and started walking up the short hill. He tried to look back across the lake once he was at the top, but the result was the same as before. There was nothing but fog and mist to see, and now it seemed there were a few rain showers to add to the dreary mix. He bundled up against the rain, driven by a wind that made it feel very cold, and walked into the building housing the RCMP regional headquarters in St. John's.

After getting directions from the reception area, he went to the third floor to meet his superior officer. Staff Sergeant Bonnie Morecombe, Director, Public Outreach, said the sign on the door, and Windflower knocked politely before going in.

"Good morning," said the officer behind the desk. "You must be Winston. I'm Bonnie Morecombe. Welcome to St. John's."

"Thank you," said Windflower. "Nice to meet you and nice to

be here."

"Let me show you around," said Morecombe. She got up from her desk, and Windflower noticed that she had a slight limp. Morecombe took a cane from beside the desk, walked out of the office and started heading down the hall, talking all the way. Windflower had to race to catch up, despite her physical impairment. Morecombe said hello to everyone along the way and popped into what seemed like every office on the floor to introduce Windflower. He tried at first to remember the names but after a while recognized that was hopeless and just smiled and shook people's hands.

They were headed to the cafeteria to get a coffee when Windflower saw a familiar face.

"Lars, is that you?" said Windflower.

"Sergeant Windflower, I heard you were in St. John's," said Corporal Lars Lundquist.

"You guys know each other?" asked Morecombe.

"We worked together on the biker case in Grand Falls," said Windflower.

"I remember that case," said Morecombe. "A lot of drugs and a lot of money recovered, as I recall."

"Yes, ma'am," said Lundquist.

"Well, I'll leave you two to get reacquainted. I'll see you back in my office," said Morecombe.

Lundquist and Windflower got their coffee and sat at a table overlooking the lake.

"There's a lake out there," said Windflower. "Somewhere."

"So they tell me," said Lundquist. "The inspector told me you were here."

"You were in Marystown?" asked Windflower, knowing that was where Inspector Ron Quigley was posted.

"Not yet," said Lundquist. "I'm here to do my weapons upgrade and then to take the mandatory supervision course."

"The anti-harassment course?" asked Windflower. "Are you getting a new assignment?"

"Didn't you know?" asked Lundquist. "I'm going to Grand Bank to replace you."

Windflower tried not to look surprised, but Lundquist picked up on it. "Didn't Inspector Quigley tell you?"

"He's very busy," said Windflower. "I'm pleased for you. Grand Bank is a nice place, too, though."

"Yeah, but it was time for a change," said Lundquist. "Plus, it felt like we were slipping back a bit. After all that work we did to clear out the bikers, they're back in full force. And the old mayor we had is gone. It just makes it hard. Maybe some new blood on our side might not be a bad idea."

"Well, I'm sure you'll do well in Grand Bank. Let's stay in touch," said Windflower.

"Sure," said Lundquist. "I'd like that."

After coffee the two men shook hands, and Windflower then headed back to the second floor where Morecombe showed him his office.

It was the standard government-issued room with a window that looked over the parking lot, a computer that had not been hooked up and a box that he discovered contained eight manuals. Each one outlined some aspect of his outreach work or the mandates and operations of the Communications Directorate of which he was now a part. His mission was to read and comprehend these tomes, and until Morecombe was satisfied he knew what he was doing, he would not be doing any outreach work. He would be doing only in-office research instead.

Just as Windflower thought his working life could not get any worse, Morecombe informed him that there was also a ten-module online course that every Communications Directorate employee was required to complete before engaging with the public. If there was anything that Windflower hated more than paperwork, it was something that required he touch more than a mouse when it came to technology.

"Don't worry," said Morecombe. "It's completely interactive, and you'll have an online tutor who will help you take the tests."

That just about did it for Windflower. "Tests?" he gasped.

"After every module there's a short comprehension test," said Morecombe. "You'll be fine. If you don't pass it the first time, they give you three more chances."

Windflower's eyes kind of glazed over at this point and so

did his brain. He didn't remember anything else Morecombe said except something about a team meeting at two o'clock later in the day. In the meantime he was alone with his manuals and a strong sense of panic at the thought of the online training ordeal coming his way. He got up, closed the door to his office and sat down to think about how he was going to survive.

He swivelled his chair around and looked out the window, hoping something would inspire him, or at least reduce the tension he felt in his chest. There wasn't much in the parking lot, but behind the RCMP offices was an apartment building. Windflower had stayed there when he was in town before. Many visiting RCMP officers used it for accommodations while they were visiting or on temporary assignments.

Windflower could see behind that building too. There was another parking lot and a large industrial garbage bin. Next to the bin Windflower saw what he was looking for. The last Christmas tree of the season was drying out and starting to turn brown beside the garbage container. Someone had hung on to it long after the twelve days of Christmas had passed. He wondered if their Christmas was as nice as the one he and his family had just had in Grand Bank.

Windflower and Sheila both loved Christmas. They loved everything about it, including all of the preparations, the anticipation and the spirit before and after. Last Christmas had been extra special for a number of reasons. First of all, Amelia Louise was almost old enough to completely enjoy the magic of the season as only a child could. She got to sit on Santa's knee at the Town of Grand Bank Christmas party, and when he asked her what she wanted, she was able, with some coaching from her mommy, to say "dollie, pleeze."

It may have also been the first real Christmas for Stella, who had come to stay with them for the holidays. Her eyes grew wide as saucers when she saw the decorated tree and all the presents underneath it on Christmas morning. She couldn't believe it when they handed her a stack to open. But she wholeheartedly got into the action after that. Windflower and Sheila had a grand time drinking their coffee and watching their kids and the two pets revel in that happy morning's activities.

So, too, had his Uncle Frank. He came for Christmas to join Windflower and his family at their insistence. They didn't want him alone at this time of year, so soon after the loss of his wife, Windflower's beloved Auntie Marie. His uncle had always liked Newfoundland, especially Grand Bank, and he made several good friends on previous visits. He stayed around until just after New Year's when he went back to his home community in Pink Lake, Alberta, where Windflower had been born and raised.

Windflower had a great chat with Uncle Frank when he drove him to St. John's for his flight.

"That was a grand Christmas," said his uncle. "Even though my heart is still heavy, I had a great time visiting with you and my friends."

"Have you thought any more about coming to live in Grand Bank. We have lots of room at the B & B," said Windflower.

"I thought you were going to sell that place," said his uncle. "What happened to that idea?"

"Kind of on the back burner for now. Sheila and I put so much time and money into it that we can't just walk away. Levi Parsons is running it for us, and Beulah and her daughter are doing the cleaning and cooking. We might just hang on to it."

"You know, I just might take you up on that. Can I get back to you in the spring?"

"Absolutely," said Windflower. "You take your time. The offer is always open to you."

Windflower was feeling pretty good after that little period of reminiscing. Now back to the box of manuals, he thought. He read his way through the introduction in the first one, which was called Welcome to the Royal Canadian Mounted Police: Mandate and Motto. That took him to lunchtime.

3

Windflower walked outside, hoping to take a short walk around the perimeter, but the rain had grown heavier and he ducked back inside. When he looked around again, he saw the raindrops grow larger and whiter. By the time he got back to his office with a sandwich from the cafeteria, it was a full-scale white-out. At first, he panicked. He hadn't even worn his winter boots or parka to work. Then almost as suddenly as it had started, the snow stopped, and he thought he could even see a glimpse of the sun.

That, too, faded. By the time he headed to the team meeting at two o'clock, the thick and impenetrable fog had returned. How quickly the weather changed in the city still amazed him, despite having lived here before. The inspector and his friend, Ron Quigley, was originally from St. John's and had told him that the only thing to expect was the unexpected. But the good news was that in most of Newfoundland and Labrador, if you didn't like the weather, you didn't have to worry. It would soon change.

The team meeting was mercifully short and to the point, exactly Windflower's kind of meeting. He met the two media relations officers, Terry Robbins and Bruce Dale, and the videographer, Steve Vaillancourt. He also got introduced to Morecombe's executive assistant, Lise Pigeon, and her administrator, Muriel Sparkes, who knew Betsy Molloy from his Grand Bank office. Well, not his Grand Bank office anymore, he thought.

After the meeting he read through manual number one, but his eyes were glazing over, and he was pretty sure that there was no way he could pass a test on the contents of what he'd just read. He was about to start again when Morecombe poked her head into his office on her way home and reminded him that he had to start scheduling his online training sessions.

"Oh yeah," he said. "I was just going to do that."

After Morecombe left, he looked up the information online and submitted his request. He got an immediate response saying that his request had been received and that he would receive further instructions. "That would be tomorrow, for further instructions, and that's it for me for today," he said to nobody in particular as he closed the computer and turned out the lights.

He was happy to be outside, although the wind had shifted and was now blowing a steady stream of wet fog into his face as he walked down the boulevard to home. He had not had the best of days, but he was hopeful that the rest of his family would cheer him up a little. That was a false hope.

When he opened the front door of his house all he heard was noise. Lady was barking, which was her universal distress signal. Stella was howling in the middle of the living room floor, and Sheila was trying to comfort a sobbing little Amelia Louise.

"Take that dog out," said Sheila, probably a little harsher than she intended. "Please," she added more softly, with half a smile as amends to Windflower.

He smiled back. "Sure," he said, keeping his words to a minimum and definitely not asking any questions. He'd made that mistake before. He'd learned to quickly get out of the line of fire or else risk being the next victim.

Lady was as pleased as Windflower to get out of the house, even though the fog had given way again to rain and that brisk St. John's wind. Lady tried to go out every time the door opened, if at all possible. Today, it was possible, so she jumped at the chance. Windflower didn't mind either. Once he finished his orientation—he almost called it his ordeal—he would get a vehicle assigned to him, and his daily walks would be less frequent. Better to take advantage now, even if the weather was less than cooperative, he thought

Windflower went up Forest Road a way and then turned down behind what people still called the Newfoundland Telephone building, even though it had changed names a half dozen times. Windflower wasn't really sure what it was called now. He cut through the parking lot and skipped through the narrow lanes that led towards the waterfront. The east end of the St. John's harbour was the main supply area for the offshore drilling rigs, and ships and cranes and trucks moved around there all day and night.

Windflower liked to stand on the hill overlooking one of the sections of the harbour and just watch the work for a while. In his mind it was almost like playing Dinky trucks except these were monstrous vehicles moving very real mountains of sand, salt and supplies. Lady seemed to like it here, too. But maybe she just liked being with him, he thought.

They walked down Water Street and turned towards Harbour Drive to see what boats were in the harbour for the night. Looking at ships that had come into shore or watching them as they were docked were also among Windflower's favoured things to do. It would have been better to get up close to the ships, but a few years ago in the after wash of the 9-11 attacks in the States, security concerns prompted local officials to put up a 10-foot-high grill fence to keep people out.

Many of the locals, especially older men who would come down in the morning for a visit and a yarn with their buddies, were quite upset that their access to the waterfront had been limited. But they were told that security trumps everything and that the cruise ships that regularly came to St. John's would not come anymore if the waterfront wasn't secured. So, the cruise ships kept coming, and all those older guys kind of just faded away from the scene.

There were none of them around this evening as Windflower and Lady strolled up to the west end container port and back. No cruise ships either. No one would visit in this weather, thought Windflower, the cold rain turning back into snow again. He and his dog walked up to Water Street and headed home. Along the way Windflower saw some more of those missing girl posters. When he stopped at one near Prescott Street, he could see that it was different. This one read "Missing: Brittney Hodder from Grand Bank, aged 15. Last seen at the Avalon Mall".

Hodder, thought Windflower. From Grand Bank. That name sounds familiar. But he couldn't place the girl or the family. Maybe Sheila would know. As the snow started to come down a little harder, he could feel Lady tugging at her leash. "Okay, girl, let's go home," he said.

4

When they got home, the house was much quieter than it had been when he left, but Windflower had also learned that this could be the most dangerous time of all, like the calm before the storm. But actually it turned out fine. In fact, it was more than fine. He could hear happy laughter from the kitchen and could also smell something absolutely delicious.

Sheila had decided to defuse her domestic situation by making a bubble bath and putting both Stella and Amelia Louise in at the same time. She had hoped that would help the girls get back to some version of normal and maybe help her survive.

Windflower went upstairs where Sheila was sitting on the bed looking utterly exhausted. He came closer and gave her a big hug.

"So what's going on?" he asked.

"Today was a disaster," said Sheila. "Amelia Louise cried and held onto my leg at the daycare and wouldn't let it go. She ran to the window, and I could see her yelling at me. She was not happy."

"It was her first day. She'll get used to the place," said Windflower.

"I don't know. Our spoiled little girl might be too much of a busy bee at the Busy Bee daycare. She was still mad at me this afternoon when I came to pick her up. The staff said she wouldn't nap, which is a problem in itself. No nap equals grouchy Amelia Louise."

Windflower nodded and rubbed Sheila's back. "Stella's day was pretty much the same, according to the staff," said Sheila. "She didn't want to leave me, wouldn't do anything they wanted in class, and she started a fight with this really big kid who sat on her."

Windflower laughed. "I'm sorry, but that's funny."

"Not to the school. That's her first warning. Three warnings and she gets suspended."

"How can you get suspended from kindergarten?"

"They don't call it that, but that's what it is. They said she may not have the social skills to thrive in this environment, and if that proves to be true, they would recommend that she be held out of school until next year."

"If that happens, we're screwed."

"Exactly," said Sheila. "Then I go to my adviser this morning, and she says they will only allow me to carry over some of my credits into this new program. And not all the ones I'm missing can be taken in person. So, I have to do some in-class sessions and some online."

"Me too," said Windflower. "They gave me a box of manuals and then said I had to take more training online. And there's a test after every module."

"That's going to be a challenge. I know your struggles with technology. Mine are more about time. I'm losing the battle already. If anything more gets added, I'm done."

"Well, I can look after these guys up here if you want to finish getting supper ready."

"Thank you, Winston. And for listening. Things will get better, I know. But it will take all of us some time to adjust. I kind of forgot about that."

"To paraphrase Tagore, 'Let us not pray to be sheltered from dangers but to be fearless in facing them.'"

"I love that. It's wonderful."

"You know what's wonderful? That smell in the kitchen. What is it?"

"It's a surprise. I'm trying something different. I hope you'll like it."

"I'm hungry enough to eat anything," said Windflower.

"Good," said Sheila. "The clean PJs are on their dressers."

Windflower got the squealing girls out of the bath and left Stella to get dressed while he looked after Amelia Louise. All three trooped down together as Sheila was putting a hot dish on the table. She also had bowls of steamed broccoli and carrots mixed together, smaller bowls of sour cream and guacamole and a tiny plate of sliced jalapeno peppers.

"Wow," said Windflower.

"Wow," said Amelia Louise.

Stella didn't say anything, but the expression on her face was almost as good as a wow.

Sheila had cooled a little of the main dish for each of the girls and added a dab of sour cream and another of guacamole to their plates along with some veggies. She scooped up a big portion of the main dish and handed it to Windflower. "You might want to add some jalapenos as well as the sour cream and guacamole. That's what the recipe called for," said Sheila.

"What is it?" asked Windflower.

"Just try it," she said.

Windflower added a few jalapeno slices on top of the cheesy casserole and took a bite. "Mmmmm," he said. "This is great." He really enjoyed the first helping, so he asked for seconds.

Sheila passed it over with a smile. "Did you notice anything?"

Windflower looked confused. "What do you mean? This is delicious."

"It's vegetarian."

"What, no meat?"

"Nope. Brown rice, onions, peppers, corn, tomatoes, black beans and cheese. Even gluten and nut-free. Not that you're worried about that. Mexican rice and beans casserole. Ready in 15 minutes. I made it on the weekend. Pretty good, eh?"

"Pretty impressive," said Windflower as he finished off his seconds. "We're not going vegan or anything are we?"

Sheila laughed. "No, Sergeant, we're not changing much at all. I just thought we could do without the ground beef all the time. If I want beef, I want a steak on the barbeque or a nice pot roast."

"Ah, that's my girl," said Windflower as he helped Sheila clear the table. Dessert was a can of tinned peaches with a dollop of whipped cream on top and strong black tea for the adults.

5

After dinner, they all watched a little TV together until first Amelia Louise and then Stella got tucked in for the night. Finally, when everything was quiet, Sheila and Windflower had the couch and the TV to themselves.

Windflower remembered the poster he saw about the missing girl. "Did you know Brittney Hodder?" he asked. "From Grand Bank."

"I think that's Chief Hodder's daughter," said Sheila. "Is something wrong?"

"She's missing. She's the second girl I saw a poster about. The other one was from St. John's."

"Oh my. That doesn't sound good. I'll call Barb Hodder in the morning. I can't imagine what she's going through. To have your daughter missing…"

"I know. And I ran into a guy I worked with in Grand Falls, Lars Lundquist. He told me he's taking over my job in Grand Bank."

"That was fast."

"Yeah, gone and forgotten already."

"Oh, Winston, you're such a baby. It sounds like Ron Quigley's looking after himself. He couldn't manage Grand Bank on his own."

"Yeah, I guess you're right. I'll give Ron a call tomorrow to check in," said Windflower. After a pause in the conversation, he asked, "Are we going to make it through this week?"

"I think this is going to be the week from hell," said Sheila. "But we'll get through it, and it will be better on the other side."

She was right on both counts. The next day didn't get any better, nor the day after that, but finally by Friday the sun was shining, and everybody seemed to have found their groove. Amelia Louise still wasn't happy about going to daycare and leaving her mommy, but Sheila reported that the histrionics were greatly reduced. Stella wasn't talking much, but at least she hadn't bitten anyone, yet. Sheila was embracing her return to school, and Windflower could see she was happy and engaged.

He wished he could say the same about himself, but he was still slogging through his manuals and getting his bearings at his new office. The rest of the team were kind and helpful, though. They even asked Windflower to join them for a drink after work on Friday at the nearby Sergeants' Mess. The mess was a private club operated by the Canadian Forces, and police officers were welcome there as guests. Windflower agreed, but he had only one beer because he didn't want Sheila to be on her own with his menagerie of little girls and pets, all of whom demanded some attention.

He was walking home in the sunshine, finally able to gaze across the lake, when his cell phone rang.

"Hey, Winston, how's she going b'y?" asked Inspector Ron Quigley. Quigley was a long-time friend and former boss. They had been friends even before Windflower got to Grand Bank, having met him in Nova Scotia on one of Windflower's first postings. It was there that Windflower got his sergeant's stripes, and Ron was rapidly moving up the ranks. They'd stayed in touch, and about three years ago their career paths crossed again when Quigley got appointed as the RCMP Inspector for the Southeast Region, which included Grand Bank.

Quigley was still there, at the HQ in Marystown, about an hour from Grand Bank when he called Windflower.

"Things are good b'y," said Windflower. "'There is nothing either good or bad but thinking makes it so.'"

"That's good," said Quigley. "And Sheila and your growing family?"

"We're all good," said Windflower. "Making adjustments. I hear you replaced me."

"Yeah," said Quigley. "Lars told me he saw you in St. John's. I meant to call before, but it's been crazy. I needed someone in Grand Bank right away, and he contacted me out of the blue to see about a transfer. It worked for me. I was in a bit of a bind because

I couldn't appoint Tizzard or Evanchuk as the supervisor since they're a couple."

Windflower thought about Eddie Tizzard and Carrie Evanchuk for a moment. They were both good cops despite their varying backgrounds. Tizzard was from the small Newfoundland community of Ramea and had been Windflower's 2IC before he had a run-in with a nasty boss. Evanchuk was from Estevan, Saskatchewan, the young sister of a family of police officers, and now pregnant with their first child.

"I understand," said Windflower. "Lars is a good cop and will be fine there."

"I think so," said Quigley. "Anyway, two things I wanted to talk to you about. One is that Bill Ford is going to be at the Miller Centre for rehab for the next few weeks. I'm hoping you can drop in to see him. His spirits are a little low right now."

"Absolutely," said Windflower. "Our house is just down the road. I can understand being down. Eddie Tizzard was the same after he got shot a few years ago. I'll certainly pop in to see Bill. When are you coming to town?"

"That's the other thing I wanted to talk to you about. We've got a missing girl, from Grand Bank."

"I saw a poster with her name on it. Brittney Hodder. Sheila thought it might be Fire Chief Hodder's daughter."

"That's the girl. The family is pretty upset. She was a kid but started hanging around with the wrong crowd, an older crew. She took off with some of them. Apparently they were going to the Avalon Mall and then to a house party in town."

"And she didn't come back," said Windflower. "I saw a poster for another missing girl, too."

"There's more," said Quigley. "We and the Constabulary in town are working together on this. We think there's a human trafficking ring operating in St. John's. That makes it a national issue and brings us in. I'm coming to St. John's to meet Detective Sergeant Langmead next week.

"I remember Langmead. What do you want me to do?"

"There's no way I can go back and forth to deal with this. I was wondering if you could be our point person on it. I know you're busy with the public outreach stuff, but I can probably pull some strings to get you released for a day or two to help us out, if you agree that is."

"I'm in," said Windflower. He didn't need any coaxing.

"Great. The meeting is at the Constabulary building at 10:00 on Tuesday. Maybe we can have coffee beforehand?"

"Sounds good. 'Farewell, my blessing season this in thee.'"

"Not bad," said Quigley. "'And this our life, exempt from public haunt, finds tongues in trees, books in the running brooks, sermons in stones, and good in everything.'"

"Where is that from?" asked Windflower. But all he could hear was Quigley laughing and then nothing as the phone went dead. I'll get him next time, thought Windflower as he smiled to himself and continued his walk home. As he got closer, the sun faded and the clouds grew darker. He didn't have to consult the weather on his phone to know a storm was on its way.

6

Sheila confirmed that there was a storm in the forecast. When Windflower arrived home, she told him there would be at least 20 centimetres of snow overnight and maybe more on Saturday and into Sunday.

"Okay," said Windflower. "We'll see what the weather is tomorrow when we get up and make our plans from there."

"I was going to go to Bannerman Park," said Sheila. "I thought it would be fun to see The Loop."

"What's The Loop?" asked Windflower.

"It's an outdoor skating rink. Not this week, but maybe soon we could get the girls some skates."

"I think Amelia Louise is a bit small for it. But I thought I saw skates in Stella's duffle bag."

"Maybe you and I can have a spin too," said Sheila with a mischievous look in her eye.

"Very funny," said Windflower. "The last time I went skating with you I nearly broke my back. No, thanks. I'll look after Amelia Louise."

Hearing her name, his littlest girl came running to him and gave him a big hug. "I luvs u," she said.

"I love you, too, sweetie," said Windflower. "Where did that come from?"

"Daycare," said Sheila. "Just before everyone leaves for the day, they have a huggin' lovin' circle at Busy Bee. Some hug and some love, and some like Amelia Louise do it all."

"I'm impressed. How was Stella's day?" he asked.

"She's very quiet and a loner apparently, but that's not grounds for discipline in kindergarten. At least not yet. I'd say better," said

Sheila. "But it's hard to tell. Anyway, I told them we'd go to the park when you got home."

"What are we waiting for?"

It took more than a few minutes to get everyone ready, dressed and out the door. But they were all happy when they finally got moving down the sidewalk to the small park next to the school a few streets away. Amelia Louise and Stella were in the large cart that Windflower was pulling along, and Sheila held Lady on her leash alongside them.

At the park the two girls ran to the swings, and Windflower helped Amelia Louise get up on hers and started to push. Sheila did the same for Stella. Soon, they had a little contest about who could get up the highest.

"Do you want to go higher?" Windflower asked Amelia Louise.

"Hiya, hiya," she said.

Sheila asked Stella the same question.

At first the four-year old just smiled. Then all of a sudden, she started screaming too. "Higher, higher."

Windflower and Sheila looked at each other, both thinking that this was a very good sign and hoping it would continue.

When they got home, Sheila made their Friday night special: hot dogs and macaroni and cheese. She had put the casserole in the oven before they left, so when they got back, they were greeted by a magical aroma. After dinner they had popcorn and watched an old movie, Bedknobs and Broomsticks, on TV.

Bedtime was now an all-hands-on-deck proposition. Windflower gave Amelia Louise her bath and read her stories while Sheila did the same for Stella. Windflower read Goodnight Moon twice, and Amelia Louise was rapt both times as she tried to find her friend, the little mouse. And because it was Friday night, she also got Llama Llama Red Pajama, a beautiful rhyming book about a llama that had trouble falling asleep.

When they finally got the girls to bed, Windflower and Sheila were content to sit in the living room and sip their tea in front of the gas fireplace.

"Ron Quigley called me today," said Windflower.

"And how is Ron?" asked Sheila.

"He seemed fine," said Windflower. "He told me the reason he brought in Lars Lundquist was because Eddie and Carrie are a couple and couldn't supervise each other."

"That makes sense. I talked to Carrie a few nights ago. She's doing well and has lost her morning sickness. I'm sure that's a big relief."

"I bet. Ron is also giving me a special assignment. That missing girl is Chief Hodder's daughter, and I guess there are more of them, too. I'll be working with the Constabulary on it."

"How will you swing that with all your training requirements?"

"Ron said he'd pave the way. I'm not one bit unhappy about it, that's for sure. 'We must take the current when it serves or lose our ventures.'"

Sheila sighed. "I'm going up. Are you taking her out?" she asked, pointing at Lady, who was staring them both down.

"I guess so," said Windflower. "We'll do a short walk. I'll be back soon."

Windflower put on Lady's leash and went out into the night. Now it was really snowing. Falling from the sky were those big, fat, deliberate flakes that promise a million more to follow. Windflower, and Lady too, often enjoyed walking in the snow, particularly at night. First, it meant fewer people on the roads and pathways, and Windflower could let Lady off the leash sometimes. But also, a nighttime snowfall was serene; for Windflower it felt much quieter and calmer than during the day, and it seemed to him that Lady felt that way too.

By the time they got back, Windflower had a heavy dusting of snow on his hat and shoulders, and Lady shook half a snowbank off her when she got into the kitchen. Windflower cleaned up and put down fresh food and water for Lady and Molly and headed up to bed. Sheila was sleeping when he got there, so he quietly undressed and slipped in beside her. He had no difficulty falling asleep. But not long after he woke in what was clearly a dream.

7

Windflower knew it was a dream because he had learned from his late Auntie Marie and his Uncle Frank how to read, interpret and sometimes even participate in the dream world. His family had long been dream weavers, people who studied the dream world and encouraged others to do the same. A Cree, Windflower had been raised in Pink Lake in Northern Alberta. Not all his people practiced dream weaving, but most believed the dream world to be as real as the one walked in.

One of the tricks Windflower had learned was to always look for his hands in a dream. That would let him know that he was having a dream, but it also allowed him to be more alive and alert during the dream itself. So tonight, he did just that. He looked down at his hands and then started to look around within his dream.

It was dark and cold. Shivering, Windflower thought he had arrived during the coldest part of the night, that time just before the dawn when the daytime creatures are still asleep and the night prowlers sneak into their beds. Even though it was dark in his dream, Windflower could still see. There was a pair of eyes glowing like coals in the dark.

Another thing he had learned about dream weaving was to ask questions of those who showed up in his dreams, especially animals because they were the ones who carried messages back and forth from and to the spirit world.

"Who are you and what do you want?" asked Windflower.

"The real question is what do you want? I'm trying to go to bed here," answered the glowing-eyed creature, which Windflower could now see was a racoon.

Windflower had heard of the racoon before. Grandfather had

told him that racoons were part of the trickster family and that they liked disguises and secrecy. Auntie Marie had said that racoons might not always be bad but that they had got so used to lying, they couldn't remember how to tell the truth.

Given all that, Windflower decided to be cautious in how he dealt with this animal. "Hey racoon," he said. "Why am I here?"

"Oh, my goodness," said the racoon. "Is this one of those existential dreams you're in? You've come to the wrong place for that, pal. You need one of those obnoxious beavers or something."

"I don't think so," said Windflower. "I was sent here, so you must have something for me. Any advice?"

The racoon walked closer to Windflower and sniffed him. "I sense danger around you," he said. "Not you personally, not your family, but someone you know. Follow this path and you will find more answers." The racoon pointed with his paw down a narrow corridor to his right.

Windflower looked but couldn't see much in the dark. The racoon held up his hand again, and it was like a light came out of it. He shone it down the corridor. Windflower still couldn't see but heard what he thought might be a girl crying. He moved closer to get a better look. And that's when he woke up. He was back in his bed with Sheila.

What the heck was that all about? he wondered. It could be somebody is in danger or it could be a trick. What were the other things that Auntie Marie had told him about racoons and dreams? One he remembered was that in its purest form the racoon symbolized curiosity, adaptability and resourcefulness, but you still had to be careful of what the racoon said. He tried to remember more, but he was too tired and was soon fast asleep again.

He could hear Sheila with the girls when he finally woke up. Saturday morning was his day to sleep in, so he took advantage of it by pulling the covers over his head and trying to get back to sleep. But he was already too awake. So instead of sleeping, he got his Richard Wagamese book off his nightstand and started reading it.

Wagamese was Ojibway, and the book was a series of meditations and teachings that he'd accumulated over the years. Windflower tried to read a few pages every day, but he actually did so more like once a week. Today he was determined to do more than try, so he cracked open the thin volume to where he'd last placed his bookmark. Today's readings focused on gratitude. That was something Windflower did actually practice every day. When he smudged with his sacred medicines, offered up tobacco for another person who might have troubles or said his prayers in the morning, he always ended with gratitude for the gifts and blessings that he had already received in his life.

As Windflower read Wagamese's stories and thoughts about gratitude, many things stuck with him. Richard Wagamese had not always had an easy life and for many years struggled with mental health and addiction issues. But his writings didn't dwell on the pain in his life. Instead, he wrote about the grace and blessings he had received by following a spiritual path. He said that it was important to be grateful for what we have now so that Creator will hear our gratitude and send more.

All of that reminded Windflower that he not only needed to be grateful, he needed to smudge this morning.

8

Windflower went downstairs where Sheila and the girls were in the kitchen making muffins. Well, Sheila was baking, and the girls were engaged in some activity that involved spraying and spattering themselves and everything in the kitchen with batter. They tried to get him to join in, but he sneaked by and grabbed a cup of coffee.

"I'll help you clean up," he said to Sheila, and he pushed open the back door and went outside, Lady right behind him. The scene was white and glorious. There was at least 10 centimetres on the ground, and it was still snowing terrifically. He brushed off a chair and sat on the deck, absorbing the wonder of the snow-filled morning. Then he unfurled his smudging kit.

As usual he put small amounts of each medicine in his shell and lit them with a wooden match. He passed the smoke over his head, his body and under his feet. Then he said his morning prayers. Again he was filled with gratitude, and he prayed for Sheila, Amelia Louise and Stella. He also prayed for his pets, the four-legged members of his family, and for his ancestors, asking that they look over him and his family throughout the day. He finished his prayers by asking for blessings for all his friends back in Grand Bank and the new ones he was meeting in St. John's. At the end, he added one more prayer, that the missing girls, including Brittney Hodder, be returned home safely to their families.

When he was finished, he gathered up his stuff and a snow-covered Lady and went inside. Sheila had somehow got two batches of muffins made and in the oven.

"They smell wonderful," said Windflower.

"Coming soon," said Sheila. "Why don't you cut us up a melon?"

Windflower grabbed the large honeydew melon and cut it into slices. "I forgot to tell you. Bill Ford is coming to St. John's to go to the Miller Centre."

"How's he doing?" asked Sheila.

"Ron said he's starting to feel pretty down. I guess the rehab is getting to him."

"I hear him. After I had my accident, it seemed like it took forever to get back to anything like normal. It's tough physically and emotionally. Your visits saved me."

"I told Ron I'd make sure to get over to see Bill. Maybe take the kids later on too. Might cheer him up."

"Might drive him crazy," said Sheila as she looked in the living room where Amelia Louise and Stella were trying to tie ribbons on Lady's head. They already had several on her tail that she was desperately trying to shake off. Molly stared at the pair from her perch atop the couch with a glare that said don't even think about doing that to me.

"Breakfast is ready," announced Sheila.

Windflower had a hot raisin bran muffin with his second cup of coffee and melon. He enjoyed that so much, he had another. He thought about a third when Sheila brought him back to reality.

"I have another surprise for you," she said. "Last week when I had my casserole spree, I also made our Saturday lunch."

"Pea soup and por' cakes?" asked Windflower, hopefully.

Windflower liked por' cakes, the little potato pancake baked in the oven. No, he loved them. He'd watched Sheila make them many times with minced pork, pork back fat and potatoes along with some baking powder and flour to bind everything together. He also loved dipping them in molasses. The saying around Grand Bank was that they were 'sum good'.

"I have them in the freezer," said Sheila. "That's one thing we can keep from Grand Bank while we're in St. John's."

"How did that tradition start in Grand Bank?" asked Windflower. "Having pea soup and por' cakes for lunch on Saturday?"

"I don't know how it became so popular," said Sheila. "Not every family did it when I was growing up. But mine did because my grandmother on my mother's side came from Point au Gaul, and they did it over there. She brought it with her to Grand Bank. Now it seems everybody there does it."

"I think it's a wonderful tradition," said Windflower. "Did you ever notice that we're always talking about the next meal when we're eating? I think we're neurotic."

Sheila laughed as she cleared away the crumbs from Amelia Louise's high chair and let her down. She and Stella ran to the living room to hunt for Lady, but the dog was hiding out in the kitchen. "Let's go out for a walk in the snow," said Sheila. "We'll bring the toboggan and take turns pulling the girls."

"Sounds great," said Windflower. He helped Sheila finish cleaning up and then went with Amelia Louise to get ready. Sheila did the same with Stella, and soon all four of them were going down the snowy sidewalk outside their house. Windflower knew there was a small hill next to the church they passed along the way the night before, and that's where he headed, pulling the toboggan with the children behind him.

When they got there, Sheila and Windflower took turns sliding down the hill with the girls, who liked it so much they wanted to stay all day. After about an hour the happy group trooped back home. Sheila warmed up their lunch while the girls played with their dollies. They tried to recruit Windflower, but he proved next to useless when it came to doll grooming, so they gave up.

Sheila served lunch, and Windflower had two por' cakes, which he dipped in molasses, and a bowl of pea soup. Afterwards it was nap time for Amelia Louise, so Windflower took her up to get her settled. Sheila stayed down with Stella and got her started with some crayons and paper.

Going up with Amelia Louise for her nap was also Windflower's way of sneaking one for himself. He laid the toddler in her crib and went to his own room where he could hear her on the monitor. But before he could tell she was sleeping, he was out cold. The next time he heard her was when she woke up.

9

The rest of the afternoon was slow as the snow continued to fall outside. When Windflower went out just before dinner, there was double the snow that had been there in the morning. Lady didn't really mind, but even she had trouble wading through to get back on the deck after doing her business.

Dinner was simple—grilled cheese and tomato soup made by Windflower. Soon he was pressured by Sheila to add some broccoli to the menu. He reluctantly agreed, but when it came time to eat, he dipped his broccoli in his soup to cover up the taste of the vegetable. Naturally, Amelia Louise followed suit by using her broccoli to splash tomato soup everywhere. Stella thought this was great fun and did the same.

Sheila and Windflower were relaxed enough to let the mess stay while they enjoyed their dinner. Afterwards, Windflower cleaned the girls and washed the floor while Sheila put away the dishes. They had dessert in the living room as they watched a nature program on TV.

Sheila took Amelia Louise and Stella upstairs and allowed them to play in the bath together while she read her book. Windflower came up after a little while and took Amelia Louise to put on her pajamas. Sheila did the same with Stella, and they all came back downstairs. Amelia Louise had her bottle, and the two little girls then watched Dora the Explorer until it was bedtime.

Tonight, Sheila read stories to Amelia Louise and Windflower had Stella. He asked her to pick a book, and after much hesitation she chose If You Give a Mouse a Cookie. It was one of her favourites and Windflower's too. The story was about a boy who gives a mouse a cookie. Of course, the mouse asks for a glass of milk to go along with the cookie and on and on. It was a lot of fun, and Stella was laughing hard at the end. Windflower had to read it three times before Stella would give him a hug and kiss him goodnight.

When he finally got downstairs, Sheila was scrolling through the movies on Netflix. Saturday night was movie night in the Windflower household, about as close as they could get to a date night anymore. It was Sheila's turn to pick.

"What about this one?" she asked, pausing on a movie called Knives Out.

"What's it about?" asked Windflower. "I don't want anything too heavy. None of those police procedurals."

"I think it's an old-fashioned murder mystery, but the reviews say it's very funny. It's got Daniel Craig and an all-star ensemble cast with Christopher Plummer and a dozen other names you'd recognize."

"Let me make the popcorn and I'll be right back."

Windflower went to the kitchen and gave both pets a treat. Lady looked at him like he was the best master in the world. Molly treated him with her usual disdain but took the treat. In her mind she deserved it for putting up with all of them.

Windflower and Sheila cuddled on the couch and watched the movie with their bowl of popcorn. It was a murder mystery and it was funny. Both laughed out loud several times during the show.

"I really enjoyed that," said Windflower when it was over. "It kept you guessing about who did it all the way through."

"It was kind of like playing Clue," said Sheila. "Plus it had this immigration theme running through it. I didn't expect that either."

"I'm going to pop out with Lady, and then I'll see you upstairs," said Windflower.

He and Lady went outside, and while the scene was still a white winter wonderland, the snow had mercifully stopped, at least for now. The street had been plowed through once, so he and the dog took the path of least resistance and walked down the centre of Forest Road. They passed not a single person and saw no cars on their way. Once Lady had satisfied the call of nature, they headed back. Windflower turned off the lights and went to bed.

Sheila snuggled in beside him and helped warm him up. He

returned the favour. Half an hour later they were both sleeping soundly, and like that old Christmas tale, not a creature or child stirred until the morning.

Sunday morning was Windflower's turn to get up and be with the girls. He would look after them early and get their breakfast while Sheila got a break and could lie in if she wanted. This morning she wanted to do just that, so Windflower was the only adult to go downstairs with the little ones.

First off, he put on a pot of coffee and let Lady out into the back. The snow had definitely stopped, and the morning looked bright and felt cold when Windflower opened the door to let the dog back in. He put on the cartoon channel for the girls and made them their secret Sunday morning treats, Pop Tarts. Sheila probably knew, but Windflower pretended that she didn't and swore the girls to secrecy with a pledge over their hearts. Amelia Louise repeated "I pledges" just to make sure she would get her Pop Tart from her daddy.

Windflower planned to make them a proper breakfast later, but this would allow everybody, especially him, to enjoy the early morning. He sipped his coffee and relaxed while Stella and Amelia Louise watched their show and tried to keep Lady away from their breakfast treat. Windflower noticed how patient Lady was, but as soon as Amelia Louise dropped a piece, the dog snatched it up. Stella laughed when she saw that happen to her little sister, but when she let a piece fall, Molly was quick to swoop in and grab it. Stella started to whine a little, but Windflower didn't take the bait and simply smiled sympathetically.

He brought a coffee and a small bowl of strawberries up to Sheila when he heard her moving around upstairs. Sheila was propped up in bed reading her book.

"Good morning, Winston, and thank you for my coffee," she said.

"You're welcome. I'm going to get breakfast going soon, if that's okay."

"Great. I'll have my shower and be right down."

Windflower went to the kitchen to start making his Sunday morning special of homemade waffles with fresh fruit. He soon had two helpers but somehow managed to get the batter made and the fruit sliced up. He pacified the two youngsters with a small bowl of fruit while he heated up the waffle iron and got the first batch on.

By the time Sheila came down, he had the second one ready for her. She sat at the table and talked to the girls while he made one for himself. When it was done, he gave another quarter to Stella and Amelia Louise and took the other half for himself. He topped it with sliced fruit and covered it in maple syrup. After a bite out of this second serving, he was ready to talk again.

"What should we do today?" he asked Sheila.

"After I come back from church and a little lunch, I thought we could go skating in Bannerman Park," said Sheila.

"That sounds great," said Windflower. "I was thinking we could barbeque a roast for supper tonight as well."

"Super. Use those spices again too. I love them."

Sheila helped Windflower clean up and then got dressed for church. Windflower didn't partake in that activity, and Amelia Louise couldn't sit still long enough. But Stella seemed to like church—at least she liked going with Sheila—and she was as quiet as a mouse there as she was everywhere else.

Everybody enjoyed this arrangement, especially Lady because she often got to go for a run with Windflower on Sunday mornings. This morning was no exception. After Sheila and Stella had gone to church, Windflower put Amelia Louise in the carrier and on his back, grabbed Lady and her leash and headed out. They didn't cover as much ground as usual today because the sidewalks were covered after the snowfall, but it was still a great day to be outside.

10

This morning Windflower ran down Forest Road, past the Miller Centre where Bill Ford would be this week, and down Kings Bridge Road beyond the former Memorial Stadium. It was no longer a stadium but a supermarket superstore of some kind. Ron Quigley, who was a townie, told him of many great nights at the stadium going to hockey games with his dad and, later in his teens, to concerts by the biggest rock groups that could be attracted to the venue.

They turned right at the boulevard and swung up through what people now called Pleasantville. The area had been an American military base during the Second World War, but few of the smaller buildings from that era remained. Windflower ran up the short hill, which of course led to another small hill and then another. He was panting by the time he got to the top. Fortunately, he was able to take the left that brought him towards Kenna's Hill, and from there it was almost completely straight down until he was back on Kings Bridge Road again.

He changed from a run to a fast walk as he felt his hamstrings tighten a little bit. That's when he saw another poster. He took a closer look. It was a different girl, again. This time the poster said "Mandy Pardy, 15, from Marystown. Last seen around Airport Heights." He was hot from running, but he shivered a little when he saw this. Another family suffering, he thought, and he grabbed Lady and ran home.

Windflower got lunch organized with Amelia Louise's help. They grabbed the rest of the cut-up fruit, heated the macaroni from Friday night and made a stack of peanut butter sandwiches. "Perfect," he said when they were finished. "Purrfect," agreed Amelia Louise.

While he was waiting for Sheila and Stella, Windflower took the roast out of the fridge and laid it on the counter. Then he took his plastic container of special spice rub out of the cupboard as well.

Windflower tried store bought rubs, and they were okay, but he preferred to make his own. He made the last batch about a month ago from a recipe that a friend had suggested. It was called a Texas-style barbeque rub, and both Windflower and Sheila had loved it from first bite. It had all the usual spices like garlic and onion powder along with black and cayenne pepper and chili powder. But what gave this rub its oomph was some strong smoked paprika that his friend had given him and a healthy portion of light brown sugar. The sugar caramelized on the beef and gave it a sweet outside crust to go along with the hot spices that penetrated the meat while it was cooking.

Windflower gave the roast a generous coat of spice and then put it in a plastic bag and back in the fridge to let the rub soak in. Sheila and Stella came in just as he was finishing up, and he called Amelia Louise to come get her lunch. The little girl came running in.

"Mila," she said.

"What did she just say?" asked Sheila.

"I think she said Mila," said Windflower.

"Mila," said Amelia Louise again.

"I think she just found her own nickname," said Windflower.

"Let's see how it goes," said Sheila. "It's probably just a phase."

"Mila, Mila, Mila," said their daughter.

"Okay," said Windflower. "If you say so. Anyway, lunch is ready. Let's eat."

After lunch and a change into outdoor clothes for everyone, the family started off towards the skating rink in Bannerman Park. They took the wagon this time so both girls could get a ride now that the sidewalks had been cleared. There were tons of people out enjoying a sunny day after the storm, and everyone seemed to be in good spirits, including the two little girls in the wagon.

"They get along well," said Windflower.

"Yeah," said Sheila. "They fight over toys and stuff from time to time, but I think Amelia Louise, or maybe it's going to be Mila now, likes having company. They're a little apart in age, but Stella doesn't seem to mind."

"I think Stella is happy too," said Windflower. "Even if she doesn't talk very much, I see her smiling and laughing sometimes."

As he spoke, Stella started laughing and Amelia Louise joined in. Soon all four of them were laughing as they turned the corner and headed into the park.

Bannerman Park was beautiful, Victorian in style and in the old part of St. John's. Its boundaries were marked by Circular Road and Rennie's Mill Road, and many older homes in the area had been turned into bed and breakfasts. It was built in the 1860s on land donated by the governor of the Colony of Newfoundland, Sir Alexander Bannerman.

It was a park for all seasons with concerts and festivals, a swimming pool in the summer and, of course, the beautiful skating rink, The Loop, in the winter. Sheila and Windflower sat on a bench, and he helped Stella put on and tie her skates. Amelia Louise 'helped' her mother until Windflower grabbed her and picked her up. Sheila and Stella moved on to the ice cautiously while Windflower and Amelia Louise watched. Sheila was trying to hold onto Stella, but the little girl slipped her grasp and to everyone's surprise started skating gracefully away. She turned back after a little while to smile at Sheila and to encourage her to catch up.

Sheila waved to Windflower and held her hands up in the air as if to say "who knew?". She then skated to meet Stella, and soon the two were skating together effortlessly around The Loop. Windflower and Amelia Louise stood on the side and waved every time they came by. After about ten laps Sheila had enough, but Stella continued to skate around by herself.

"Wow," said Windflower when Sheila came over and sat on the bench to take her skates off. "I wasn't expecting that. She's really good."

"She's a better skater than I am," said Sheila. "I wonder if her mother was a skater. Because she certainly has talent. We should see about getting her into a club. I know she's young, but she's so good."

"Absolutely," said Windflower as he watched little Stella pass by them again. "That's if we can ever get her off the ice."

They did manage to get her off the ice and everybody back in the wagon and on the road home. When they got there, Amelia Louise went for her nap, and maybe not surprisingly, given the amount of skating she had just done, Stella went for one too.

11

When the girls were both down, Windflower took the roast out of the fridge. He went outside and turned on the barbeque, lighting only one side. When this was hot, he put the roast on the cool side of the barbeque and closed the cover. It was about a two- kilogram roast, so he figured it would probably take about 90 minutes or so, and then he would check it with a meat thermometer to see if it was done. The challenge was to have the outside burned a little while keeping the core a medium rare, the way Sheila and he liked it.

He went back inside and sat with Sheila in the peace and quiet of their living room. She was reading her book and he picked up the newspaper. The local paper, The Telegram, wasn't much during the week, but on the weekend it had a lot more news and commentary. He liked reading the columns but today started at the news section in front.

He saw one story on page two and read the headline out loud, "Girls Missing. Families Worried."

"That's what you're going to be working on," said Sheila, lifting her eyes from her book.

Windflower continued, "There are five known cases of missing teenage girls. There is now another, this one from Marystown. Mandy Pardy, age 15, was last seen at the Walmart in Marystown."

"That's where the taxi picks up and drops off," said Sheila. "I know some of the Pardys from over there. One's a fabulous accordion player, Earl Pardy, but he's not married."

"Whoever the family is, I bet they're worried sick," said Windflower.

"When I talked to Barb Hodder, she started crying and couldn't stop. What is going on in the world?"

"It's pretty scary right now. Maybe I'll give Ron Quigley a call to see if I can find out more."

Windflower walked out to the kitchen and called Quigley. There was no answer, so he left a message. He couldn't stop thinking about the latest girl and all the others, so he found his medicines and took out a little tobacco. Lady followed him as he went outside. He said a short prayer for all the missing girls and laid the tobacco on the ground. That was one of his other traditions.

For many generations of his people, and Indigenous people all over North America, natural tobacco was an integral part of their community. It was used in rituals, ceremonies and prayers and seen as a sacred plant with healing and spiritual benefits. For these reasons they treated it with great respect. It was also believed to be a gateway to Creator and the spirit world. Windflower used it to ask for help for people in trouble and to acknowledge people who had passed.

Today, he offered it for the well-being of the missing girls. It couldn't hurt, and maybe it would even help. Windflower went back inside and started getting the rest of dinner ready. He peeled potatoes and got the broccoli and carrots ready to go. An hour later he could hear the girls stirring upstairs as he was going out to check the roast on the barbeque. When he lifted the lid, he was almost swept away by the scent of the roasting meat and the sweet and spicy smells of the pepper and brown sugar sinking into the meat.

He checked the thermometer. The roast was making good progress. Back inside, he worked on the potatoes and other veggies. He heard Sheila shepherding the girls into another joint bath and then a lot of giggling. He would be able to finish everything off while they had their bath, he thought, and everyone would get to bed early to be ready for work, school and daycare the next day.

Once the potatoes were cooked, he called out to Sheila that dinner would soon be ready. He mashed up the potatoes and added butter, a little milk and a clove of minced garlic. The carrots only needed a little butter and some dried ginger, and they were ready. He put the broccoli on to steam and went to get the roast.

When he came back in, Sheila was already moving to get the

girls some potatoes and veggies. Windflower then carved up the roast—a nice outside slice for himself to taste the brown sugar and two smaller outer portions that Sheila would cut up for Stella and Amelia Louise. Then he took two very pink slices from the centre, one for Sheila and one for him, to complement the meat that what was already on the adults' plates.

He took one bite and was lost in meat heaven. When he came back to earth, Sheila was struggling to stop Lady from grabbing an overboard piece of meat from Amelia Louise and losing the battle.

"I love this roast beef. You have outdone yourself, Sergeant," said Sheila.

"We aim to please," said Windflower as he finished off his meat and cut another small slice.

After dinner Windflower cleaned up and put away the barbeque while Sheila got the girls a small bowl of ice cream for dessert. The adults had hoped for an early night, but the late naptime ruled that out. Instead, they let the two girls run around and play in their pajamas until they tired themselves out. But they had only one story each before being tucked into their beds.

Windflower had just settled in with Sheila to have another cup of tea when the phone rang. It was Ron Quigley. He motioned to Sheila that he would take the call in the kitchen and said hello to the inspector.

"Hey, Sergeant, how are you tonight? You called?" said Quigley.

"Yeah, I saw in the paper that there's another girl missing. Five, that's crazy," said Windflower.

"I know," said Quigley. "And the latest is from Marystown. I'm glad you called. There's been another development. We were tracking a crew of guys who we thought might be involved in this. Now one of them is dead."

12

Do we know the dead guy?" asked Windflower

"We sure do," said Quigley. "It's Freddy Hawkins."

"The lawyer?" asked Windflower. "I knew he represented a lot of low-lifes, but I thought he was clean."

"He was, relatively," said Quigley. "But if you keep going to the barbershop, eventually you'll get a haircut. I talked to him a few days ago. He said he was 'engaged peripherally' in something. That's how he described it. But he wanted out. Said it was bikers and girls."

"Now he's gone. Any leads?"

"Well, we have an idea about who might be involved. After we pushed the Angels out last year, the local wannabees picked up the slack. But there's a bit of a turf war going on too. I hear from Langmead that the Outlaws are trying to move into St. John's. This whole thing is getting out of hand."

"What do you want me to do?"

"I'm glad you asked," said Quigley. "I want to pull you off your assignment. You can stay in St. John's, and it would be helpful to have support from the comms directorate, but I'm going to need you to run the investigation full-time from our side. There are five missing girls now that we know of, and there may be more. We have to get a handle on this right away."

"I'm okay with that. You'll have to pull some strings with my boss, though."

"No worries," said the inspector. "I'm going to call Superintendent Majesky in Halifax. This has to take priority over your training."

"Let me know," said Windflower. "I'm in your hands. 'We

cannot all be masters.'"

"'When the sea was calm all boats alike showed mastership in floating,'" replied Quigley.

Windflower tried to think up a quick response, but the phone was dead. He went back inside. Sheila had gone up to bed, and he followed her. After a long and full day he was happy to fall asleep.

His sleep, however, did not last long. He woke up again in dreamland. This time it was much more familiar terrain. He was back in a clearing in the woods outside his old home in Pink Lake. It was the autumn of the year, and the Manitoba maples and willow trees were in full fall splendour. The air was crisp with the first early frost, and Windflower could see his breath when he blew out.

He was a little surprised, but happy, when his Auntie Marie walked out of the forest and came closer to him. His aunt had died late last year, but he had learned that the dreamworld was the place where both sides of living could make contact and communicate.

"I hear you had a visit with our friend racoon," said Auntie Marie.

"Was he coming as a messenger or as a trickster?" asked Windflower. "I heard a girl's cry."

"That's not for me to say," said Auntie Marie. "You have the power of discernment. Use it wisely. But I will say this. Sometimes we can ignore the messenger, but we should never discount the message. Now come walk with me to the lake."

Windflower followed his aunt through a narrow path in the forest that seemed to part before her. When he looked around, it was closing fast behind him. He hurried to catch up and found her sitting on a log overlooking the lake.

"Come sit beside me," said his aunt. Windflower sat down on the log.

"Look at the water," said Auntie Marie. "It looks calm, like nothing is moving. But you can see here where it laps the shore, and underneath the water everything is alive and moving. Nothing stands still."

When she stopped speaking, a large trout breached the water and grabbed an insect floating on top.

"That's what happens when you stand still," she said. "I see you,

Winston, trying to hold back the waters and pretend that nothing is changing when all around you the old is passing and the new is trying to sprout. Pay attention, you have a lot of information but little wisdom. Your teachers are ready when you are." His aunt snapped her fingers and vanished. Windflower woke with a start and sat up in bed.

"Are you okay?" asked Sheila right after she had woken up beside him.

"I will be," said Windflower. "I just have to go to the bathroom." He padded off, washed his face in cold water and stared in the mirror. He thought about what his aunt had said in his dream and what it all meant. He was still thinking about it when he got back into bed. But he couldn't figure it out. The only way he could get back to sleep was to let go of that thinking. And the only way to do that was to have a plan about what he'd do next. It came to him. He'd call his Uncle Frank in the morning. With that decision made, he reached for Sheila, and she held him tightly. He didn't think about anything else until he woke in the morning.

Every morning in their household was hectic, but Monday mornings tended to be the craziest of the week. Both Windflower and Sheila had accepted that and learned to just go with the flow. The girls were a handful, but with two of them managing one each, they got by.

While they were eating their oatmeal for breakfast, Windflower had a chance to fill Sheila in on the previous evening's conversation with Inspector Quigley.

"Oh my goodness," said Sheila. "Freddy Hawkins? I guess he did one too many side deals."

"Yeah, but I kinda liked him," said Windflower. "He was the lawyer of last defence. That's how he saw himself anyway. He made the system work. Without duty lawyers like Freddy, we would always be in court. He wasn't harmless, but 'it hurts not the tongue to give fair words.'"

"'He that dies pays all debts,'" said Sheila.

"Very good," said Windflower. "And true. I'm going into work today, but I have been given a reprieve from my technological nightmare. Ron is assigning me full time to the missing girls' case.

And I guess to the Freddy Hawkins murder as well."

"Will you have to go back to Grand Bank? 'Cause that might be a problem."

"No, at least not yet. I'm going to start working with Langmead at the Constabulary, and I can check in with Ron and Marystown as needed. My first task today was supposed to have my car assigned. I hope that's still on."

"Okay. Let's get everybody organized. You go with Stella. I got her," Sheila said, grabbing Amelia Louise and wiping her face with a damp cloth. She let her down on the floor and then had to run and catch her. Windflower already had Stella, and he put the squealing four-year-old over his shoulder and carried her upstairs where her clothes were laid out on her bed. He left her to dress while he shaved and put on his uniform.

Minutes later everyone was out the door with Windflower waving goodbye. He stayed behind so he could walk Lady and then make sure everything was turned off. Walking just a few blocks was not nearly enough for Lady, and she looked at Windflower with baleful eyes. "Sorry, girl," he said as he filled her bowl and Molly's, too, before starting off on his walk to work.

It was a nice sunny January morning, not hot and not too cold, especially for a brisk walk. But Windflower could feel the wind starting to blow. It wasn't a cold wind, like the ones that swooped down from the Arctic on Pink Lake in Northern Alberta, but a smooth, warm breeze. That wasn't a sign of good weather on the way though. In fact, it probably meant the direct opposite. Most of the storms crossing over Newfoundland came from the Eastern Seaboard of the United States. This time of year, that meant more snow and likely lots of it.

Windflower turned his collar up against the wind as if to try to deflect the storm. It was pointless. He could feel it coming, and when he looked up in the sky, he saw the clouds darken. 'Barren winter, with his wrathful nipping cold' is coming again, he thought. And not a darn thing we can do about it.

13

When Windflower got to work, there was a note to go see his boss immediately. He walked to her office and said good morning to her admin, Muriel Sparkes.

"Good morning, Sergeant," said Muriel. "Is everything okay? If you need anything just let me know."

"I'm fine, thanks," said Windflower. "Is she in?"

"She's on a call right now, but she should be free soon. Betsy tells me you've got a beautiful daughter," said Muriel.

"We have two girls now," said Windflower, and he showed Muriel some pictures on his phone. She was oohing and aahing at the pictures when Morecombe came out of her office.

"Good to see someone's having fun," said Morecombe. "Come in, Sergeant."

Windflower winked at Muriel and walked in behind Morecombe. She closed the door behind him.

"You've been given a new assignment," she said. "But you probably already know that. I have also been instructed to put our section at your disposal if you need us in your work."

"Thank you, ma'am," said Windflower.

"Five missing girls, maybe more. Two homicides," said Morecombe.

"Two? I only heard about one."

"Last night, here in St. John's. Reports said it might be a targeted shooting. It was a biker, but I don't have any more information. Do you have a contact at the RNC?"

"At the Constabulary? Yes, Detective Carl Langmead. We were supposed to meet tomorrow, but I'll call him today."

"Okay. You're free to assume your new assignment. You can pick up your training once that's completed. Let me know if there's anything you need."

"Thank you, ma'am. I was supposed to get a car today. I'll really need one to get around town."

"All I have right now is the public outreach van," said Morecombe. "That's your assigned vehicle. Muriel has your keys."

"I'm sure it'll be fine. Thank you," said Windflower.

"Here are your keys and your gas card," said Muriel after Windflower had left Morecombe's office. "If you'll just sign these papers." She handed Windflower a form that had to be initialled in four places and signed twice.

"Signing my life away," said Windflower as Muriel looked on.

"It's in the lot out back," she said. "You can't miss it."

Windflower walked out to the parking lot. Muriel was right. He couldn't miss it.

It was a white panel van with the RCMP stripes and logos prominently displayed all over it. Plus, there was foot-high lettering that said "RCMP Public Outreach: Helping Your Community." That and the full light package made it pretty easy to spot in a crowd, or to gather one if that's what you were interested in. That was definitely not what Windflower was interested in. He was starting what was sure to be a very difficult investigation that would require him to tread carefully, not boldly.

He thought about going back in and getting another car, but then he figured he might as well make the best of it. It would take days, if not weeks, to find another vehicle. He didn't have that kind of time. He sat in the van and looked around. At least it was clean and full of gas, and it had an online computer and an RCMP radio set. That's all he really needed. He pulled out his phone and called Langmead. Maybe he could fill him in on the latest death.

He found the general number for the Constabulary.

"Welcome to the Royal Newfoundland Constabulary," was the answer he got. He punched zero when the voice started giving him options. That took him right to the operator. He asked for Langmead, was directed to his voice mail and left a message. He's probably up to his neck in the murder, thought Windflower, so maybe I'll go for a drive while I'm waiting to hear back.

Windflower drove out of the RCMP parking lot and headed east. One of his favourite drives around St. John's was the one that took him around the coastline starting at Logy Bay. He turned off the main highway just past the city dump and started moving closer to the ocean. He passed by Memorial University's ocean sciences lab at Logy Bay, which he'd often visited to look at the marine specimens and then watch the seals playing out back.

He continued along the rugged coastline and towering cliffs and stopped at Middle Cove Beach to take a look around. He got out and stared at the ocean as it churned up waves and peaks of white foam. There was starting to be some white stuff floating around in the air too, so he decided to head back. As he was getting into his van, a couple stopped beside him. They waved and he smiled. Before he could leave, the man tapped on his window.

"Could we get a picture with you?" he asked.

"Sure," said Windflower, and he went to stand next to their car.

"No," the man said. "Can we take a selfie with you and the van?"

"Okay," said Windflower as the man and his wife stood next to him and snapped a few pictures on their phone.

"Thank you," said the woman when they were finished. "Too bad you didn't have your red serge uniform on with the hat. That would have been perfect."

Windflower smiled and got into his van. He realized that he may be on a murder investigation and looking for missing girls, but to the public he was the RCMP's community representative. This was going to be interesting, he thought. Very interesting.

His cell phone rang as he was about to leave. It was Langmead.

"Good morning, Carl," said Windflower. Just then he noticed the man and his wife were outside his van, and it looked like they were taking a video of him. "Excuse me for one sec," he said to Langmead.

"Can I help you?" he asked the couple.

"No, we're fine," said the man. "We're just filming the RCMP in action."

Windflower thought about telling him to go somewhere not very nice, but he resisted. "I have to leave now," he said, and he put the van into drive and went a little way up the road. He pulled over and picked up his phone.

"Are you okay?" asked Langmead.

"I will be," said Windflower.

14

Some guy and his wife wanted to take pictures of me talking to you on the phone," said Windflower to Langmead. "The lady even wondered where my dress uniform was."

Langmead laughed. "I can assure you we don't have that issue at the RNC. Most places we show up, people run away. How are you doing, anyway? Haven't spoken to you in quite a while. I hear you're in St. John's now."

"Temporarily," said Windflower. "But I'm doing well. My wife is back in school at Memorial, and we have a two-year old and a four-year old, as well. So, we're busy. You?"

"Busy, too," said Langmead. "Two boys, both in hockey. Got me run ragged b'y."

Windflower laughed. "What's the story on the latest vic?" he asked.

"Reggie Windsor," said Langmead. "He was an Outlaw prospect. Looked like he was moving up the food chain. They don't have anybody on the ground here, so they use the locals to conduct their business. They're fighting over the drug scene in St. John's with the original hoods, the ones supplied and backed by the Angels. Looks like Windsor got squeezed."

"Was he connected to the missing girls?"

"They run two of the strip clubs in town. Now the city has approved massage parlours too. Those are prime locations for trafficking."

"Did you hear about Freddy Hawkins?"

"Yeah, I just got an email from your boss, the inspector. He said we're still meeting tomorrow. That good for you?"

"Yeah, I'm good," said Windflower. "I'm going to see what I can find out about Freddy's death and the two girls missing from the Burin Peninsula."

"Okay, we'll see you tomorrow," said Langmead. "Good thing you're in St. John's now. Another storm coming on tonight."

After Windflower hung up, he could see that the snow had moved from a few flickering flakes into a steadier stream of white stuff. And the wind was picking up too. He drove down into Torbay and back into St. John's. He stopped for coffee at the Tim Hortons drive-through on Torbay Road. He ordered his coffee black, no sugar. He'd given up the milk and sugar some time ago and now couldn't stand the taste of a double-double.

He also ordered a partridgeberry muffin and sat in his van in the parking lot to enjoy his snack. A car drove by and waved at him. He waved back. Then another car, then another. After about 12 cars waving, he decided to leave. I hope I don't need to sneak up on anybody, he thought.

He drove back to the RCMP building in the White Hills, parked his van and went inside to his office. He phoned the Marystown RCMP, but Quigley was out. Then he remembered that Smithson was in Marystown.

Constable Rick Smithson was an energetic young officer Windflower had first met while working on that case out in Grand Falls with Lars Lundquist. Windflower had requested him to be posted in Grand Bank because he was a whiz with technology, and Windflower certainly was not. Over time he got to know Smithson a little and liked a whole lot about this young man.

One thing they had in common was a love of classical music. Windflower hadn't even heard much classical music before he got to Grand Bank, which seemed like a strange place to develop what many locals might consider an exotic taste. But Windflower got introduced to and educated in this form of music through Herb Stoodley, a really good friend in Grand Bank. Once Windflower knew that Smithson had studied music in university, they became close as well.

Now Smithson was working in Marystown. Just like Windflower had scooped him up from Grand Bank for his technical expertise, Inspector Ron Quigley had done the same for his office in Marystown. Windflower decided to call Smithson's cell phone.

"Sarge, how are you? How are things in the big city?" asked Smithson. He might have asked a hundred other questions, but Windflower cut him off short.

"I need your help," said Windflower. "I've been assigned to the Freddy Hawkins murder and the missing girls. Who's managing that file in your office?"

"I was on the missing girls," said Smithson. "But the inspector said you were going to handle the Hawkins case."

"Excellent," said Windflower. "So, you'll be working with me on both files. Tell me about the girls first."

"I've talked to the families. They're pretty upset. We haven't mentioned anything about human trafficking yet."

"I guess you better go back and tell them we've opened a file on all the missing girls and we're worried that it might be part of a ring. This will likely be all over the news soon, so it would be better if they heard it from you. Have you talked to their friends?"

"We've tried, but they're teenage girls, and they don't even want to be seen with us. Evanchuk had better luck with the Grand Bank girl. You should probably talk to her too."

"Okay. What I think we'd like to know is who they were hanging around with in the period before they went missing."

"Well, in Marystown that would be the local bikers," said Smithson. "They have a clubhouse on back of the old mall, where Riffs is. Used to be a club of some sort."

"The Pink Lady, a strip club. Shuttered long ago, around the time I first came to the area. Even then there were suspicions that Hells Angels were running the girls through there as part of their Atlantic circuit. What about Freddy Hawkins?"

"We don't have much yet, other than he was shot several times at his home. He lives alone, so no witnesses. I can go talk to the neighbours and see if somebody saw anything."

"Great," said Windflower. "Keep me posted."

"Nice working with you again, Sarge," said Smithson.

"Me too. Me too."

Windflower had barely hung up when his cell phone rang.

"Hello, Nephew," said Uncle Frank.

15

"Uncle Frank, nice to hear from you. How are you?" said Windflower.

"I am doing well," said his uncle. "I miss you and my friends in Grand Bank though. I had such a nice Christmas with you and your family. How is everybody?"

"We're all well, thank you. Sheila is back in school, and the girls are adjusting to their new lives in St. John's."

"And you, how are you doing? This is another transition for you."

"I'm okay, although I am glad you called. I've been having some interesting dreams lately."

"I know," said Uncle Frank. "You forget that we do have the power to enter other people's dreams, not to interfere but to monitor. I wasn't really looking for you. I was trying to reach your aunt."

"She came, too, in another dream. But it is the racoon dream that still puzzles me. What do you think it means?"

"You keep seeking answers outside of you when you have them in your heart already. It's your dreamworld. What do you suppose it means? Trust your intuition, my boy. Don't think, but let it come. Let it flow."

Windflower sat back in his chair and took a deep breath. "Well, it feels like a part of my life is in some kind of trouble and is calling out for help."

"Good," said his uncle. "Keep going."

"But maybe part of me is trying to cover that up and pretend that it's not happening, or that it's not real," said Windflower.

"That's the trickster part of you. Racoon can sometimes be a symbol of that part of us that wants to keep us in unhealthy situations or habits. Psychologists might call that false ego or something like that. But we trick ourselves into not trusting our heart and letting our minds run the show."

Windflower sat silent again for a few moments.

Uncle Frank continued. "The other thing to try and notice is when the things in your dreams start showing up on this side of the fence, in this world."

"Like a trickster?" asked Windflower.

"I think you're getting it, my boy. Anyway, I gotta go. I got some beef stew brewing on the stove, and there's a big snow coming tonight."

"Same here. Not the stew, just the snow. Thank you, Uncle. I love you. Call anytime."

"Goodbye," said Uncle Frank. "Give my love to Sheila and the girls."

After hanging up Windflower went to the cafeteria, picked up a sandwich for lunch and brought it back to his desk. He ate his sandwich with the rest of his coffee that he had warmed up in the microwave. He was hoping to go for a walk, but the snow had switched from intermittent to full speed, and the beginnings of snow drifts were circulating around the parking lot.

He called Sheila to check in, but there was no answer. He figured she might still be at school. He left a message and called Grand Bank instead.

Grand Bank was the small town that had been his home for the last nine years or so. He transferred in after a stint at the airport in Halifax where his work had led to his promotion to sergeant. He'd fallen in love with the place and with one beautiful Sheila Hillier, who at the time was the proprietor of the Mug-Up café. Normally he would have been rotated years ago, but circumstances and knowing the inspector personally had allowed him to continue running the RCMP detachment there.

Grand Bank was a special place with a long and proud history. It's been recorded that French fishermen were living in the small community on the southeast coast of Newfoundland at least as far back as 1640. They called the community Grand Banc, which got changed to Grand Bank when the British took over after one of a series of wars between the European powers. But its major claim to fame was as the traditional capital of the Banks Fishery that started in the 1880s and led rise to the famous Grand Bank schooners built and operated out of the town.

Today things were much different, but Grand Bank was still a very important place for Windflower. And it always would be. He was thinking about how much he missed it already when he heard Betsy Molloy answer the phone at the Grand Bank RCMP Detachment.

"Good morning, Betsy, how are you?" said Windflower.

"Sergeant, it's so nice to hear from you. Muriel says you're getting all squared away in St. John's," said Betsy. "We miss you very much. Corporal Lundquist is very nice, but he's just not you, sir."

"Thank you, Betsy, you're very kind. You'll like working with Corporal Lundquist. He's very professional. Are you getting the snow today?"

"Not too much. We don't get as much snow down here as in town."

"True. Is Constable Evanchuk there?"

"Yes, sir, I'll just put you through," said Betsy. "I hope you can help find those missing girls. Muriel told me you were looking after it. I said if anybody could find them, it would be Sergeant Windflower."

"Thank you, Betsy," said Windflower.

The next voice he heard was that of Constable Carrie Evanchuk.

"Good morning, Sergeant. Nice to hear from you, but I wish it was under better conditions. I'm guessing you want to talk about the missing girl."

"Yes, I do," said Windflower. "But first, how are you and that little baby growing inside you? And how's Eddie?" Evanchuk was about five months pregnant according to Windflower's very inaccurate reckoning, and Eddie was his former 2IC. Eddie Tizzard was almost like a son, or certainly a younger brother, to Windflower. Tizzard had struggled with being a Mountie after a series of unfortunate events that culminated in him being demoted and leaving the Force for a while. Now he was back, at least for the time being, and was partnered with Evanchuk at the RCMP in Grand Bank.

"The baby is fine and growing. Kicking me more than I'd like right now. But everything appears normal and on track. And Eddie is the same as ever," said Evanchuk.

"Great. So tell me about the missing girl from Grand Bank, Brittney Hodder," said Windflower, looking at his notes.

"It's all very sad," said Evanchuk. "The parents are heartbroken, and I almost hate going to see them. They keep searching my eyes for a sign when they see me. At first I thought they were looking for hope, but now they're expecting the worst. I've talked to her friends. They're almost useless. Some of them even seem envious that Brittney may be off on some glamorous adventure. But I did find one person who was helpful, a teacher, Kirk Pressland."

"What did he tell you?" asked Windflower.

"For some reason the Hodder girl confided in him. Something about male teachers that high school girls seem to trust. She told him that she was going to be an exotic dancer, that a guy she knew could set it up and even provide fake ID so she could get into clubs."

"Didn't the teacher try to talk her out of it? And why didn't he tell the parents?"

"He said he told her it was a crazy idea. But he never thought she would actually go through with it. That's why he kept her secret. He wanted her to continue to confide in him so he could stop her from doing anything stupid. It was a judgment call on his part. Bad judgment, I guess."

"Wow. Did he have any idea who the guy was?"

"He didn't know, but he thought a male student at the high school was involved. I'm asking around, but it's even harder getting the boys to talk than it is the girls. Eddie had an idea about maybe pulling a few of them in to talk to them at the office, but Lars, I mean Corporal Lundquist, suggested that might not be a great idea."

"Given what we know right now, he's probably right," said Windflower. "But if there was a suspicion of any of them dealing drugs, it might be a different story. I'm sure in that case the corporal would be fine with taking Eddie's approach."

"I'll talk to Corporal Lundquist when he comes back in," said Evanchuk. "Anything else for now?"

"No, but do let me know if you find out more. We've got a meeting tomorrow with the RNC to try to share as much as we have with each other, although what we have so far is that we only know there are five missing girls and two murders."

"That's awful about Freddy Hawkins. He was a bit creepy, but he didn't deserve to die."

"I agree. But 'golden lads and girls all must, as chimney-sweepers, come to dust.' Call me if you hear anything."

16

After Windflower hung up from Evanchuk, he looked out the window again. It was still snowing, maybe heavier than before. The difference this time was that almost all the cars were gone, except for his van, which stood out more than ever surrounded by all that white. He looked around the offices nearby, but everyone was gone. Obviously, he'd missed the memo about going home early. But he got the message now.

He packed up his stuff and was in the van when Sheila called to ask him to pick up pizza for supper.

"Absolutely," said Windflower. "You call Venice Pizza right now, and I'll pick it up on the way home. See you soon."

He drove through the streets that were filling with snow and the several cars that were now stuck in the spots where they'd been parked all day. He stopped once to give somebody a hand pushing their car out of a snowbank. It was the least he could do with an RCMP van that almost screamed "we're here to help." The pizzeria was busy, but he managed to find a parking spot in a nearby street and was soon on his way home with a small cheese pizza for Stella and Amelia Louise and a large combination for him and Sheila.

He was delighted that he managed to squeeze his van in the driveway behind Sheila's car, and everybody was equally happy to see him when he got in the door.

"You're just happy for the pizza," said Windflower.

"Well, there is that," said Sheila as she got the excited girls their drink and pizza. She gave Windflower half of the small Caesar salad that she'd picked up on her way home and a large slice of pizza.

Nobody spoke for the next few minutes until it was time for more pizza. Once they had that, everybody, except Stella, started talking at once.

"I talked to Uncle Frank today and Smithson and Carrie Evanchuk too," said Windflower.

"You've been busy," said Sheila. "And what's with the van? Are you going to be in a parade or something?"

"Pawade, pawade," said Amelia Louise, and she started laughing. Soon, Stella and Sheila were laughing too. Even Lady looked like she was laughing as she frantically wagged her tail. Only Molly didn't seem impressed. That would be un-catlike.

"Very funny," said Windflower. "It's only temporary, at least I hope it is. It feels like I am driving around in a fishbowl, and everybody can look in and see me. Everybody waves to me like I'm their personal police officer."

"What part of outreach don't you understand, Sergeant?" asked Sheila. "Anyway, Uncle Frank first. How is he?"

"Frank is good," said Windflower, reaching for the second last piece of pizza. "He said he misses Grand Bank and to give you a hug. Smithson is good too. I recruited him to help me on my case."

"He'd be happy about that," said Sheila. "He worships you like a puppy dog looks up to her mistress." With that Lady turned her attention away from the hopes of a scrap of pizza crust from Stella back to Sheila.

"No, we have a working relationship," said Windflower.

"Yeah, like master and slave. How is Carrie?"

"She's good too. Says she feels better and the baby is kicking. I got her working for me as well."

"Pretty soon you'll have the whole Grand Bank crew in action."

"I hadn't planned it that way, but I like the sound of it," agreed Windflower. "Anyway, Evanchuk's been talking to a teacher at the school who knew the Hodder girl. He said that he thinks one of the boys in school might be mixed up in all this."

"I'm not surprised. Teenage girls are unpredictable, but teenage boys are crazy and reckless. Do they know which one?"

"Not yet. But Evanchuk is going to get Tizzard to help her."

"How's the new guy doing in Grand Bank?"

"Lars will be okay. Betsy said he's nice but not as good as me."

Sheila laughed. "Another one under your spell," she said.

Windflower pretended he was insulted. "'But if it be a sin to covet honour, I am the most offending soul alive.'"

"Please," said Sheila.

"Pleeze," repeated Amelia Louise.

"Now you're turning my own daughter on me," said Windflower. "Can't a man get a little respect in his own house?"

"Pleeze," said Amelia Louise again.

"Exactly," said Sheila. "'And whatever praises itself but in the deed, devours the deed in the praise.'"

"Oooh, that hurts," said Windflower.

"No cry, Daddy," said Amelia Louise.

"Okay, who wants some cake?" asked Sheila. "Raise your hand."

Everybody raised their hand, and Sheila went to the fridge and pulled out a large white cardboard box. Everyone cheered and then cheered again when she took the chocolate cake out and started cutting it up. There were smaller pieces for Stella and Amelia Louise and a large one for Windflower.

"None for you?" asked Windflower.

"I'll have mine with my tea once we get them settled down," said Sheila. "It looks like we might have a snow day tomorrow. I don't have classes 'til after lunch, so I think I'll stay here in the morning with the girls. I can get Mo from down the street to come in the afternoon."

"I've got a meeting in the morning, but I'm not sure if Ron can get here through the snow. He may have a problem getting here in time for the meeting. I'll give him a call. Maybe we can shift the meeting to the afternoon, and we can all have a snow day, or at least a snow morning."

"Schnow, schnow, schnow," started Amelia Louise, and before long all of them were sing-songing along. Even the normally quiet Stella clapped her hands to join in the fun.

Sheila took the girls upstairs while Windflower cleaned up the dishes and let Lady out in the back. The collie struggled to get through the snow but managed to accomplish her mission and get back to the doorway. Windflower brushed a lot of the snow off her, but she still managed to spray quite a bit on the kitchen floor. Windflower wiped that up and went upstairs for story time.

Sheila had the girls in the adults' bedroom and was reading to Stella from a book suitable for her age, and Amelia Louise was watching them intently. Windflower picked up Amelia Louise and carried her over his head, much to her delight, to her bedroom.

"You pick a story tonight," he said as he plopped her in front of the shelf that held her books. Amelia Louise took her time and started pulling out all the books.

"Just one," said Windflower, holding up one single index finger.

The little girl hemmed and hawed and looked back at her dad. He held up his finger again. "One book," he said.

Finally, Amelia Louise picked a book and handed it to him. "Mila hippo," she said.

"That's pretty clear," said Windflower. "And a very good choice." The Hiccupotamus was a story about a group of friends—a centipede, an elephant and a rhinoceros—that tries to help cure a hippo's case of hiccups. Amelia Louise loved the book and would hic, hic, hic along with the hippo every time. After three times through, she was ready to stop, and Windflower kissed her goodnight and put her to bed.

17

Sheila was downstairs having her cake, and Windflower joined her with a cup of tea before taking Lady out for her last walk of the evening. The snow was starting to thin a little, but the wind kept whipping it up in their faces. That made for an unpleasant and rather short walk. When he got back, Sheila had gone upstairs, and Windflower was starting to turn out the lights when his cell phone rang.

"Hey, Ron, how's she going b'y?" asked Windflower.

"It's going rather slowly I'm afraid," said Quigley. "I'm going to bunk down for the night in Whitbourne. It was fine coming up from Marystown, but I hit the snow at Swift Current and have been struggling ever since. They've closed the highway just east of here, so I guess I'm stuck."

"It's still snowing a lot here," said Windflower, "though it's easing off a bit. We got a lot on the ground. It's the second storm in a week. I suspect I'll be snowed in tomorrow morning."

"Let's push our meeting off 'til the afternoon," said Quigley. "I'll call Langmead."

"That would be better for me. I've been talking to some people down in Marystown and Grand Bank about the situation."

"That's what I hear. Smithson said he had to help you out."

"It's very kind of you to allow him. It looks like another turf war, but as usual there appears to be a lot of willing participants in the community. Evanchuk told me she thinks some of the high school boys are involved. She and Tizzard are going to dig deeper. It'll be interesting to see what Langmead and the RNC have to say."

"Indeed. I'll send you a text to confirm the time."

"Perfect," said Windflower. "Drive safely."

"'Fortune, good night. Smile once more. Turn thy wheel,'" said Quigley.

All Windflower could think of to say in return was 'to die, to sleep; to sleep: perchance to dream,' but that seemed a bit weird, so he just said goodnight instead.

He couldn't figure out why that came into his head until he woke up a few hours later in a dream.

The racoon was back. Windflower could see his eyes in the darkness.

"What do you want?" asked the racoon.

"It's my dream. I get to ask the questions," said Windflower.

"Who are you? Some kind of trickster?" said the racoon, and he started to cackle like an old woman.

"What are you? A witch?" asked Windflower.

"I tell you what. I'll give you three questions."

"Do you promise to tell the truth?"

"That's one." And the racoon started to cackle again but stopped short when he saw the look on Windflower's face.

"Is there a girl or girls in danger?" asked Windflower.

"Yes," said the racoon.

"Where are they?"

The racoon studied Windflower closely. "I'm not supposed to talk about things that are happening over there."

"You said three questions. You didn't make conditions," said Windflower.

The racoon grumbled under his breath. "I can give it to you in a riddle."

"No, no more games."

"You want it or not?"

"Give it to me," said Windflower wearily.

"Under a bridge by the river that sings, hangs a life in the balance by a soft silver thread. And over the brook past the watery fowl, is a clue to where she is living right now." And with that the racoon started running down a dark hallway. Windflower followed as fast as he could, but he was losing ground and finally collapsed on the hallway floor.

He woke in his bed drenched in sweat and panting.

"Are you all right?" asked Sheila.

"I think so," said Windflower. "It was just a dream."

But he knew that it was more than a dream. It was a message, one he had to figure out quickly. But he couldn't do that right now. Sheila moved towards him and held him. Despite his anxious state, just having her beside him calmed him enough to fall asleep.

But when he woke in the morning, the dream was the first thing on his mind. He snuck out of bed and checked outside. The snow was still falling. It was much lighter than before though, and the good news was that the wind had finally died down. The bad news was the six-foot drift across his driveway and no sign city services had even attempted to plow the road. Definitely a snow day, he thought.

Windflower got the coffee ready—lots of it—and plugged in the percolator. He put on his coat and boots and pushed his way out the back door with Lady at his heels. He hadn't brought his smudge kit with him this morning. Instead, he brought a pipe. But it wasn't just any pipe. It was his Auntie Marie's pipe, and before she died, she had asked Uncle Frank to give it to Windflower.

It was a beautiful ceremonial pipe with a long wooden handle and a catlinite, or pipestone, bowl. Auntie Marie had told Windflower that she used the pipe to connect to Creator and to the spirit world. He had only used it once before, but he felt that it would be a good morning to use it again. He put a small amount of sacred tobacco into the bowl and lit it. He gave a few puffs to get it going and then let the smoke from the pipe curl around him.

The backyard and even all the snow almost started to melt in the vapours. He could feel something, maybe someone, near him, but it was all very vague, more like a sensation than anything else. He took a deep breath and remembered what his aunt had told him about not trying to see but to feel instead. He closed his eyes and felt a hand on his shoulder and another touching his face. Finally, a message came, not in words but in a kind of emotion. Use your heart and not your head.

He let himself drift and allowed his heart to feel. First, he felt a tightening all around him and tried to move his hands, but they were tied behind his back. He looked around him and saw a window.

He pulled himself up and looked out. He saw water flowing and a bridge in the distance. He heard voices, and they sounded like they were coming towards him. A door opened, and in a blinding light everything vanished.

Windflower rubbed his eyes and tried to figure out if what he had just experienced was real or if he'd somehow imagined all of it. But as he came more and more out of the dream-like state, he felt his Auntie beside him and her voice in his ear, as though she were telling him that she was with him on the journey. When he finally came back to his normal self, Lady was staring at him with a worried dog look on her face. "I'm okay, girl," he said. "Let's go inside."

18

Windflower poured himself a cup of coffee and heard activity from upstairs. When he went up, Sheila was still in bed, but Stella and Amelia Louise were playing with their dolls in Stella's bedroom.

"Mila dolly," said Amelia Louise. "Daddy dolly?" she asked as she put the most battered Barbie at his feet.

What was a dad to do? Windflower sat on the floor and played with his girls until Sheila woke and came to see what all the noise was about.

"We're playing dollies, obviously," said Windflower. "There's coffee."

Sheila went for a coffee while Windflower continued his games with the children. Next was dress-up, and Stella went through her closet and dressers to find things that Amelia Louise could wear. There was quite a lot, and by the time Sheila came back up to see about breakfast, there was a huge pile on the floor.

"What are you doing?" she asked Windflower.

"Playing dress-up?" said Windflower a little carefully. "How about if I make breakfast? Scrambled eggs with some of that smoked salmon we have left?"

"If you couldn't cook, we'd have to throw you out," said Sheila. "Go."

Windflower cooked the eggs with smoked salmon and sliced some strawberries and bananas while he was waiting for the toast. When it was all done, he called out, "Breakfast is ready."

All he could hear were feet scrambling across the ceiling above him and then a thundering like galloping hooves coming down the stairs from the two girls followed by Sheila.

"This is delish," said Sheila.

"Mila delish," said Amelia Louise.

"It's her new version of 'mine'," said Windflower. "Maybe having Stella around has helped her become a little grabby."

"That's just the phase she's going through," said Sheila. "And we're not calling her Mila. It sounds too old for a little girl."

"Mila, Mila, Mila," said Amelia Louise, as if to contradict her mom.

"If you say so," said Windflower. "Hey, since it's an official snow day and school is cancelled, why don't we stay in our pajamas."

"You are such a kid," said Sheila. "'Woe to the land that's governed by a child.'"

"'The most sophisticated people I know—inside they are all children.'"

"Mister Rogers?" asked Sheila.

"Close," said Windflower. "Jim Henson from the Muppets. But let's ask the experts, shall we? PJs? What do you guys think?" he asked the girls.

"Mila peejay," said Amelia Louise.

"See, it's unanimous," said Windflower when Stella shook her head yes. "We can leave our pajamas on, and when we go out, we'll put our snowsuits on over them."

"You go put on a show for them while I clean up," said Sheila. "Then we can all go outside and make a snowman."

Windflower found Blue's Clues on TV, and he and the girls settled in on the couch together. When Sheila was finished, she joined them with another cup of coffee for herself and Windflower.

"I love these days," said Windflower. "It's kind of like we stole them from reality to live out our fantasies."

"Well, not exactly my fantasy, but I know what you mean. Sometimes we're so busy we don't have the time—or we forgot why we have it—to share it like this," said Sheila.

"I guess it's about how we use it," said Windflower. "Tagore said, 'The butterfly counts not months but moments, and has time enough.'"

"That's beautiful," said Sheila. "Now, let's go play in the snow."

"Schnow, schnow, schnow," was started again by Amelia Louise, and she led everybody upstairs to put on sweaters over their pajamas and back downstairs to put on their snowsuits.

It took Windflower and Sheila both to keep Amelia Louise still enough to get her suit on, and when they looked over, Stella was sitting on a chair, patiently waiting for them.

"Amazing," said Windflower. "You got dressed all by yourself."

Stella smiled in return.

"That's one of the first things they teach them in kindergarten," said Sheila. "How to put their snowsuit and jackets on and how to tie up their shoes."

"Stella probably already got that lesson from some of her other foster homes," said Windflower. "They wouldn't want to be bothered with that all the time."

"Okay, let's go," said Sheila, and she opened the door to the backyard. Well, she tried to open the door to the backyard. There was so much snow out back that Windflower had to take a shovel and walk around to clear enough for Sheila and the girls to get out and for a none-too-patient Lady to escape.

Amelia Louise, dressed like a mummy and wrapped from head to toe, tumbled over the back steps and fell into the snow. She got up laughing, and thought it was so much fun that she did it again. And again and again, with Stella right beside her every time.

Windflower and Sheila started rolling a big snowball for the base of their snowman, or as Sheila suggested, their snowwoman. Given that it was a woman, Windflower said they could make it a little smaller, and everyone agreed. Stella and Amelia Louise 'helped' a lot, but despite that, their mounds of snow eventually started to take shape, and the snowwoman was ready for decoration.

Sheila went inside and came back with three large black felt circles from her craft basket for the snowwoman's buttons, a few old hats to choose from, including a sou'wester, and a large carrot for the nose. The girls pushed the felt buttons into the snow, and Windflower secured them. The girls and Sheila decided it was a Newfoundland snowwoman, so they opted for the sou'wester. Amelia Louise got lifted up to put the hat on Mildred, as she was christened. And Stella was assigned the task of putting the carrot in for her nose, but first they had to chase Lady, who thought for sure that this was her treat for the taking.

Once Stella had put the nose on Mildred, they all stood back to admire their work.

"Not bad," said Sheila. "I've seen better and I've seen worse."

"I think she's perfect," said Windflower.

"Purrfect," echoed Amelia Louise.

19

Back in the house Windflower made everyone hot chocolate with marshmallows, and Sheila got the kids ready for a bath. Windflower helped clean up the mess they'd made in the kitchen and hallway and was going upstairs when the phone rang.

"Hey, Winston, how's she going b'y?" asked Quigley.

"It's great," said Windflower.

"We're on at one o'clock with Langmead. I'm just getting into town now," said Quigley.

"Okay. But can you pick me up? I don't think I can get out of my driveway. I've got a service, but he isn't here yet. And I'd say there's a couple of hours worth of shovelling out there."

"No worries. I'll be there in about an hour. You're on Forest Road, right?"

Windflower gave him the number and hung up. He looked around on the fridge for the snow clearing number and called it.

"Due to the high demand for service, we may have some delays in getting to your call today. Please be patient, and we will be there as soon as we can," was the message.

Windflower went upstairs where Sheila was just taking the girls out of the bath. "Ron called and he's going to pick me up. I called the snow guys, and they say it's slow but they're coming."

"Okay," said Sheila. "If they don't come by the time I'm ready, I'll get a taxi. Mo is coming over soon."

"Excellent," said Windflower. "I'm going to have my shower and get dressed."

Almost an hour later Windflower was sitting in the living room while the girls built something out of their massive box of Lego. The doorbell rang, and he could see it was Mo, the girl from a few doors down whom Sheila had recruited as their babysitter. She'd been over once before and the girls loved her. They ran to the door with Lady to greet her.

"Mo's here," Windflower called to Sheila as he brought the teenager into the living room. Immediately she started playing Lego with Stella and Amelia Louise. "Oh, you're building a rocket ship," said Mo.

"I knew that," said Windflower as he heard a car outside. He checked and it was Quigley. He waved to him and told Sheila he was leaving. He gave the two girls a kiss on the top of their heads and walked to the door. Only Lady followed him out. He went back and gave her a Milk Bone biscuit for her loyalty. And because Molly was staring him down, he gave her a treat too. "I'm not afraid of you," he said to Molly. But she simply turned her back to him and held her tail in the air.

"You got lots of snow," said Quigley.

"It's the second dump this week," said Windflower. "What is with this place and snow?"

"We get lots in St. John's," said Quigley. "I can remember as a kid walking to school on top of snowbanks that were as high as the telephone wires. The good news about the weather here is that it will change sooner than you think."

"I know about that. We can get all four seasons in one day."

"This snow will be all gone by the end of the week except for the few piles that are stacked up. It's going to rain starting tomorrow and rain, drizzle and fog for the rest of the week."

"That's something to look forward to. RDF for the whole week."

"Let's go for coffee before the meeting. There's a Tim's right next to the cop shop."

"I know the spot. I've been there before."

Quigley drove them up Kings Bridge Road and then onto Military Road on the other side of Bannerman Park. They went up past the Basilica and close to The Rooms, the provincial museum and archives. "Have you been up there yet?" asked Quigley.

"Not this time around," said Windflower. "But I want to take the girls soon. Amelia Louise is a bit small, but Stella would really like it."

"How's she fitting in with your little family?" asked Quigley.

"She's been really good, especially with Amelia Louise. But she doesn't talk much, hardly at all."

"Have you taken her to see somebody?"

"Not yet. It's not that she can't talk. We've heard her. It's that she usually won't."

"Here's our stop," said Quigley as he slid into a parking spot near the door at the Tim Hortons on Harvey Road. The two Mounties went in and Quigley treated by buying their coffee. Windflower secured a table for them at the window and took a seat facing out. The view was stunning. From his perch he could see right out into St. John's Harbour. He even watched a pilot boat bring a container ship in through The Narrows.

"What a view," said Ron Quigley. "And we're sitting in a coffee shop to get it."

"It's pretty amazing," said Windflower. "That's called The Narrows, right?"

"Right. It's the only entrance by sea to St. John's and at its narrowest point is only 61 metres across. That pilot ship out there is doing what's called 'threading the eye of the needle' to bring that container ship to port. It has served this city well over the years, first by stopping pirates who wanted to loot and plunder, and then in the Second World War, they put a steel mesh across The Narrows to keep out the German U-Boats."

The men finished their coffee and drove the short distance to the nearby Royal Newfoundland Constabulary building. The building itself was new, but the RNC, or Constabulary, had been around a long time. Windflower read a plaque on the wall that claimed that the RNC was the oldest police force in Canada, dating back to 1729. But it only officially became Newfoundland Constabulary in 1871. The Queen then granted the prefix "Royal" to it in 1979.

"So it started even before the RCMP," said Windflower. "I didn't know that."

"Yeah," said Quigley. "The forerunner to the Mounties, the North-West Mounted Police, wasn't formed until about 1873. In 1904 it became Royal, and only in 1920 did it officially become the Royal Canadian Mounted Police."

The two got out of Quigley's vehicle and lifted their collars against the cold. Once inside, the senior Mountie got them their visitors' badges and an escort to Langmead's office on the third floor.

20

Langmead brought Windflower and Quigley to a small boardroom on the floor. Two other RNC officers were waiting for them.

"Brian Hayes and Anne Marie Foote, meet Inspector Ron Quigley and Sergeant Winston Windflower. Hayes and Foote have been working with me on this file," said Langmead. "Hayes is on gangs and drugs, and Foote is our new person on human trafficking."

"Why don't you tell us what you have first?" said Quigley. "And we'll fill in our pieces. Sergeant Windflower just got assigned, so he's getting up to speed."

"Okay. Hayes, you go first," said Langmead.

"We have some local bikers but not a major gang situation yet in St. John's," said Hayes. "The Avalon Riders, who are the puppets for the Outlaws, do some dealing, and there's a number of smaller operators who connect back up with their suppliers. Years ago they would've been quasi-independent too. But now everybody has backup. What's developed is almost a free market, except that the bikers, Angels and Outlaws, each supply and try to control about half of the independents. And both of them would like to have more of the pot. That's likely what happened to Reggie Windsor."

"And the girls?" asked Quigley.

"We haven't been really able to deal with that aspect," said Hayes. "We've had our hands full with the drugs. All we know is that like everything else, the Angels were running that operation too, and the Outlaws were trying to move in, but Foote can talk more about that."

Foote took her cue. "Ever since the offshore oil boom, there's been a growing sex trade," she said. "We've always had strip clubs and some escorts, but it really took off once there was real money here. The Angels were running all the girls on the East Coast for years and were supplying the scene here, but when it got big, they started recruiting locally as well. Now what happens is we have both Outlaws and Angels trying to recruit girls and stealing them from each other."

Langmead jumped in. "That's also when we started seeing the biker disputes spill out into the open. The local bikers were all Angels affiliates, and the Outlaws, as you know, set up out in Grand Falls and started creeping eastwards."

"They're everywhere now," said Quigley. "Even down in our area. Last year we even had some skinheads trying to get involved in the meth trade."

"I guess business is tough, so they're fighting over everything, including the girls," said Langmead. "Tell them how this whole thing works," he said to Foote.

"Both crews have been actively recruiting local girls, some from St. John's but most from outside of town," said Foote. "They give them booze and drugs, show them the party and then ask them to work. Usually it starts with stripping, which is a bit of a grind but not unbearable, and then they're asked to service specific clients. As they get more experienced, they're moved into escort agencies or massage parlours full time. By then, it's no longer a choice."

"We've also had a targeted shooting and a few drive-bys," said Langmead. "One dead and several more in hospital."

"We've got two dead guys," said Quigley. "A local biker and a lawyer who likely got himself in too deep with the wrong people. Sergeant Windflower just started his investigation."

"Not much to go on yet," said Windflower. "Still early days. But we've got a few people to talk to about the missing girls. We think that some local boys are involved in recruiting."

"Not surprised," said Foote. "The boys think it's some kind of game, and they do it for kicks and a bag of dope or a case of beer. We had one case here in St. John's where one guy set up his girlfriend as an escort and got her to recruit a few of her friends."

"And we talked to a girl who got out," said Langmead. "She got picked up in Ottawa and told the police she was being trafficked. She was from Corner Brook and started out when she was just fifteen. She was nineteen when she finally got back home."

"They take them to Quebec and run them through the small-town circuit where there's few questions asked," said Foote. "Then they move 'em into Montreal and Ottawa. That's Angels territory. But now with the Outlaws, they send them to Toronto where they work out of massage parlours and airport hotels."

"So, it looks like we know roughly how they operate," said Quigley. "Now we need to figure out how to stop them."

"Do we know if any of the missing girls are still in the area?" asked Windflower.

"We're not really sure," said Langmead.

"So why don't we check all the airport records to make sure? We have a techie guy who can search the records for us," said Windflower. "If you send Constable Rick Smithson in Marystown a list of the girls and the approximate date they were reported missing, along with a photograph, he can start the search."

"That's good," said Langmead. "Hayes, will you look after that? From our end we'll start pulling in all the usual suspects, anybody connected to the bikers that we can lean on. If any of them are still here, there should be somebody who knows something."

"And I think it's time to rachet up the media and the public on this," said Quigley. "If you guys want, I can have our comms section work with you to put together a media release about us working together."

"I like that idea," said Langmead. "Foote, you work with Windflower to set that up."

"I think this is a very good move," said Foote. "Because I think this is just the beginning of a local recruitment drive, and we'll need everybody to be vigilant, especially parents and family members."

"Okay, are we good for now?" asked Quigley.

"We're good," said Langmead. "Here's my cell," he said to Windflower as he handed him a card. Windflower passed one back to him.

"Look forward to working with you all," said Quigley, and he stood to leave, stopping to shake hands with all the RNC officers on the way out. Windflower did the same and followed Quigley and Langmead to the elevator.

"We'll talk," said Langmead as he left them at the elevator and went back to the boardroom.

"That went well," said Quigley while they walked out the front door of the Constabulary building. "I'm hungry. Do you want to have lunch?"

"I can eat," said Windflower. "I can always eat."

"Fish and chips?"

"Perfect."

21

They left Quigley's car in the parking lot, walked down Harvey Road and turned up Freshwater Road.

"I know where we're going," said Windflower. "Leo's."

Leo's Restaurant had been around for a long time. Ron Quigley had introduced it to Windflower a few years back, and a trip to St. John's was not complete without a visit for the fabulous fish and chips.

The two ordered the same: fish and chips with dressing and gravy. It was a St. John's thing, Quigley had explained to him, the dressing and gravy concoction. But Windflower loved it when he first tried it. The dressing soaked up the gravy and was a perfect fit for the fish and golden-brown french fries.

"I used to live up around the corner on Mayor Avenue," said Quigley. "My mom would send me down for fish and chips every Friday. But we were always in this area, riding our bikes or on the way back and forth to school. In the summer we would see local fishermen come up to the back door here with codfish that had been caught in the morning. That's how fresh it was."

"Wow," said Windflower as the waitress brought them their order. Their plates were barely visible under two huge pieces of deep-fried cod with a mound of fries topped with another mound of gravy and dressing. Windflower poured malt vinegar over it all and added a hefty hand of salt. Then he tried one fry and dipped it in the gravy.

"Man, this is wonderful," he said.

"The fish is super good today," said Quigley. "It tastes fresh. They must have a local supplier."

"Yeah, sometimes the local shops in Grand Bank can get some

fresh codfish too," said Windflower. "Not too many people fishing there anymore, but there's still quite a few in Fortune. They have quotas for their fish and have to send it to designated plants for processing. But a little is reserved for the restaurants and takeouts."

"People gotta have their fish and chips b'y."

There wasn't much more talking as they worked through their plates of food. At the end Windflower paid. "My treat," said Windflower. Quigley thanked him, and they walked back to his car at the Constabulary.

"Can I get a lift home?" asked Windflower.

"Sure, your car should be unburied by now," said Quigley. "Oh, nice move to commandeer Smithson, by the way."

"I need him, Inspector."

"We all need him. I just thought it was smooth to voluntell me that he was going to be working with you full-time."

"The Inspector doth protest too much, me thinks," said Windflower. "You are the one who assigned me and then offered this joint work with the Constabulary."

"Fair enough," said Quigley. "Just remember that I did you a favour. It is sharper than a serpent's tooth to have a thankless Sergeant."

Quigley laughed as he turned right and drove down Forest Road to Windflower's house. They passed the Miller Centre again. "Bill Ford is coming tomorrow," he said. "Weather permitting, of course."

"Great," said Windflower. "I'll go by and see him. If he stays over, I'll bring the girls on the weekend."

"Oh he's moving in. Depending on how the rehab goes, it could be anywhere from a few weeks to a few months. Here's your stop. And it looks like you're in luck. The driveway's clear."

"Thank you, Ron. I'm sorry, I forgot to ask earlier, but you're welcome to come for dinner."

"Thank you, but I'm heading back right now. Maybe next time. Wish me luck on the roads."

Windflower waved goodbye to Quigley and got his keys out to start his van. Sheila's car was still there, so she must have taken a taxi to school. He could call and pick her up. He brushed the snow off the two vehicles. He decided not to go inside because that might just cause a disruption for Mo, and he was sure she had everything under control. He started the van and drove to his office.

When he got there, he called Sheila and made plans to pick her up at the university at five. Next, he went to see Morecombe to talk about his meeting with the RNC and to see about getting help with the joint media release. Quigley had already talked to her.

"I'm assigning Terry Robbins to work with you," said Morecombe. "But just so you know, Sergeant, I don't work for Inspector Quigley or you."

"Okay," said Windflower.

"Great, I'll send Robbins over to see you in the morning."

"Super." Windflower smiled at Morecombe as he walked away and then said a friendly hello to Muriel. No point getting into a rock-throwing contest here, he thought. He didn't even know where the rock pile was located. When he got back to his office, his cell phone rang.

"Eddie Tizzard, how are you?" he asked.

"B'y if I was any better, I'd be dead in heaven," said Tizzard. "How's life in the big city?"

"So far, so good," said Windflower. "I just had lunch with Inspector Quigley. Fish and chips."

"Leo's? I love that place," said Tizzard. "I'm not jealous of much in St, John's, but I am about that. Anyway, I wanted to call you about the boys in Grand Bank who might be involved with the missing girl. I talked to the school principal."

"What did he have to say?"

"It wasn't so much what he said as what he's prepared to do. He's going to make an announcement over the public address system in the school asking if anyone knows anything about Brittney Hodder to come forward."

"That will shake them up."

"Yeah. After he makes the announcement, we're going to go in, and we're going to pull out all the kids we suspect of dealing drugs at the school. Just to talk to them. Let them know we're watching. We're hoping all that will spook the other kids to start naming the guilty parties."

"Good strategy."

"We have a small issue here, though. You'll need to talk to Lars, I mean Corporal Lundquist. He's questioning why we're doing so much on this when it's your case."

"Okay, I'll talk to him," said Windflower. "I talked to Carrie, and she seems to be doing well."

"She's great. I can hardly wait to get home to feel the baby kick," said Tizzard.

"Boy or girl, do you know yet?"

"We've decided we don't want to know. I have a feeling it's a girl, and Carrie is sure it's a boy. We'll have to wait to paint their room until after they're born."

"Well, good luck. Let me know how it goes at the school."

Windflower almost said "I miss you" as hung up the call. Because he really did miss Eddie and the Grand Bank detachment. He thought about what was going on with Lundquist and also about his recent encounter with Morecombe. It wasn't shaping up to be the spirit of cooperation he'd been hoping for. And it was certainly something to watch as he moved forward.

He didn't have much time to think about that, though, because his cell phone rang. It was Smithson.

22

Hey, Sarge. I just got this info dump from St. John's. What exactly do you want me to do with it?" asked Smithson.

"Let me open my computer and we can talk," said Windflower. He flipped open his laptop, powered up and found the email from Hayes. It was stark and a little chilling to see the pictures of the five missing girls all together. "Okay, got it," he said.

"So, what do you want me to do?" asked Smithson again.

"Can you check the airports in Gander and St. John's from a week before the date the girls went missing up 'til now? See if any of these names show up in the passenger manifests. Check the ferry in Port-aux-Basques too. They may have used that route."

"Okay. Have these girls been put on the wire across Canada?"

"I don't know. Check and see, and if they haven't, can you get them up? Maybe somebody has seen them. Good point."

"Also, I talked to Evanchuk, and she is going to come here to Marystown and help me talk to some of the girls Mandy Pardy hung around with."

"That's good. Maybe check out some of the boys as well. We think some boys in Grand Bank might be involved in this," said Windflower. "Anything more on Freddy Hawkins?"

"One of the neighbours heard a motorcycle in the area the night Hawkins died. She said she couldn't see the person's face, but it was a man with some kind of lettering on his jacket."

"Keep digging. Let me know if you find anything from your airport searches. It would be good to know for sure if any or all of them have already been shipped out."

"There could be another possibility," said Smithson.

"We're not even going to consider that until we rule everything else out," said Windflower. "Talk to you soon."

He couldn't go there. Not even think about that. Not yet. In his mind this was still a rescue operation. They would go to recovery if they had to. But not yet.

Windflower spent the last hours at work going through the information and the files sent by the RNC. Maybe he could see something that others missed. Maybe a pattern. Maybe a clue. But nothing. Just before five o'clock he closed his computer and drove to the university to pick up Sheila.

He drove up Elizabeth Avenue and turned into the campus of Memorial University of Newfoundland, commonly known as MUN. He went to the back and pulled into the library entrance. The QE II, or Queen Elizabeth II Library, was the main library on campus, and it was huge, towering over the parkway. Windflower watched the main entrance, and when he saw Sheila emerge, he drove to the door to get her.

Windflower thought Sheila looked beautiful as she came across the sidewalk and got into the car, and he told her so.

"That's very nice, Winston. Flattery will get you everywhere," she said. "I thought I could drop by the supermarket on the way home and pick up a roast chicken and a salad for dinner. Are you hungry?"

Windflower didn't want to own up to his fish and chips, but he also didn't want to lie, so he told the truth. "I can always eat," he said.

"Great, that's supper then, and enough for lunches in the morning too. Anything new with you?"

"Lots of meetings and stuff. I saw Ron Quigley, and he's going back tonight. I talked to Tizzard and Smithson too. And Bill Ford is coming to the Miller Centre tomorrow."

"Wow, there's lots going on. How's Eddie?"

"He sounded great. He's really excited about becoming a dad. I'm going to try to get over to see Bill tomorrow. I was thinking about taking the girls over on the weekend."

"That sounds okay," said Sheila as they pulled up to the door of the supermarket. "I'll be right back."

True to her word she was back in a flash with a chicken and a large box of salad. "I'll cut up some cucumber and carrots for the girls too," she said.

Minutes later they were at their house, and while Sheila organized their meal, Windflower paid Mo and helped extricate her from two clingy little girls. Once Mo was free, they grabbed Windflower and held him hostage until supper was on the table.

After dinner Windflower took Lady for a long walk around the neighbourhood all the way up to the hotel, around Government House and back down Empire Avenue to home. Both Lady and Windflower were grateful for the exercise and fresh air. When they got back, he read to Stella while Sheila looked after duties with Amelia Louise.

Tonight for some reason Stella wanted one of Amelia Louise's books, Goodnight Moon. Windflower and Stella had to sneak it out of the younger girl's room so she wouldn't notice. Stella liked that game, and she loved the book. She got Windflower to read it twice and then settled down for the night. But Windflower noticed, not for the first time, that as much as Stella enjoyed the book, she pointed to the mouse and the cow and the moon without saying any of the words.

Windflower went downstairs and put on the kettle to boil while he waited for Sheila. When it was ready, he put a tea bag in the pot and brought the tray with two cups out to the living room. Sheila joined him soon after.

"Stella doesn't really talk at all," said Windflower. "Maybe we should have her see somebody?"

"I talked to her teacher earlier this week. She said that she would monitor Stella and let me know if there was any progress. She said she had another child last year with a similar problem. She said that child had something called selective mutism."

"What is that?" asked Windflower.

"She gave me a handout. I'll go find it," said Sheila. She came back soon after with a sheet of paper. "It says that children who have selective mutism have difficulty speaking in social situations, like school for example. But when they feel safe, like at home, they may not have any difficulty at all."

"I guess that means she still isn't fully comfortable around us yet. That's understandable. It hasn't been that long."

"Exactly. Let's wait and see how it goes at school. She's still adjusting. I will keep in contact with the teacher."

"Okay."

"I'm going to bed. Will you turn everything off?"

"I will," said Windflower as he carried the tea tray back to the kitchen. He let Lady out for her final turn in the backyard. When he opened the door, a mild and pleasant wind blew in. That's nice, thought Windflower, until he opened it a little further to let Lady back in and got hit in the face with a driving rain. Lady shook herself and sprayed him to finish him off. Windflower laughed and went to bed.

Sheila was in bed reading but turned the light out and moved towards him when he got in. Windflower relaxed and listened to the rain on the roof sing him to sleep. That night, there were no dreams, only lots of sleep until the alarm went off to signal the start of a new day.

Windflower made coffee and started the girls' lunches while Sheila got the children's clothes organized upstairs. He made them each a chicken sandwich on a dinner roll and added a juice pack, a box of raisins and some carrot sticks. He also started the oatmeal, and while Sheila saw that Stella and Amelia Louise ate, he got dressed. Then he switched off with Sheila again, looking after the girls and helping them get dressed while she got ready.

After a lot of hustle and bustle and then dawdling and delaying, they managed to get both girls into the car with Sheila, and she drove off. Windflower breathed a short sigh of relief and then ate his breakfast and took Lady for a short walk down the road to the new development of houses at the eastern part of Quidi Vidi Lake. It was short and wet as the rain continued to pelt, and the wind caused sheets of water to stream across the road and down the hill.

Back at the house Windflower towelled a vey wet Lady and changed his very wet trousers. Finally, he was ready again, and he and his big, bright van headed down Forest Road to his office.

23

It rained steadily as Windflower drove to work, and once in the parking lot, he had to run to prevent getting soaked again, all while manoeuvring his way around puddles so he wouldn't splash murky water up onto his clean trousers. He picked up a coffee from the cafeteria and politely said good morning to a sea of unfamiliar faces.

When he got to his office, there was a note taped to his door. "Call me when you get in," it read. It was signed "T.R. Ext. 421". Windflower racked his brain to think about who T.R. was and finally remembered Terry Robbins from the comms team. He called the number, and Robbins said he'd be up soon.

That gave Windflower a chance to organize his office and his thoughts. He had printed off all the material that he'd got from the RNC and laid it on his desk.

"Morning," said Robbins. "Great day for ducks."

"Indeed," said Windflower. "Are you from around here?"

Robbins laughed. "About as far away as you can get. I'm from Athabasca, Alberta."

"No way," said Windflower. "I'm from Pink Lake, west of Hondo on highway two."

"My father worked at Athabasca University, and my mom was a nurse. We were almost neighbours. Isn't that funny?"

"Sure is. How long you been here?"

"Arrived last year from HQ. I came because I heard there might be a retirement soon."

"Morecombe?"

Robbins nodded. "But it looks like she changed her mind," he said. "I don't really mind. I like the lifestyle here. Laid back. Not much happening really."

"Me too," said Windflower. "Been in Grand Bank for a while now. I love it. Or should I say I loves it b'y."

"I think you got that Newfie thing down. So, what are we working on?"

Windflower gave Robbins a quick update. He handed him all the materials and told him to go through the stack. "Make a copy and bring mine back. I'm still going through it, trying to find something that'll help us. I'm also going to call Foote at the Constab to see if she can come over after lunch for a meeting. Your ideas about how to best get this out to the public and the media would be appreciated."

Robbins went off to do his assignment, and Windflower called Foote at the RNC. She said she would come over at one o'clock for the meeting. Next, Windflower called Ron Quigley.

"Good morning, Inspector. You make it back okay?"

"No problems," said Quigley. "Is it raining there?"

"Coming down buckets."

"Told ya. It'll clean up the snow for you. Anyway, you didn't call about the weather. I talked to your boss, Morecombe. She was barely civil."

"Yeah, she wasn't very happy about me getting reassigned," said Windflower. "I hear she was supposed to retire but is not going to now for some reason."

"Maybe she should go anyway," said Quigley. "It's hard enough without having to fight inside as well."

"Speaking of which, there appears to be some resistance from Lundquist about me using resources for this case. Seems like a common theme."

"Don't worry about Lars. I'll talk to him. I think he might be struggling with managing Tizzard and Evanchuk because they're one unit. He's used to more of a chain-of-command style."

"That will not work in Grand Bank. Trust me."

"'Love all, trust a few, do wrong to none,'" said Quigley.

"'To thine ownself be true,'" replied Windflower. He would have loved to have sparred quotes with Quigley all morning, but he had an incoming call. "Sorry, Ron, gotta go."

"Good morning, Eddie. What's up?" asked Windflower as he picked up the other call.

"Things are great, Sarge. But we've got a bit of a situation going on. And quite frankly, Corporal Lundquist is not helping," said Tizzard.

"What's going on?"

"Well, the principal made the announcement first thing this morning, and I guess there was quite a buzz going around the school. Carrie went over to talk again to some of the girls, and then I came in later and rounded up the three or four boys we thought were dealing drugs. I have them over here, and I guess one of the parents is freaking out and talking about civil liberties and getting a lawyer, and Lundquist started agreeing with him."

"What? In front of the parent?"

"Yeah. I tried to pull him aside and talk to him, but he wouldn't listen. He released all the kids before we could even talk to them."

"Is he there now?"

"Yeah, his car is out in front. I had to go out and blow off some steam."

"Go have a coffee," Windflower told Tizzard. "I'll call him."

Windflower called the Grand Bank RCMP Detachment and got Betsy on the line.

"Good morning, Sergeant. How nice to hear from you. Muriel says you are so handsome."

Windflower smiled. "Thank you, Betsy. I'm doing well. Is Corporal Lundquist around?"

"One moment please," she said.

"Lundquist here."

"Good morning, Lars. It's Winston Windflower."

"How can I help you, Sergeant?"

"Well, I think there's been some misunderstanding," said Windflower. "I have been giving direction to your officers at the request of Inspector Quigley."

"Inspector Quigley explained that to me this morning," said Lundquist.

"Then why are you interfering in Tizzard's work with the school?"

"He had no authority to hold those boys for questioning. I was responding to a complaint from the community, one of the parents."

"You may have jeopardized this investigation, Corporal. Let me remind you that we have two missing girls and a dead man in this region, plus more in St. John's. It's not a time for legal niceties or interference in our work. Do I make myself clear?" Windflower's voice rose at the end despite his attempts to stay calm and under control.

"I understand your position," said Lundquist. "But I would remind you that I do not report to you and that I have the responsibility of maintaining good relations with the community in Grand Bank."

Windflower wished he could have reached through the telephone and grabbed Lundquist by the neck. It was a good thing he wasn't close enough to do it or they would've both been in big trouble. He paused and tried to breathe. Then as calmly as he could, he responded.

"Thank you, Corporal. I will follow up with Inspector Quigley."

Then he hung up.

24

Windflower wanted to go for a walk to let his head and his heart settle down, but the downpour outside continued. Instead, he called the Miller Centre and asked if Bill Ford had been brought in. When he heard Ford had come in that morning, he grabbed his hat and coat and negotiated his way to the van.

He drove up through town and stopped at another place that Quigley had told him about called Fabulous Foods. It was a little hole-in-the-wall place that had a couple of tables but mostly featured a variety of home-cooked lunches and baked goodies. Windflower's favourite lunch there was a turkey roll and chips deluxe. The turkey roll was actually a half-moon shaped pastry filled with stuffing and the ends of hams all ground up together. Warm, they were a delight. The chips deluxe was french fries, gravy, a square of dressing and green peas in a tin foil plate.

Windflower ordered two of each, and then thinking about Sheila and the girls, got a lemon meringue pie and a package of freshly made apricot squares. That would make for a great lunch for Bill and himself and still give him a peace offering to take home later.

As he headed back down towards Forest Road and the Miller Centre, his mind turned to Bill and the years they had known each other. Bill and he were friends and old fishing buddies. Ford had introduced Windflower to salmon fishing. They had spent many hours in Central and Western Newfoundland fishing on the powerful Gander and Exploits rivers. Ford was a nice man and a good cop who went to Marystown to finish off his career but last year got ambushed and shot. He was now in recovery and rehab mode. Windflower was looking forward to seeing him and to the delicious lunch that was steaming in the bag next to him.

Despite the rain, people kept waving to him in the streets. He realized that it was the van and recognized that this would be his lot in life while he was driving around. Better be on his best behaviour, he thought. He pulled up in the Miller Centre parking lot, found a spot relatively close to the door and went in.

The Miller Centre was an old military hospital that had become the general hospital for the St. John's area in the 1880s and over the years had expanded its facilities to include a nursing school, a residence for veterans and an extensive rehabilitation section. It was named after Doctor Leonard Miller, an influential doctor who had helped develop the province's medical system and had served as its Deputy Minister of Health for a number of years.

Windflower checked in at reception and was directed to Bill Ford's room on the fourth floor. The elevator was crowded, and Windflower could sense people sniffing his lunch as he gripped it tightly until his floor. He suspected that their cafeteria might have healthier food than his, but none as tasty. He knocked and walked into Ford's room where a technician was hooking up Ford's bedside TV.

"The life of royalty, eh?" said Windflower as the technician finished connecting the cable and left.

"Good to see you, Winston. How are you and your family?" asked Ford.

"We're all good," said Windflower. "If you'd like I can bring the girls over on the weekend. But be forewarned, they are a handful, especially Amelia Louise."

"That would be great. Something to break the monotony. What have you got in that bag that smells so good?"

"Have you had lunch?" asked Windflower, opening the paper bag and taking the tops off the tinfoil containers.

"Nothing like that," said Ford. "I had some kind of mystery meat with canned peas and carrots and Jell-O for dessert. I like Jell-O, but I have a feeling that's what I get for dessert every day."

"Well, maybe rice pudding every other day. Anyway, here's a knife and fork. Dig in."

"This is so good. I love the girls at the clinic back home and in the hospital at Burin, but they don't serve anything like this in there. Where did you get this stuff?"

"Another one of Quigley's secrets. I love these turkey rolls, and the gravy is out of this world."

Windflower finished up his lunch and looked over at Ford and his half-eaten meal. "Not hungry?" he asked.

"Hard to get up an appetite when you're laying around all the time," said Ford. "I'm trying not to complain because I know it could be much worse. But I am impatient."

"I hear ya. Some wise man once said, 'He that can have patience can have what he will.'"

"In that case I'm ready to go home now."

"You haven't lost your sense of humour. You want me to pack this up for you for later?"

"Save me that turkey roll, but you can throw the chips out. Maybe put them in the garbage outside so I don't get in trouble."

"Absolutely. You'll be up and at 'em soon enough, Bill. I bet you can't wait for spring to get your line in the water."

"Man, that would be so great," said Ford. "As soon as I can, I'm going trouting, and God willing, I am going to get to Labrador in the fall. That's what I dream of when I go to sleep every night."

"That's a pleasant thought," said Windflower. "If you go to Labrador, I'm in. I'll have to clear it at home, but I'm in."

"Thank you, Winston, and thank you for coming. You made my day."

"Okay, we'll see you on the weekend. If you need anything, let me know."

Windflower carried the garbage out and deposited it in the container near the front entrance. It was still raining and blowing as he dodged the rain and ran to his van. He called Sheila on his way back to work to tell her he was bringing home dessert, but there was no answer, so he left a message.

25

Terry Robbins and RNC's Anne Marie Foote were waiting for Windflower when he got back to his office. Robbins suggested they move to the small boardroom where they could spread out.

"Why don't you run through all of this one more time so that we're all on the same page?" said Windflower.

Foote stood and spent half an hour walking through each case and then gave an overview of what they knew about human trafficking in the province. Robbins asked questions and took notes, which Windflower appreciated since he learned better when he could just listen to absorb the information. He explained this to a teacher once who said that he might be able to learn by assmosis, which is what he called Windflower's learning style, but that if he wanted to pass, he would also have to study.

"Okay," said Robbins. "It seems to me the main points we want to convey are that these girls didn't go off missing all of a sudden and that someone must have seen them somewhere along the way."

"And that this stuff is happening right here in St. John's and across Newfoundland," said Foote. "Yes, we have to find the missing girls. And I think that once we go public, we'll find there's more. But we also have to get the message out to parents, teachers and school counsellors that this could happen to anyone."

"That's a good point," said Windflower. "We're doing as much prevention work as we are investigating. Robbins, why don't you take a crack at a first draft and send it to both of us and Detective Langmead at the RNC. Foote, can you work on setting up a media conference for tomorrow afternoon with me and whomever you want from your side. As we're there to provide support to the RNC, you should take the lead."

Both officers nodded and left to carry out their tasks, and Windflower went back to his office. Sheila called shortly afterwards.

"I was thinking we could take out a casserole tonight for supper," said Sheila. "Put on some veggies, and we'll be good to go."

"And I got dessert," said Windflower.

"Where did you get it?"

"Fabulous Foods."

"I'll bet you got lunch there too, didn't you?"

"I had to pick up something for me and Bill Ford."

"Did you see him? How is Bill?"

"He's okay. Bored, impatient, just like you'd expect," said Windflower. "I told him if he got well enough to go salmon fishing in Labrador, I'd go with him in the fall. That seemed to cheer him up."

"Probably cheered you up too," said Sheila, laughing. "You can do that trip if I can do a shopping trip to Toronto."

"I think I've just been had for a lot of money, but it's a deal. I'll see you at home."

Windflower noticed that his in-basket had been filled with paper while he was away. That was something that seemed to never change, he thought. Today's mail brought brochures and inter-office memos about security after hours and a big thick envelope of forms from human resources. He had to complete a bunch of forms so his personnel files could be transferred to the St. John's offices. There were forms to fill out to update all his personal and professional information, and even some asking him what courses he had taken recently and which ones he would like to apply for in the coming months.

He sank beneath the weight of all the paper for about an hour until he was finally released when his cell phone rang. It was Smithson.

"Hey, Smithson, whaddya got for me?" asked Windflower.

"I got good news and bad," said Smithson. "Which do you want first?"

"Gimme the bad news. Get it out of the way."

"It appears that nobody sent the info on the missing girls out on the wire. Not from us and not from the RNC."

"That means nobody outside of Newfoundland has been

looking for them? Do we even know if they're still here?"

"I haven't been able to find all of them on the passenger lists, but at least two were booked for flights to Montreal, both from the St. John's area."

"That's your good news?"

"No, Sarge. The good news is that one of those girls, Larissa Murphy, was stopped by the Ottawa police in a sweep of the Byward Market area. She claimed to be 16, and they didn't have anything on her so let her go. But they recorded her name. I searched their records and found it in the files."

"So, we know that at least one girl is in the Ottawa area," said Windflower. "Anything else?"

"No, but I'm still digging," said Smithson. "And all the girls and their pictures are up on our database. I've sent it directly to HQ and to both Montreal and Ottawa police to ask them to look out for them."

"Good work. Keep at it and let me know if anything else turns up."

After the call, Robbins came by Windflower's office to hand him a draft of the press release. "I sent it to your email but thought you would want a printed copy too."

"I would," said Windflower. "If you want me to read something, paper is best. I'll take a look at this, thanks. In the meantime, can you talk to Foote? Tell her we've found Larissa Murphy, or at least we have an idea where she is."

"Where is she?" asked Robbins.

"She was seen in Ottawa. Stopped by the police. But they didn't have any reason to hold her. They didn't know she was missing."

"Didn't the RNC put the names and pics out on the wire?"

"I guess not, and we didn't either. They're up there now, and we'll be contacting the Ottawa and Montreal police as well."

"Okay. I'll talk to Foote. Maybe she could call the parents and tell them too."

"Great idea," said Windflower.

"And I have a contact on the Ottawa police if you need it. It's my brother," said Robbins.

"I thought you said your family was from Alberta," said

Windflower.

"They are. But Scottie went to university in Ottawa. He was going into law school but applied to the Ottawa Police Service and got accepted. Been there for four years now."

"If you can talk to your brother that would be good. Better yet, can you ask him to call me?"

"No worries," said Robbins. "I'll call Foote and check in with you again on the press release. Then I'll call Scottie."

"Thanks," said Windflower. He picked up the press release, went over it and then made a couple of minor suggestions to Robbins in an email. Then he went back to reading and filling out the forms from HR. He was just signing the last in the package when Foote called from the Royal Newfoundland Constabulary.

26

"We've talked to Larissa Murphy's family, and if we want, they can come to the press conference with us tomorrow," said Foote. "They have been cooperating with us all the way through this. What do you think?"

"I think it's a great idea," said Windflower. "We used this once before with a missing girl in Grand Bank. It's a great strategy for getting attention and public support."

"Okay, I'll set that up," she said. "We'll do it in the chief's boardroom tomorrow at one o'clock if that's okay with you. The chief wants to be there."

"Perfect. I've sent my suggestions on the press release to Robbins, so we should be good to go from here. See you tomorrow."

Robbins came back a few minutes later with a new version of the press release and a draft statement for Windflower's part in the press conference.

"Leave that with me," said Windflower. "I'll run through it tonight. I talked to Foote. She's going to bring some of Larissa Murphy's family tomorrow."

"That's super," said Robbins. "From a PR perspective it makes for great TV, and that means more people will hear about the missing girls and possibly have more information for us. We'll have to get them in and out quickly, so the reporters don't have an opportunity to ask them questions. I've seen that go really badly."

"Agreed," said Windflower. "I'll let you work that out with Foote so she can look after the family. And we're on for one o'clock. We can go over together if you want."

"Sure. By the way, I called my brother and left a message. If you give me your cell phone number, I'll pass it on when he calls back."

Windflower scribbled his number on a scrap of paper and handed it to Robbins.

“Thanks,” said Robbins. “I’ll call Foote and finalize everything, and then I’m heading out for the night.”

“Me too,” said Windflower. He put his draft statement for the press conference in his briefcase, turned off the lights and went outside. Of course, it was raining. But Windflower wanted to look on the bright side of things. For now, at least, the wind had died down a bit, and while the rain was steady, it wasn’t torrential. And as Quigley had suggested, it was melting the snow. The snow was down substantially from the morning and more would be washed away overnight. The disappearing snow was a minor miracle, thought Windflower, but in the absence of a major one, he and St. John’s would take it.

He drove home slowly through the predictable mini-traffic jam resulting from the rain but still managed to pull into the driveway within 15 minutes. All in all, not much of a rush hour, he thought, remembering the stop-and-go traffic on the bridges in Halifax and his brief glimpse of Vancouver gridlock. As soon as he opened the front door of his house, his thoughts of bumper-to-bumper traffic were quickly replaced by another. What was that wonderful smell?

Windflower didn’t have to announce his arrival; a scampering dog and two small girls screaming did that job for him. He laid down his briefcase and his bag of desserts to be surrounded by his happy crew. He fell to the floor in mock surrender as the girls and Lady nearly smothered him in hugs and kisses.

“I love you all too,” said Windflower as he picked up Stella in one arm and Amelia Louise in the other. Lady had to settle for circling his legs. “That smells delicious,” he said. “Some kind of fish?”

“Scallop casserole,” said Sheila from the kitchen where she was chopping broccoli and carrots. “It’ll be ready when the veggies are done. Put those desserts in the fridge before one of them gets at them.”

Windflower did as he was told, kissing the back of Sheila’s neck as he went by. “I love you, beautiful,” he said.

“Thank you. That’s very kind,” said Sheila. “I appreciate the sentiment."

"It must be crazy for you right now," he said. "How are you holding up?"

"It's hard. But now that we've got everybody on a routine, I think it'll get better. Why don't you get changed before supper?"

Windflower had company as he went upstairs, but he managed to distract them by pulling out Stella's box of Lego and getting them started on building something. He changed into jeans and an RCMP sweatshirt, and when he came back, all the girls, Lady included, were happily engaged in what looked like some kind of construction business. What exactly was being built had yet to be determined, but it kept them entertained until Sheila called everyone for supper.

She had dished up a small portion of the casserole for Stella and Amelia Louise and was setting Windflower's larger plate on the table when he came down.

"It looks gorgeous," said Windflower. "And it smells divine," he added as he waited for it to cool a little. "I'll have to get you to show me how to make these casseroles."

"This one is easy," said Sheila. "I had a small bag of scallops left, and you just basically boil them and then sauté the onions, celery and mushrooms, add a can of cream of mushroom soup and some milk, and you're nearly done. Sprinkle some breadcrumbs over the top and bake for 25 minutes. Simple."

"And delicious," he said as he savoured the first forkful. That plate of food went down so well that he determined he needed a second, smaller helping.

"Now it's time for dessert," said Sheila, and she took the lemon meringue pie out of the fridge. "I thought I'd save the squares for lunches."

"Oooh," said Windflower as she laid the pie on the table and cut him a slice.

"Oooh," said Amelia Louise as she got her piece. Stella said nothing but gave a wide smile when Sheila gave her a piece.

Windflower looked at Sheila, and she smiled at him. "We'll talk later," she said.

After she was a few mouthfuls into her pie, Sheila declared the pie fabulous.

"That's why they call it Fabulous Foods," said Windflower.

"Ha, ha, ha," she said.

"Ha, ha, ha," repeated Amelia Louise.

After dinner and cleanup Sheila took the girls for their bath, and Windflower let Lady out in the backyard. "Sorry, girl, we'll go for our walk later," he said. He watched as Lady slipped and slid across the ice that had completely covered the backyard. That gave him an idea. He'd talk to Sheila about it later.

27

Once bath time, story time and quieting-down time were over, Windflower and Sheila finally got to sit in the living room to enjoy a break and a cup of tea.

"I did some research at the library on why Stella doesn't speak," said Sheila. "She may or may not have selective mutism. That's for an expert to say. But she is certainly what anyone would call a reluctant speaker."

"Is that even a thing?" he asked.

"What I read said that until there is a diagnosis, all cases should be considered reluctant speakers. I also saw that kids with selective mutism often talk at home, but not at school. Stella doesn't talk hardly at all, anywhere."

"That is true. Can we get her in to see a speech pathologist at school?"

"There's a waiting list. They only have three speech pathologists for all the kindergarten and primary schools in St. John's. Will be at least a month. At least she's not getting into too much trouble."

"That's a good thing," said Windflower. "I do have an idea."

"Oh no," said Sheila, feigning horror. "I've heard some of your ideas before. Have you thought this one out before you decide to launch into it?"

Windflower reacted in his own version of make-believe, which actually looked really, really weird, and Sheila started laughing.

"Wait 'til you hear it," he pleaded. "What about a backyard skating rink?"

Sheila tried to muffle her giggles, and then a snort snuck out. She gave up and just broke down laughing.

"What's so funny?" asked Windflower.

"First of all, do you know how to do it?" asked Sheila once her laughing fit had subsided.

"I can look it up on YouTube."

"You could, but you're not exactly a handyman. There are a few holes left in the plaster from the time you tried to hang pictures in the B & B. And there're wires still hanging out of that socket where you were going to replace the light in the B & B basement."

"Okay, I could ask somebody for help."

"You could, or you could forget the fact that it's hard to get enough nights for the ice to freeze, should you get that far. And every time it snows, which it does a lot around here, you would have to be out there to shovel it off. I certainly won't be doing that."

"I'm still going to look it up," said Windflower, now determined more than ever. "I'll take Lady out one more time."

Sheila gathered up the tea things and went to the kitchen while Windflower grabbed Lady and her leash and headed out the door. "C'mon, girl," he said. "We'll mark her down as undecided." Lady wagged her tail enthusiastically in response.

"Yeah, you understand," he said. "Thank you for your support," and he gave the dog a quick but appreciative scratch behind an ear.

The rain had lessened a bit, for which both man and dog were grateful. Windflower stepped around as many large puddles as he could. Lady didn't bother and looked surprised when Windflower jerked from side to side. By the time they got back, she was fairly dry on top but completely soaked on the bottom. Windflower dried her off as best he could and laid down a fresh towel on her bed. He was finishing up filling the pets' bowls when his cell phone rang. It was an unknown number.

"Windflower," he said.

"Hi, Sergeant. It's Scott Robbins. My brother, Terry, asked me to call. Is this a good time?"

"Yeah, it's great," said Windflower. "Thanks for calling. I don't know how much your brother told you, but we're working together with the local cops on a number of missing girls."

"He did say that. He also mentioned one girl in particular, Larissa Murphy," said Scott Robbins. "I've had a look at the report involving her. She was questioned and noted but not picked up because she claimed to be of age. We don't ask for ID anymore, unless we have a reason to hold them."

"What's the area like she was stopped in?" asked Windflower.

"It's the Byward Market. I work in the guns and gangs unit, and we're down there all the time. It's a hotbed for drugs and prostitution. Lots of homeless kids. Lots of violence, mostly on each other. We've stopped arresting the young people, if we can. Mostly we just see if they're safe, but not many of them talk to us."

"Are there any other notes on the file or anything about whom she might be with or hanging around with?"

"I talked to the officer who stopped her. He says she was with a crew of young people, mostly known as low-level drug dealers. Unfortunately, that's who hangs around down there. It's safer to be on the streets with them than in any of the shelters."

"Okay, thanks," said Windflower. "Did you see the notice about the other missing girls from Newfoundland?"

"Yeah. We're on it now. If your girl or any of the others show up on our radar, we'll let you know."

"Thanks. We appreciate that."

Windflower went into the living room, fished out his draft statement for tomorrow's press conference and had a look at it. It was offering the RCMP's support for the efforts to find the missing girls and echoing the call for the public to come forward. The only thing missing was to add Inspector Ron Quigley's name as a member of the new RNC-RCMP task force working on the investigation. He sent a text to Terry Robbins about that, with a note telling him that he'd talked to his brother. He closed everything up and turned off all the lights.

Then he stopped before he went to bed to say another silent prayer for Larissa and all the other missing girls. How would he feel if it were Amelia Louise or Stella missing? He walked upstairs and went into each girl's bedroom and kissed them both on the forehead. Sheila was sleeping, so he quietly undressed and slipped in beside her. Unconsciously, she reached for him. Very consciously, he reached back.

28

Windflower was still lying there as he heard Sheila rouse the girls. Amelia Louise came willingly, while it sounded like Stella offered more resistance to leaving her warm bed. Windflower went downstairs, let Lady out back and put the coffee on to perk. He sliced some fruit into bowls and put half a dozen muffins in tin foil and in the oven to warm. He let Lady back in, managed to squeeze two small cups of coffee out of the still perking coffee maker and brought them upstairs.

"Here you go," he said to Sheila as he passed her one of the cups.

"Thanks," said Sheila. "Stella's moving a bit slowly this morning. Maybe you can get her going."

Windflower went in to see Stella, who had managed to get out of bed but just barely. Her clothes were lying on the bed next to her. Windflower tried to move her and her clothes closer together and was immediately rebuffed. He tried another tack.

"I'll read you a story if you put your clothes on," he said. It was a bribe, but things were getting desperate.

Stella went to the bookcase and started looking at a book. Progress, thought Windflower. Then he saw what book she had selected. It was I Am Too Absolutely Small for School. It was a book that had been recommended to Sheila to help kids adjust to going to school for the first time. It told the story of Lola, who wasn't sure about school, and how her older brother helped persuade her that school would be fun.

Windflower read the story and got Stella moving towards her clothes but couldn't get her fully dressed. Time for the cavalry, he thought, and he called Sheila.

Sheila came and started talking softly to Stella. That was Windflower's cue to leave. He went downstairs with Amelia Louise and got her a muffin and some fruit. While she was eating, he made the girls' lunches—sliced cheese and lettuce sandwich, a banana and a special apricot square for dessert. He put a square in a baggie for Sheila and another wrapped square in his briefcase for later.

Minutes later Sheila came down with Stella and everybody had their breakfast.

"What did you do?" asked Windflower.

"I told her that if she got dressed and ready for school, we might go skating again this weekend," Sheila said. "I said you were going to build her and Amelia Louise a skating rink."

Windflower stared at her dumfounded. "I'll never understand women," he said finally. "But I do understand what Shakespeare said."

"What did the Bard have to say?"

"'Women speak two languages—one of which is verbal.'"

"Hmmm...doesn't sound like him, really. But I reserve the right to change my mind. Women were so long without any rights, we intend to use them whenever we get a chance."

"Is that Gloria Steinem?"

"It's vintage Sheila Hillier, Sergeant. Now let's get this crew on the road before we have any other roadblocks, shall we?"

"Yes, ma'am." Windflower got Amelia Louise dressed while Sheila got herself and Stella organized. He helped her load the car and kissed her goodbye. He noticed that the rain had stopped and went back in to call Lady for a walk. Better check the temperature to see if it would be cold enough to build a rink, he thought.

He and Lady had a pleasant walk around the neighbourhood, and as he was passing along the houses on his side of Forest Road, he noticed something interesting. He went closer to take a look, and his first glance was confirmed. One of his neighbours had a rink in their backyard. There wasn't any ice on it, but it had boards all around, and when he got even closer, he could see that there was some kind of covering on the bottom. So, that's how they do it.

"Can I help you?" came a voice from the back door of the house.

"Oh, sorry. I was just admiring your rink," said Windflower.

"We live up the road."

"I've seen you and your dog before," said the man, walking towards him. "I'm Wilf Pittman."

"Nice to meet you," said Windflower. "I'm Winston Windflower, and this is Lady."

Pittman came closer to pet Lady and offered his hand to Windflower. "Welcome to the neighbourhood."

"Thanks very much. Is it a lot of work?" Windflower asked, pointing to the rink.

"Not too much to set up," said Pittman. "I use two-by-twelve boards to build the walls. Frame it out like a sandbox. I used to have a big one when the kids were around. Now I just do a small one for my grandkids when they come by."

"What do you use for the bottom?"

"I use a tarp. But most people just spray the water directly on the ground. You pour it in layers once the weather gets cold enough. You just need a couple of consecutive nights well below zero, and you have a rink in no time."

"I'm guessing the hard part is keeping it clean."

Pittman laughed. "That is a challenge around here, that's for sure. But I have a little blower and lots of time since I retired."

"Well, thanks for the tips. Nice to meet you."

"Same here. If you decide to build one, let me know, and I'll come and give you a hand. I got lots of free time."

"Thanks a lot," said Windflower. He was fairly humming as he walked back the last few steps with Lady.

"Won't Sheila be surprised when I build that rink?" he asked Lady. She looked at him strangely. "You wouldn't understand." What she did understand, though, was the Milk Bone biscuit he offered her. Molly also understood that treats were being handed out and showed up to demand her share. Windflower handed it over and headed off to work.

There were still plenty of puddles from all the rain, and he had to be careful not to splash any pedestrians along the way, especially because he was driving the RCMP van. Wouldn't do to have the Mounties muck up someone's clothes.

He managed that successfully and even got a parking spot

that didn't have a deep pool of water to navigate. He walked to the building, noting that the wind had changed direction and now had a distinctly cool, northern flavour. Not many people around here would be cheered by that news, but it raised Windflower's already-high spirits up another notch.

It was a good thing he was in a positive mood when he got to his office because somebody else probably was not. Taped on his door was a note that said "SEE ME!!" all in caps. It was signed, or more precisely, scrawled, "Morecombe". He calmly took the note down and went to the cafeteria to get his coffee mug filled. No point of going into battle without some fuel, he thought.

29

He saw Terry Robbins sitting at a table with some other officers and waved good morning. Robbins approached him as he was standing in line to pay.

"She's on a tear this morning," said Robbins.

"So I gathered from her note on my door," said Windflower.

"It's because I'm working with you," said Robbins. "She had some project for me to work on, but when I told her I had to help you with the media this afternoon, she freaked."

"Thanks for the heads-up. Your brother was helpful too."

"I talked to him again last night. If our girls are still around Ottawa, he said they'd find them. The other thing he said was that if Larissa Murphy was on the street, then she may have got away from the really bad guys."

"That's good news, isn't it?" asked Windflower.

"Maybe, or maybe not," said Robbins. "Scottie said those bad guys don't often let people go voluntarily."

"So, Larissa may be on the run?"

"And maybe out of the frying pan into the fire."

"Okay, and thanks for the warning about Morecombe."

Windflower left the cafeteria and walked to Morecombe's office. Muriel greeted him with her usual smile and escorted him right in.

"It's one thing for you to be out gallivanting around on this special project. It's quite another to be dragging my staff into it," barked Morecombe.

"Didn't Inspector Quigley tell you that he would be needing some comms help?" asked Windflower.

"He might have authority over you, and he might run the

southeast region, but he doesn't run me or this section." Morecombe was now red-faced and shouting.

"I thought we were all on the same side here." Windflower thought that was probably not the best thing to have said, judging by the response it elicited from his boss.

Morecombe stood and grabbed her cane to steady herself. Then she screamed at Windflower. "If you want to access any of my staff, you come to me first. Is that clear, Sergeant?"

Windflower nodded and left Morecombe's office.

That wasn't a great way to start the day, he thought as he passed an ashen-looking Muriel on the way out. But he had learned not to take on other people's problems. And Morecombe clearly had some. He would talk to Quigley later, but first he had a more important task. He had to research making backyard skating rinks on YouTube.

He was into his third video and feeling confident that he had a handle on this rink-making thing when his cell phone rang. It was Evanchuk.

"Hi Sarge. I wanted to give you an update on Marystown," said Evanchuk. "I went over yesterday, and Smithson and I went to the high school. We asked around about Mandy Pardy."

"What did you find out?" asked Windflower.

"Not too much about her in particular, but we did find another girl who'd been approached but decided against going. She waited until we were leaving the school property to come up to us. She asked for my number, and I called her last night. She's pretty scared. She says that she's already been warned that they will hurt her and her family if she talks to anybody."

"Who are they? Do we know?"

"She wouldn't say, but I'm pretty sure it's the bikers."

"I can see why she's scared," said Windflower. "Any way to get her to talk?"

"Smithson is going to talk to the principal. Maybe he or one of the teachers could help us get through to her."

"Maybe get the parents involved too."

"We'll need somebody to run interference on that side. I'm sure the last thing she wants is her parents knowing about all this."

"Let Smithson be the bad guy on this, and maybe you can still keep her trust. Let me know how it goes. And we found one of the girls in Ottawa. Well, not really found her, but we know she's there."

"That's good news," said Evanchuk. "If one is there, maybe there's more."

"Okay, thanks," said Windflower as he hung up the phone. Time to bite the bullet, he thought. He had Morecombe breathing down his neck here and Lundquist squeezing him at the other end. He phoned Ron Quigley.

"Winston, nice to hear from you, but I'm swamped. Remember that 'brevity is the soul of wit,'" said Quigley.

"Got it," said Windflower. "Morecombe is upset that I've asked one of her staff to help me with the media stuff, and Lundquist is a pain in my nether parts. I need you to fix both."

"You're on your own with Morecombe, but her bark is much worse than her bite. And what's the deal with Lars?"

"I need him to get out of the way of the investigation. You need to talk to him."

"Okay," said Quigley. "Thirty-second update?"

"Media this afternoon. RNC chief will be there. You're on the joint task force too. There's a sighting of one missing girl in Ottawa, and we've got a potential whistleblower in Marystown," said Windflower.

"Perfect. I'll call you after the press conference to see how it went. Don't worry, I'll look after Lundquist."

"'Modest doubt is called the beacon of the wise,'" said Windflower, but as usual Quigley was gone.

30

The rest of the morning went by quickly, and Windflower only had time to grab another coffee and eat his apricot square for lunch. Robbins came by just after one, and they drove together to the RNC building. Along the way people continued to wave to Windflower and he waved back.

"It's the van," said Robbins. "That's why none of us will drive it unless we have a specific event to attend that calls for it."

"So, you left it for me," said Windflower. "Thanks a lot."

"Well, it is your job," said Robbins. "Public Outreach Coordinator."

"That's what people keep telling me," said Windflower, waving to a lady who was crossing the street near the Basilica. He parked in the visitor section and walked to the reception desk with Robbins.

They were met by Brian Hayes from gangs and drugs, and he got their badges.

"Detective Sergeant Langmead is briefing the chief, and Foote is with the family," said Hayes. He led them down the corridor on the main floor past the chief's boardroom where some of the media had already assembled.

"Come in here," he said as he brought them into the chief's suite of offices. There was a small boardroom next to the main office, and Windflower and Robbins took a seat. A few minutes later Langmead came to greet them and to bring them in to meet his boss.

"Chief Gordon, this is Sergeant Winston Windflower," said Langmead.

"Nice to meet you, sir," said Windflower as he shook the chief's hand. "This is my associate, Corporal Terry Robbins from communications."

"Sit down, sit down," said Gordon. "We appreciate your help on this. Superintendent Majesky speaks highly of you. Anything new from your end?"

"Thank you, sir. We're happy to help out. I don't know if Detective Sergeant Langmead had a chance to tell you yet, but we do know that at least one of the girls is in Ottawa," said Windflower. "We've also got a girl in Marystown who claims she was being recruited. We're following up on both leads."

"We've also got some news," said Langmead. "Hayes, why don't you tell everybody what you've heard."

"It looks like the bikers, on both sides, have decided to fight it out openly in St. John's," said Hayes. "Our sources tell us that they are recruiting bodies and are even sending some people in."

"We can help you track them at the airport if you want," said Windflower.

"That'll be good," said Hayes. "We can't really stop them unless we have cause. But we certainly need to know who's coming in."

"They're not fighting about the girls, are they?" asked Chief Gordon.

"Not really," said Hayes. "This is about the drugs, sir, and who will control the market."

"But we may be able to put a dent in them through the girls," said Windflower. "Human trafficking is getting easier to prosecute than drugs."

"Good point," said the chief. "I can see why Majesky likes you. I like the way you think, Windflower."

"Can we meet with the family now?" asked Langmead.

"Bring them in," said Gordon.

Hayes went to another room and was soon back with Foote and Larissa Murphy's parents. The father was dressed in his best suit and trying to look stoic, but he only succeeded in giving off a deer-in-the-headlights look. The mother simply looked distraught and devastated.

Only the chief spoke to the parents, and he used a kind and gentle tone. Like a gentleman, thought Windflower. It was easy to see why he was chief. After he spoke, he asked Foote to run through their part with them again.

"The chief will make his statement, which I showed you already," said Foote. "Then Sergeant Windflower from the RCMP will speak. After that I will bring the two of you up and introduce both of you. Mary, you read your statement, and then I will bring both of you back down and bring you outside. Okay?"

The parents both nodded. "We will do whatever we can to help find Larissa," said Mrs. Murphy. Her husband held her tightly, and she leaned into him.

An officer from the Constabulary media team came into the chief's office.

"We're ready when you are, sir," he said.

Chief Gordon led the way out into the large boardroom followed by Windflower and the other RNC officers. Foote stayed behind with Larissa Murphy's parents. They would be spared the cameras and flashing lights on the way in.

The chief strode to the podium and greeted the media representatives. He talked about why they were there and the joint task force that had been created to find the missing girls. As he spoke, the images of the girls flashed up behind him. Windflower thought he heard a gasp from the back of the room when the Murphy girl's photo came up.

The chief introduced Windflower and moved aside to let him come to the podium. Windflower had his statement in front of him, but he had memorized it and gave it as loudly and clearly as he could. Chief Gordon thanked Windflower and the RCMP and then spoke about one of the main reasons for holding the press conference.

"We need the help of the public to find these missing girls and to bring them back safely to their families. Somebody out there knows something or may have seen something. If you have, please call the number on the screen behind me. Their families miss them and want them home."

He signalled to Foote to bring Mr. and Mrs. Murphy up to the front. The chief introduced them and invited Mary Murphy to speak.

She came to the podium with her husband at her side. She

had a paper with her statement on it in her hands. Windflower saw her hands tremble as she laid it on the podium in front of her. She looked out into the bright lights and then started to read her statement.

"Our daughter, Larissa, is missing, and we are afraid. There are four other families that are just as afraid today. We don't know where our daughters are, and we want them to come home. If you have seen our Larissa or any of the other girls, please let the police know. We need your help. If it was your daughter…." Mary Murphy's voice trailed away and Foote came to her side and guided her and her husband to the back of the room and out the door.

"We need your help," said Chief Gordon. "Please help us find Larissa and the other girls. We'll now take questions."

The next 20 minutes were a bit of a blur as the reporters peppered the chief with all sorts of questions about the missing girls and the investigation to date. Near the end one of them asked if he thought the missing girls were still alive.

"We have no reason to suspect that they are not alive and well," said the chief. "But just last night we received information that at least one of the girls may be outside the province. Sergeant Windflower, would you comment on that, please."

"Yes," said Windflower. "We have received information that one of the missing girls was spotted in Ottawa. We are still following up on that. We are also actively investigating all information about sightings of the missing girls in the St. John's area to learn as much as we can about their possible current whereabouts. I would echo Chief Gordon's suggestion to please let us know if anyone has seen these girls in your area. It may save their lives."

Windflower stood back, and the chief gave him a positive nod.

Chief Gordon took a few more questions, and then the RNC's media person stepped forward and stood next to him. He knew that was his cue to say thank you and leave. Windflower followed him out and back into his office.

He could hear Foote trying to comfort Larissa's parents in the small boardroom. He went closer and stepped inside, Terry Robbins following him. Mary Murphy was crying inconsolably in her husband's arms.

"I just want to thank you for what you did today," said Windflower. "I know it was hard, but in my experience that really works to get information. And if we can get more information, we can find them. You know that Larissa has been spotted in Ottawa. Last night I spoke to one of the officers who works in that area. It was my colleague Terry's brother. He said the whole Ottawa police force will be looking for Larissa." Terry Robbins nodded as if to support that view.

"Thank you, Sergeant," said the mother. "It was so hard to see Larissa's picture and all those other poor girls." She started crying again.

"You did a great job today," said Windflower. "Stay strong. Larissa will need you when she gets back home."

Robbins and Windflower said goodbye to the other officers and walked back down the corridor to the front entrance.

31

Let's get a coffee before we head back," said Windflower.

"Great idea," said Robbins. "I'll even buy."

"Even better," said Windflower as he drove to the coffee shop. A few minutes later they had their coffees and were driving back across town to RCMP regional headquarters. Windflower phoned Ron Quigley and left a message about the press conference and then called Sheila.

"Hey, Winston, what's up?" asked Sheila.

He could hear noises in the background. They were distinctly Amelia Louise-type noises. "Are you home?" he asked.

"Not only am I home, but I am slaving over a hot stove to cook your dinner. It's my half day at university, and I picked up the girls early today. Since I have time, I'm cooking a chicken for supper."

"That, my dear, sounds absolutely wonderful. You are the best wife in the world."

"'He does me double wrong that wounds me with the flatteries of his tongue.'"

"Oh you are so wrong, although that is a great quote. I can assure you that 'nothing flatters a man as much as the happiness of his wife; he is always proud of himself as the source of it.'"

"That's not Shakespeare," said Sheila. "Is it?"

"Samuel Johnson," said Windflower. "I'll be home soon."

Windflower walked to his van feeling the air growing colder around him. He checked the sky for warning signs, but it was clear and blue. He checked the weather on his phone. His app had an icicle symbol. To almost everybody else in St. John's, that was bad news. To Windflower, it felt like his lucky charm. He needed the weather to be cold, really cold, to put his plan into effect.

He was smiling as he drove the short distance home and made sure to wave to everyone he saw along the way. That was his job, he realized. Part of public outreach was to be out in the community as a partner, not only as someone looking after the community or keeping people safe. For his new job as a police officer and a public outreach coordinator, he had to do it all together. So, he waved at everybody, even those who didn't look like they wanted to be waved at. He made more of an effort with those people, just in case.

He was still smiling when he got home, and the greeting from Lady and his girls made that smile even wider. With a girl on each arm, he went to the kitchen and gave Sheila a kiss on the cheek. She had her apron on and was making gravy.

"Get changed and cleaned up," she said. "Supper is almost ready."

"Yes, ma'am," said Windflower, and he marched upstairs with a troop of two and one dog behind him. Minutes later they paraded back down, and Windflower helped the girls get settled at the table.

Sheila had laid the steaming chicken on the table, and Windflower did his best to carve up most of the bird. He cut up a piece each for Stella and Amelia Louise and put it on their plates. He gave Sheila a crispy wing and a slice of breast and took a leg and two slices for himself. Sheila passed out the carrots, mashed potatoes and corn and poured a little gravy over everything.

"Mmmm," said Windflower.

"Mmmm," repeated Amelia Louise.

When he finally came up for air, Windflower complimented Sheila on dinner and asked about her day.

"I had a good day," she said. "Thursday's my best day of the week at school. I only have one class, and it's economics, which I really enjoy. Plus, I get to do some research or study at the library and still have time to do a few things for myself. How did the media stuff go today?"

"I think the press conference went well. Did I tell you one of the missing girls was spotted in the Ottawa area?" asked Windflower.

"No, I don't think so," said Sheila.

"That's another long story. But in any case, that girl's parents were part of the conference."

"Oh my goodness. How did that go?"

"The mother spoke, and she was amazing. But it was so hard for her to do. So hard to watch, too. I tried to reassure her and her husband afterwards, but I can understand why they're worried."

"I'd be out of my mind."

Windflower and Sheila paused and looked at their own little girls. "You'll do your best to find them," said Sheila.

"I'll try," said Windflower. "Oh, I met one of our neighbours this morning, Wilf Pittman from a few doors down. He's got a skating rink in his backyard. Well, not right now, but he's got the boards up and everything. He said he'd help me if I wanted to build my own."

"You're really going to do this?" asked Sheila.

"I'm going to try. I have to talk to Wilf this weekend, but if it stays cold, you never know."

"That is true. With you, we never know." She made a circle around her head with her finger accompanied by a cuckoo sound.

"Cu cu," said Amelia Louise.

"You'll all be surprised," said Windflower.

"I'd be happy if you just do the dishes," said Sheila.

After a dessert of cookies and the remainder of the squares chopped up, Windflower cleaned up while Sheila went to the living room with the girls. He took Lady for her walk as Sheila gave the girls their bath.

The walk was short but pleasant, and Windflower would have been more than pleased to see his new friend down the road, but no lights were on at the Pittman house. When he got back, it was story time. Tonight he had Amelia Louise, and she picked The Very Hungry Caterpillar. It was a classic children's book about a caterpillar that one day hatched out of a tiny egg and came out very hungry. Throughout the book the caterpillar keeps eating everything in sight. When he is finally full, he makes himself a cocoon and goes to sleep. When he wakes up a few weeks later, he is transformed into a butterfly.

Both Windflower and Amelia Louise absolutely loved that book, and Windflower didn't mind at all reading it three times for his daughter before she was ready to go to sleep. He kissed her goodnight and went downstairs. He and Sheila shared one more cup of tea and watched the news.

"There you are," said Sheila, pointing to the TV where Windflower could be seen following the chief into the briefing room. They didn't show Windflower delivering his statement, but they did show a lot of the chief and, of course, Mary Murphy.

"That was amazing," said Sheila. "That woman was so strong to do that."

"I don't know where she got that strength. But every time I see a woman, a mother, in that role, she rises to the challenge," said Windflower.

"'A woman with a voice is by definition a strong woman,'" said Sheila. "'But the search to find that voice can be remarkably difficult.'"

"That's a pretty good quote," said Windflower.

"That's Melinda Gates," said Sheila. "I'll see you upstairs."

32

Windflower turned off the lights and said goodnight to Lady, who then rolled over on her belly to get a rub. Molly pushed up against him and demanded to be stroked as well. "You don't have to be so pushy," said Windflower. Molly just looked at him with a quizzical gaze as if to say, you have no idea about cats, do you? She almost sneered when Windflower said that he wasn't afraid of her.

He was still muttering to himself about the cat as he was getting into bed.

"What are you talking about?" asked Sheila.

Rather than admit he was struggling with dealing with a cat, he stayed silent and snuggled in. "Let's go to sleep. It's been a long day."

Sheila fell asleep quickly, but Windflower stayed awake for a few minutes plotting out his backyard rink. He was trying to measure it in his mind when he, too, fell asleep. Unlike Sheila, who stayed sleeping peacefully, Windflower was soon awake in another dream.

This time it was just him, and he was back in Grand Bank. He walked along the wharf and all the way down to the beach. It was a fine day, but there was clearly something missing. He didn't see a soul along the way. The Mug-Up café was there, and the door was open, but there was nobody inside, not even the owners, Herb and Moira Stoodley.

He kept walking down by the brook and neared the water where the ducks would usually come to be fed. But today there were no ducks, even none of the ever-present seagulls. No, that wasn't true. There was one duck, and he or she was swimming right towards him.

Windflower tried to remember what he knew about ducks and their symbolism in his native culture. But all that came to his mind was how good duck tasted. He quickly shook that idea from his mind. Wouldn't be helpful if this duck wanted to talk to him, and he was thinking about dinner. Luckily, he remembered that the duck had special powers in and with the water and could clearly see things that others often missed.

"Good day, duck. How is the water today?" asked Windflower.

"It's cold and wet," said the duck. "That's what you wanted to ask me?" The duck started to paddle away.

"Wait, wait," said Windflower. "Thank you for coming. I am honoured by your presence." Windflower had learned that flattery worked almost as well over here as in the earthly world.

"That's better," said the duck.

"What can you see that I cannot?" asked Windflower.

"You are seeking someone, I believe. She is not here, but someone over on the other side knows where she is."

"Can you show me?"

"If you can follow me, I can," said the duck, and it started swimming to the other side of the brook.

Windflower got in the water. The duck was right. It was cold, very cold. He started swimming behind the duck, but as he got closer, the water kind of dried up, and he was left shivering in the cold air.

"Winston, you're as cold as ice," said Sheila. "Are you okay?"

Windflower didn't know what to say. He just grabbed Sheila and held her as close as he could. "It's just a dream," he said as he started to warm up, though he wondered if some of it was real. He was still wondering that when the alarm clock went off in the morning.

As difficult as Monday was in the Windflower household, Friday was the exact opposite. It was a good day for everybody, even the children and the pets. Yes, even Molly seemed to be in a good mood, as good a mood as a cat would let on to being in anyway. The Friday morning routine—making lunches, eating breakfast and getting dressed—was the same as other mornings but somehow more fun and enjoyable. Amelia Louise was dressed in no time after breakfast and was sitting quietly with her dollies in the living room while Windflower made chicken sandwiches for the lunches.

With Friday much smoother than any other day of the week, Windflower got his whole crew out the door and into Sheila's car in record time. He sipped his coffee and watched Sheila drive away.

He took Lady for a tour of the neighbourhood, hoping again to see his new buddy, Wilf, but still there was no sign of him and no car in his driveway. Windflower was a little disappointed, but there was all weekend to find him. He could stake out his house. He was a Mountie after all.

Back at his own house, he grabbed his smudging gear and went outside. Might as well take advantage of the few extra minutes, he thought. Lady, his constant outdoor companion, came along to see what he was up to.

He took out his bowl and filled it with a pinch of each medicine and lit it with a wooden match. He let the smoke envelop him, and he passed it all over with his eagle feather. When he was finished, he closed his eyes and asked for guidance about his recent dream. He allowed himself to feel rather than think, focusing on what it might have been like had he followed the duck all the way to the other side.

A large white house came into his vision. It was a house that he recalled from his times feeding the ducks. It had a black Ford-150 pickup in the driveway. Whatever he was supposed to find, it was in that house. He came back to reality shivering as much as he had during the night. But this time it wasn't from cold. It was from anticipation. He hurried back inside and quickly got ready for work. After grabbing his lunch he hopped in the van. He couldn't wait to get into the office to see if he could learn anything about the house and what might be in it.

He thought back to the dream with the racoon. How did that go again? Oh yeah. "Over the brook past the watery fowl is a clue to where she is living right now." He was so distracted by his thoughts that he almost forgot he was driving. And what he was driving. He nearly missed seeing a lady trying to cross at the intersection but luckily recovered quickly enough to allow her to pass and to give her a smile and a good morning.

There were no more incidents as he continued his drive and parked the van at the RCMP building. He grabbed a coffee to fill up his mug and went to his office. No notes on his door this morning. He hoped that was also a good omen. He started to write out his notes when his cell phone rang.

33

Good morning, Sarge," said Smithson. "How are you today?"

"I'm good," said Windflower. "It's Friday and the sun is shining. What more can a man ask for?"

"That's great," said Smithson. "I wanted to tell you that it looks like we're making some progress with the girl that approached Evanchuk. I talked to the principal, who then sent me to see the school counsellor. He's going to reach out to the family and try to set up a meeting."

"Good work," said Windflower. "Anything else?"

"I went back to the neighbourhood where Freddy Hawkins was killed and talked to the people who lived next door. The man told me they didn't know anything, but his wife came out later and spoke to me privately. She said they heard an argument and shots fired, but her husband had told her to shut up or they might get killed. She said 'ain't nobody going to tell me to shut up.' Those were her exact words."

"Can she identify the people who were involved?"

"She said there were two of them, one guy with a beard and 'dat ting on his back' and another younger guy. She also said that if we found them, she would go to court and tell the judge what she knew. 'No point in livin' in fear. I's too old for dat stuff'."

"Excellent. Sounds like you got a live-wire witness. What's next?"

"The boss told me we had to round up all the bikers and wannabes and bring them all in," said Smithson. "Said he heard that there might be a gang war coming, and the more we can get off the street right now, the better. There's lots of breaches and unpaid fines to pick them up on, and as we get them in here, we'll discover even more outstanding offences. I thought I'd go see all of them while they're here to see if we can't identify our guys."

"Good," said Windflower. "I heard the same news in St. John's. They're on the lookout for guys being shipped in to be part of the action."

"Our people at the airport could probably help with that. We could even set up a remote surveillance system if they wanted."

"That would be great. They could use the help. Why don't you call Brian Hayes at the Constabulary? He's their gangs and drugs guy."

"Will do. I'll talk to you later."

"Okay, thanks."

Windflower put down the phone and started thinking again about the white house in his dream. He needed to talk to somebody in Grand Bank. He phoned Eddie Tizzard and left a message. He worked away at the papers on his desk, and an hour later Tizzard phoned him back

"Eddie, I need your help," said Windflower.

"Sure," said Tizzard. "But my instructions are that whenever I receive a request from an outside source, I am to make a request in writing to my superior officer."

Windflower almost spit out his coffee. "Where are you? Stalag 19?"

"Orders from Corporal Lundquist," said Tizzard.

"Okay, thank you for the information. Now let me ask you some questions instead, if you think that would fit under your new protocols."

"He didn't say nothing about questions. Shoot."

"Is there a big white house across the brook in Grand Bank?"

"Yes, that's old Skipper Foley's. But I don't think anybody has been living there for years. It's been for sale for as long as I can remember."

"In the course of your regular duties, could you go by that house to see if anybody has been in there recently? And if there are signs of activity, could you call me during your break time?"

"I could do that. I have to do my regular patrol around town, and today I need to visit that very neighbourhood. What a coincidence."

"What a coincidence indeed. Thank you, Eddie."

Windflower was on his way to get another cup of coffee when his cell phone rang. It was a familiar and welcome voice.

"Winston, how's she gettin' on b'y?" asked Herb Stoodley.

"Herb, how nice to hear from you. Are you in town?" asked Windflower. Herb had been a great friend to Windflower over the years, and as a former Crown Attorney, he loved to talk about the law, justice and policing issues.

"No, but I'm coming in Monday to do our monthly run," said Stoodley. "I was hoping we could get together for a coffee and a chat."

"That would be great. What time could you be available? I'll try to make myself free."

"Probably around two if that works for you. I can come down near you. Costco is up in Dannyland now out in the west end."

"What's Dannyland?" asked Windflower.

"You know, Galway, the new development that the former premier is building out almost in Mount Pearl."

"Oh yeah, up on the hill. How about meeting me at the Tim Hortons on Harvey Road?"

"I know that place. And I'll bring a couple of CDs for you."

"Super. What are they?"

"That'll be my surprise. How are Sheila and the girls? Moira and I desperately miss little Amelia Louise."

"They're great, and I'm sure she misses you too. Give my love to Moira. See you Monday."

Windflower wondered if Sheila would be able to join them if she didn't have a class. It would be their own little Grand Bank reunion. After getting through some tedious paperwork and even more tedious emails, he started off to the cafeteria to get another coffee, this time to go with his lunch. He pulled out his cell phone to talk to her about Herb's visit.

"Hi Winston, I can't talk right now. I'm driving to the school. I'll call you back," said Sheila.

"Okay," said Windflower, wondering what that was all about. He continued to the cafeteria, got his coffee and ate his chicken sandwich and tried to relax for a few minutes. Sheila called him back.

"I'm still at the school. Now I'm waiting to see the vice-principal," said Sheila.

"What's going on?" asked Windflower.

"I don't know yet. I got a message while I was in class to call Marjorie Simms, the vice-principal. When I called back, she said that there'd been some problem with Stella. That she was okay, but she'd been really upset. I don't have all the details, but Marjorie said that Stella was crying and in a fetal position in the class. They brought her to the safe office, and she's lying down there now. I went in to check on her, and she was sleeping."

"None of that sounds good. Do you want me to come over there?"

"No, let me talk to the vice-principal, and if there's anything else, I'll call you. She looked okay when I saw her. But she had clearly been crying, and her hair was all upset. You know how fussy she is about that."

"I do," said Windflower. "Every morning it costs an extra ten minutes while she tries to fix her hair just right."

Sheila laughed, despite being upset. "It's a girl thing," she said. "Here comes Marjorie now. I'll call you."

Windflower decided to forego the coffee and went back to his office where Robbins was waiting for him. He looked out of breath. "There's more of them," said Robbins.

"More of whom?" asked Windflower.

"Four more missing girls. I just talked to Foote. She said they now have reports of four more missing girls. They came in as reports following the press conference. I guess that part of the public appeal is working."

"Okay, thanks. I'll check in with Langmead." Windflower picked up the phone in record time and called the Royal Newfoundland Constabulary.

34

Morning, Carl," said Windflower. "I hear there's some news."

"Yeah, and still coming in," said Langmead. "We now have five more reports of missing girls, some back six months. Three from St. John's, one from CBS, and one from Corner Brook."

"What's CBS?" asked Windflower.

"Conception Bay South. It's everything from Topsail all the way up through Kelligrews to Seal Cove. They amalgamated a few years ago," explained the detective sergeant. "Anyway, the calls started coming in right after the press conference. It's good news, but it means we have to start backtracking all these new cases. Plus, we must have a hundred tips on where people saw the first five girls. Gonna be a long weekend."

"Sounds like it. We're working on getting some of the locals to talk about the girls down our way. A few promising leads, including a girl who claims she was offered and refused a chance to join up. And we're still trying to get more info about the Murphy girl in Ottawa. One of our media guys, Terry Robbins, has a brother on the Ottawa force. They're going to dig around a bit more for us."

"That's good," said Langmead. "Hayes tells me that Smithson called him and offered to help with the airport watch. Thanks for that. We're stretched so thin that we're barely treading water right now."

"No problem," said Windflower. "I'm around on the weekend if you need me."

After hanging up, Windflower realized how lucky he felt. He would be around on the weekend with his wife and family instead of working on a case or following up leads. Another reminder to be grateful, he thought, and he said a silent thank you prayer to

Creator. He had learned from his Uncle Frank and Auntie Marie that all prayers should start with thank you. They said Creator will hear your gratefulness for abundance and always send more. If you prayed for what you wanted, Creator may only hear the wanting and give you more of that.

He was grateful, too, when his phone rang, and he saw that it was Sheila.

"We're going for ice cream," said Sheila. "Somebody told me there's a great place down on Kings Road that we're going to try out."

"I take it Stella is doing better," said Windflower.

"She will be after ice cream, and so will I," said Sheila. "I can't really talk now, but I'll fill you in when I get home."

"Stella's not in any trouble or anything, is she?"

"No, no, it's not that. I'll tell you later."

Windflower felt a bit relieved that Stella wasn't in any kind of trouble. She sure didn't need that right now. He pushed around the paper on his desk for a little while and thought about another cup of coffee, but he was woken out of his semi-slumber by a call from Tizzard.

"There's definitely been someone in there," said Tizzard. "The boards that were nailed up in back are gone, and the lock is broken. I haven't gone inside, though. I'm trying to find a reason to go in or figure out if I should get a green light from Lundquist first."

"Maybe talk to the neighbours and see if they've seen anybody around the house," said Windflower.

"Okay, I'll do that," said Tizzard.

Windflower hung up and decided to get that coffee after all. He managed to get the last order in before the cafeteria closed for the day. A medium coffee and a date square would get him to supper time.

He was sitting in his office with his feet up enjoying his snack when Morecombe came by.

"Must be nice," she said, her arms folded. Windflower had seen that posture many times. It usually meant the other person was defensive and more than often, dangerous. His training told him to try to defuse this situation before it went sideways.

Windflower laid down his snack. "I'd buy you one, but they were closing down," he said.

Morecombe didn't seem to know how to respond to that, so he kept going. "Listen, we seem to have got off track lately. I know you must be under a lot of pressure."

"You don't know what's going on with me," said Morecombe.

"That's true," said Windflower. "But I'm no threat to you. I'm here for a year, and then I almost certainly am going back to Grand Bank". Morecombe stayed silent as if she didn't know what to say next. A light went on for Windflower.

"I don't want your job, if that's what you're thinking," said Windflower. "I'm not an office guy. I can do this job, and I'll do it really well once I get trained and figure it out. In the meantime, I'd like to make it as pleasant as I can around here for me and for you. Whaddya say?"

The last question hung in the air like a helium balloon until Morecombe finally popped it.

"I don't know," she finally said. "I'll think about it. But I still don't want you poaching my staff. Got it?"

"Got it. Have a good weekend," he said to Morecombe's back as she was leaving. She waved back.

An opening, a small one but an opening, Windflower thought. He spent as long as he could shuffling papers until it was time to close everything up and walk to his van. He was even growing to like that vehicle.

Bill Ford, who'd had his struggles with the bottle over the years and was now clean again, always told him that acceptance is the answer. That didn't mean you had to tolerate bad behaviour or bad people, just to accept that was the way things were and move on.

Time to move on home, he thought.

Home was a wonderful, beautiful chaos. Windflower was very happy to walk in the door where he was quickly surrounded and held prisoner by two little girls and a frantic collie.

Sheila was stirring a pot of soup on the stove and went to be part of the greeting party. "Let's go for a quick walk before supper," she said. "It'll be good for all of us to stretch our legs. I'll leave the soup on simmer."

35

Windflower ran up, got changed and was back down in a flash. He got the wagon, took Lady by the leash and went outside followed by Amelia Louise, Stella and Sheila. All of them seemed in good spirits bundled up against the cold. The girls begged for a ride in the wagon and Windflower agreed. That would give the adults a chance to talk.

"So, what happened at school?" he asked as they walked along.

"I guess Stella got frightened in class and got really upset," said Sheila.

"Did something happen or someone hurt her?"

"The teacher told the vice-principal that the day was going along smoothly and they were planning on going outside for playtime. Just before, as they were getting their coats on, the janitor had come into the room to replace a light bulb, and that's when Stella started crying, and then it only got worse."

"What did the janitor do?"

"Change the light bulb? I don't know. Why?"

"Maybe the presence of a strange man in the classroom frightened her."

"Or maybe he looked like someone she knew."

"Like her father?" asked Windflower. They knew who Stella's father was. Paul Spurrell was a now-dead drug dealer. Her mother had been a drug addict who died in a car crash just before Stella's father was killed by his rivals.

"I don't know," said Sheila. "But she was pretty upset. They are going to have her see somebody at school who knows about this stuff. And if there is any good news, they are also moving her up on the wait list for the speech pathologist."

"That is good news. Let's make sure we keep an extra eye on her. I think she really needs us right now."

"What we really need right now is to go home and have supper."

Windflower cheered, and the girls cheered along. They came up the east end of Forest Road and passed by Wilf Pittman's house. And this time there was a car in the driveway, and the lights were on.

"That's where Wilf lives," said Windflower. "I may drop by to see him on the weekend."

Sheila just smiled and squeezed his hand.

Back at the house Sheila popped a tray of chicken fingers in the oven, and Windflower sliced up celery and carrot sticks. Along with Sheila's chicken rice soup, that made for a delicious, if not entirely nutritious, supper. Tonight's movie was E.T, and Windflower made the requisite bowl of popcorn to share among them. Lady and Molly lay in wait to fight over whatever fell onto the carpet.

After the movie, they let the girls run around until they were tired enough for bed, and then Windflower and Sheila finished off the popcorn with a glass of wine. They tried to watch another movie, but neither had the stamina. It had been a full and long week, and Sheila went to have a bath while Windflower took Lady for her final turn around the block.

The night was crystal clear, and even with the lights of the city, the sky exploded in a million stars. The moon was full and bright, and Windflower thought back to his teachings about Grandmother Moon and the 13 moons of his culture. The January moon was called many names including the Spirit Moon and the Freezing or Frost Exploding Moon, from the sound the trees make when the cold temperatures freeze their branches.

In his Cree culture Grandmother Moon watched over the earth and all its creatures. She looked after the waters and the tides and called women to be the water keepers. But everyone could pray to Grandmother Moon, and as he gazed up at her fullness tonight, Windflower prayed for all the women in his life, starting with Sheila and his daughters.

He also prayed for Larissa Murphy, Brittney Hodder, Mandy Pardy and all the other missing girls. He finished with a prayer for

Mary Murphy and all the girls' mothers. They would be going to bed tonight worried about their daughters. He prayed that they be given peace and that he be given strength to help bring their daughters home safely. He pulled Lady's leash gently and led her home. He closed everything up and said goodnight to his pets. When he got upstairs, Sheila was asleep with her book as her pillow. He gently took it away, put the real pillow under her head and turned out the lights. Soon, the whole house became silent as everyone slept.

Sheila got up when she heard the girls playing in Amelia Louise's room. Windflower felt her stir, but he lay there as this was his morning to sleep in. He tried to go back to sleep but couldn't manage that. So, he picked up his Richard Wagamese book of meditations. This morning's reading was another of the many conversations Wagamese has in the book with an elder that he calls Old Woman. In the conversation Old Woman tells him to always be a gentleman.

Wagamese asks if that means he should be polite. No, says Old Woman. Be a gentle man, and act softly and kindly to yourself and others. She says to be like grass. It might get flattened when it is stepped on, but as soon as the pressure is released, it springs back up. Grass is humble, accepting and soft, and that makes it strong.

Windflower thought about how he could be like grass in his own life and especially in his work. He also thought about a saying from the Dalai Lama about kindness. 'Be kind whenever possible. It's always possible.' With that positive thought in his head, Windflower went downstairs to greet the day.

36

Sheila was already in the kitchen cutting up fruit, and the girls were lying on the living room floor in their pajamas watching cartoons.

"There's coffee," said Sheila.

"You are a princess," said Windflower.

"Queen," said Sheila

"You are the queen of my heart," said Windflower, grabbing a cup of coffee.

"I'd rather have a slave. Take these out to them, please." Sheila handed her husband two small bowls of fruit.

"Yes, your majesty," he said. Windflower brought the fruit to the girls and kissed them both on the top of their heads. When he came back, he took his smudging kit from the shelf in the porch. "I'm going outside for a minute," he told Sheila.

The morning was sunny but cold, and to Windflower it seemed like perfect weather for a skating rink. Lady was more interested in the hard ground. She was sure she had buried something somewhere, and now she couldn't get to it. In desperation she rolled around the ground over the spot where she hoped to retrieve her lost item. That didn't really help, but it looked like she felt better as she jumped up and started exploring other parts of the garden.

Windflower took out all his stuff and laid it on the deck. He lit his mixture and watched the smoke billow and then drift away in the cold air. He managed to get some of it around him and let the medicines seep into his hair and around his body. Then he did his morning prayers. First of all, he offered a prayer of gratitude for the many gifts he had been given. Then he asked that he be gentle and kind in all his thoughts, words and actions.

He prayed for his ancestors, both living and on the other side, that they have peaceful journeys wherever their paths led. Finally, and he knew he didn't do this nearly enough, he thanked his four-legged allies, not just the ones who lived with him but his spirit animals as well. Those were the ones he met as he travelled along the water or through the bush and those that came to him in dreams like the racoon and the duck. They were helping him; sometimes he could see how. By being grateful for them, they would come back and bring him more gifts. So, he prayed for their health and well-being too.

He packed up his things and called Lady, who was happy to get back inside out of the cold. Sheila was in the kitchen with two little helpers. She had an enormous bowl of dough that must have been sitting out all night because it had risen, and she and the girls were kneading it. Well, Sheila was kneading whereas the girls treated it more like play dough and made different shapes out of the small pieces Sheila had given them.

"You're making bread?" asked Windflower. "That's wonderful."

"Yes, and they're making their own special bread creatures," said Sheila. "I'll put these in, and then I thought I could make toutons for breakfast."

Windflower loved a lot of foods, but toutons were one of his favourites. Every culture had its own version of fried bread, and Newfoundlanders were no exception. You simply took leftover dough and fried it up with butter or pork fat. Windflower watched as Sheila put her loaves into the oven along with the doughy creatures that Stella and Amelia Louise had made.

Then, while Windflower cleaned up the little girls' hands and faces, scrubbing them free of sticky dough, Sheila heated butter in the frying pan and cooked up a series of small pancake-sized toutons. When they were nicely browned and cooked through, she put them on plates for the girls. They had to wait until they cooled, but then Windflower gave them the treats along with a large spoon of molasses to dip them in.

Soon after, Sheila had the second order ready, and she and Windflower sat down to enjoy their Saturday delicacy.

"I love toutons," said Windflower.

"Mila luvs em," said Amelia Louise.

"Good girl," said Windflower. "They are the ultimate comfort food."

"Yeah, I used to love going to visit my Grandmother Irene," said Sheila. "Mom didn't make much bread. She'd rather get it from the store. But Grandmother Irene was always baking. She'd always have some leftover dough to make toutons, and we'd always go home with a fresh loaf of bread."

"It reminds me a bit of my early days back home when my mom would fry up bannock for us," said Windflower. "We didn't have molasses, but we did have maple syrup. Man, that was good. But I think that these toutons might be even better."

"I thought you baked bannock in the oven."

"You can, and my Auntie Marie often did that. But many days it was cooked in a pan over a fire, and if you didn't have a pan, you used a stick."

One more small touton split between the girls and another each for Windflower and Sheila completed the meal. After cleaning up, Windflower suggested that he take the girls over to see Bill Ford.

"Might as well go now while they have lots of good energy," he said. "The walk will help them burn off some of that sugar."

"I'll stay and mind the bread," said Sheila, happy for the chance to get a break.

Windflower dressed the girls and once again was forced to relent on the wagon. Better to give them a ride than listen to them all the way there and back, he thought. Windflower walked up to the Miller Centre while pulling the girls along and left the wagon at reception, and then they went straight to Bill Ford's room.

Bill was watching TV, and he smiled broadly at Windflower and the girls as they came in.

"This is Amelia Louise, and this is Stella," said Windflower. "And this is my friend Bill."

37

The two girls stuck to Windflower like glue, so he kind of dragged and pulled them closer to Ford's bed.

"Maybe they'd like to watch TV," said Ford. "Let's see if I can find a good show." He ran through the channels on his remote control until he got to the children's stations. "How about Thomas?" he asked. "I remember watching that show with my daughter."

The two girls crept closer, pulling Windflower along with them. He settled them together in a large chair, and he took another chair on the other side of the bed.

"She's so much bigger," said Ford.

"Yeah, I guess it's been a while since you saw her," said Windflower. "How are things going here? They treating you okay?"

"They are very nice. Except for the physiotherapist. He runs me hard, like a drill sergeant. But I don't really mind. That's why I'm here. I just want my life back, as much as I can anyway."

"You'll have lots of life left. Get fixed up here and then sit back and enjoy your pension. I thought about something you taught me the other day."

"What? Like don't get shot?"

Windflower laughed. "Well, maybe that too," he said. "But I was thinking about acceptance and how it was the answer to all my problems. And it really helped me."

"I'm not ungrateful, you know," said Ford. "That's the other piece to go along with acceptance. A grateful heart has no room for self-pity or regrets. I'm ready to move on. It's just a lot of pain and effort right now."

"Stick with it."

Windflower noticed the program on TV had ended, and the

girls were starting to explore the room. He tried to stop them, but it was like playing whack-a-mole. He'd catch Stella and get her to put something down only to have Amelia Louise grab something else. Ford was laughing so hard, he was almost crying.

"That's the most fun I've had in a long time," he said.

"We're always entertained," said Windflower, joining in the laughter. "We should be going."

"Well, thank you for coming," said Ford. "And thank you to you too, Amelia Louise and Stella. Would you girls like a sucker?"

"Sucka," said Amelia Louise, and Stella's eyes grew very wide.

Ford reached over to his table and opened the drawer. He reached in and pulled out two of those large circular rainbow suckers and handed them to Windflower. "You decide when they can have them," he said.

"Like I have any choice." Windflower unwrapped the suckers and handed them over. "Say thank you," he said to the girls.

"Tank you," said Amelia Louise as loudly as she could.

Then Windflower heard Stella speak as well. "Thank you for my sucker," she said.

Windflower looked a little stunned. "She doesn't normally speak. I mean she can speak, but she doesn't do it very often. She must like you."

"I like her too," said Ford. "Come back and visit me again soon."

The girls were quite happy with themselves and their suckers on the ride back. Windflower was happy that his friend seemed in better spirits. Everyone was happy when they came into the house and smelled the homemade bread that was sitting on the kitchen counter.

"Let's have a slice of fresh bread with butter and molasses for lunch," said Windflower.

"Such a kid," said Sheila, but she sliced the bread and passed it around.

"This is so good," said Windflower.

"Sum good," said Amelia Louise.

"Stella said thank you to Bill for a sucker," Windflower told Sheila. "So did Amelia Louise, but I was surprised when Stella did too."

"Interesting," said Sheila. "She must really like him."

Stella just smiled and kept eating her lunch.

After everyone had their fill, Sheila announced that she had to go to the mall. "I'm assuming you don't want to go. I'll take the girls," she said.

"Perfect. I'll take her for a walk," he added, pointing to Lady, who so far was shut out of the dropped bread category.

"And organize something for supper," said Sheila.

After the girls and Sheila had left, Windflower cleaned up and took Lady down the road towards the end of Quidi Vidi Lake. This was where the rowing boats would turn around when they took back to the waters again in the spring for practice gearing up to the summer regatta. It was certainly something to look forward to, thought Windflower. It was a nice, pleasant day, and Windflower could feel it getting just a little milder on the way back. The wind had changed again, this time to a more southern breeze. That was great for anybody hoping for a mild spell, but it could ruin his grand scheme, his rink of dreams. He was a little put out by the thought of his dreams being dashed, but his spirits were raised when he saw Wilf Pittman in his driveway unloading groceries.

"Hey, Winston," said Pittman. "How's she going b'y?"

"It's going good," said Windflower. "Wanna hand?"

"No, thanks. This is my last bag," said Pittman. "It's easy shopping when it's only for one."

"Your wife?" asked Windflower.

"Passed away last year. Cancer. I was happy to let her go at the end. But I really miss her. It's like a hole in my heart, you know."

"I just lost my favourite Auntie. She was like a mother to me. It's hard."

"Yes b'y. So, you still thinking about a rink for your backyard?"

"Yeah, but it feels like it's getting mild again."

"And then it'll get cold. You gotta be ready for it. Want a hand?"

"Absolutely," said Windflower. "Come have a look. I have to admit that I don't know much about putting one together."

"No worries b'y," said Pittman. "I'll put this bag in the house and come with you."

Wilf Pittman walked along with Windflower and Lady and

went to the backyard. "You got a nice size yard. But you want to leave enough room to get around and for our friend here to move," he said, pointing to Lady. "Have you got a measuring tape?"

Windflower went inside and came back with the tape. Pittman took it and then walked around the yard, taking a few measurements here and there. "I think five boards along the side and two at the ends should do it," he reported. "I have some extra at the house if you want to borrow them."

"I can pay you for them," said Windflower.

"Don't worry about that. You can mow my lawn for me when I go up to the cabin. Come on with me, and we'll bring a few back at a time."

Windflower could not believe his luck. The two men carried a few boards at a time until all of them were lying in the backyard. "They look ready for action," said Windflower.

"When you're ready, just tap them together and put a few nails in. The ice will hold everything together," said Pittman. "Have you thought about using a tarp?"

"I think so," said Windflower.

"Good man. Get a big one that will cover as much of the space as possible and you'll be good to go."

"This is great. I really appreciate it. Can I offer you a cold beer?"

"No thanks b'y. I had to give that up after Lucy died. I was using it to cope. But I'd love a cup a tea."

"No problem," said Windflower.

38

Windflower and Wilf Pittman were sitting in the kitchen drinking tea and having a brownie when Sheila came home with the girls. After introductions she joined them at the kitchen table. The girls seemed to have found a new burst of energy. The house grew very loud, very quickly, but Pittman seemed to enjoy the company.

"I love having my grandkids come over," he said. "They have kept me going, that's for sure."

"I see you've got some lumber out back," said Sheila.

"That's from Wilf," said Windflower. "All I need now is a tarp, and I'll be in business."

"And a few cold nights," said Sheila. "The forecast is calling for more snow right now and then maybe freezing rain."

"That's all ice is, freezing rain," said Pittman. "Anyway, I should be going. Thanks for the tea and the snack."

"No, thank you," said Windflower.

"Would you like a loaf of bread?" asked Sheila as Pittman was leaving.

The older man paused, and he looked like he was going to cry. "I haven't had homemade bread since Lucy died," he said.

"I'll put it in a bag for you," said Sheila.

Wilf Pittman said his goodbyes and walked back down Forest Road to his house, clutching his bread under his arm.

"What a nice man," said Sheila.

"He is indeed," said Windflower. "And we're going to have a skating rink. Yay!"

"Yay. Yay," said Amelia Louise. She didn't really know why her dad was celebrating, but she was clearly happy with the news, whatever it was, and was soon marching around the house with her arms up in the air. Lady, Stella and even Windflower joined in the fun.

"So, what's for supper?" asked Sheila as she cut up some apples for a snack.

Windflower went down to the basement and rummaged around the freezer. He came back with two packages. He displayed them triumphantly to Sheila. "Cod tongues and fried fish, a true Newfoundlander's dream," he pronounced.

"That sounds great," said Sheila. As she was speaking, Amelia Louise and Stella were starting to bicker over a toy in the living room. Soon, both of them were crying.

"You take her for a nap, and I'll look after Stella," said Sheila.

Windflower put his frozen packages in the sink to thaw and carried a whiny Amelia Louise up to her room. Sheila gave Stella some paper and crayons to keep her happy.

Windflower read Amelia Louise one short story and then laid her in her crib. He thought she would fuss a bit, but she must have been really tired because he couldn't hear a peep from the monitor after just a few minutes. He was tired, too, and laid down on his bed. He closed his eyes, and before he knew it, he was fast asleep.

His sleep, however, was uneven and fitful. Sometimes afternoon naps were like that. It also usually meant that he would have some interaction with the dream world. Today was no exception. He woke in his dream near a frozen lake back home in Pink Lake. The day was crisp and cold, so cold that he could see his breath in the air. He walked out onto the ice, and he could hear it crack, but it did not budge under his weight. That meant it was early in winter before the heavy ice set solidly on top of the lake.

But from the middle of the ice, a giant crack appeared, and he started to move back towards land. Then realizing it was a dream and that he was probably not in real danger, he paused and stood absolutely still. As he did, a cloud of steam rose from an ever-widening hole in the middle of the lake and out came a beaver.

"Hello, beaver," said Windflower. "It's nice to see you again."

"Oh, you remember me. That's good," said the beaver.

"I do remember you," said Windflower. "You are the holder of great wisdom."

"You are getting better at this," said the beaver. "What do you want?"

Windflower thought about this for a moment. "I would like to know where to look for a missing girl," he said finally.

"I thought the racoon already told you. Under a bridge by the river that sings, hangs a life in the balance by a soft silver thread."

"But what does that mean? I need help."

"That's good. The first step to solving a problem is to admit you have one. The second is to ask for help. Ask and you shall receive."

The beaver disappeared into another cloud of steam that kept getting bigger and bigger until everything but mist disappeared. Then Windflower could slowly start to make out something in the distance. It was a bridge, and water was running rapidly below it. He looked around to see what else might be nearby. He saw a large white church and then what looked like the outskirts of a park. He tried to move closer to get a better look, but as he did, the ice below him began to crack and fall apart, and he woke up in his bed at home. He shook himself awake and heard Amelia Louise on the monitor and got up to see how she was doing.

She was back to her pleasant smiling self. She and Windflower almost danced on their way downstairs. Windflower was a little fuzzy headed from his nap and his dream. But he made up his mind to try to process that later. Now, he had a supper to cook.

39

The fried fish was easy. Windflower had made it dozens of times. Dry the fish well, coat it in flour, add salt and pepper, and fry it with salted pork. His special addition was a heavy hand of cayenne pepper to spice up the fish. The pork was cut into very small pieces and fried crisply to make what people around there called scrunchions. They were poured on top of the fried codfish to add an extra zing to the meal. He decided he would make some garlic mashed potatoes, ginger carrots and some maple Brussels sprouts to fill out the meal.

He could do the same with the cod tongues, he thought. They were certainly considered a prized delicacy in these parts. Or maybe something different. He started looking around for a recipe on his phone. He found one that looked interesting, baked cod tongues. Perfect. He checked to make sure he had all the ingredients and got to work getting everything ready. He put the bag of cod tongues in a bowl of warm water and made sure they were completely thawed out.

After that he washed and dried them and put one layer of them in a buttered casserole dish. He covered them with cracker crumbs, sliced onions, salt, pepper, savoury and a couple of teaspoons of butter. He laid another layer of cod tongues and covered them too. At the end he topped the mixture off with the remaining crumbs and a little more butter and covered it all with milk. It would take over an hour to cook, so he put the dish in the oven and went to join Sheila and the girls in the living room.

They were watching figure skating on TV. Stella had her eyes glued to the screen while Amelia Louise looked like she was doing an audition for the Ice Capades.

"She really likes it, doesn't she?" asked Windflower, nodding at Stella, who was lost in the skating competition.

"She does indeed," said Sheila. "I was hoping we could get to The Loop again tomorrow, but I think there might be too much snow."

"You can still skate in the snow."

"I don't think they will clean it off if we get a lot. Look outside. It's already started."

Windflower took a glance out the window and could see many, many fat white flakes coming down. "She will be very disappointed," he said. "Maybe we could take both of them to Bowring Park. We haven't been there in a long time."

"That's a great idea," said Sheila. "I don't think I've ever been there in the winter."

"Okay then, that's a plan."

"So, what's the plan for supper? I can smell something delicious already."

"It's a new recipe. I hope you like it."

Windflower went back into the kitchen to get everything else moving. He peeled the potatoes and carrots and sliced the ends off the Brussels sprouts. He cut the pork into tiny pieces and got that frying on the stove and laid out a plate of flour that had been sprinkled with salt and black pepper. Then he added his usual dose of cayenne pepper.

Once the vegetables were boiling, he moved the fried pork scrunchions to the side of the cast iron pan, carefully placed two pieces of cod in the fat and let them sizzle for five minutes on each side. Then he put the rest of the fish in the pan. While that was cooking, he mashed up the potatoes and put in his butter and milk and garlic shavings. He sliced some fresh ginger and added it with a dab of butter to the carrots. Finally, he poured a dollop of maple syrup over the Brussels sprouts along with another dab of butter. "That's a lot of butter in all of this," he said to himself.

"What did you say?" asked Sheila. "And is supper almost ready?"

"Ready to go," said Windflower. "Send in the troops."

Sheila got the girls organized while Windflower took the casserole dish out of the oven.

"Oh my God, that smells great," said Sheila.

Windflower put all the veggies in serving bowls and laid them on the table. Then, he served up a piece of fried fish for everybody.

Sheila doled out the veggies and dug into the baked cod tongues. The aroma of fish, onions and butter soon filled the room. She poured a helping on her plate to let it cool before she handed it off to her daughters and gave Windflower a ladleful.

"Oh, that is good," said Windflower as he tasted the piping hot cod tongue dish. "I've always wondered what cod tongues would taste like without frying them up."

"They are good," said Sheila. "But so is the fish. Do you like the fish?" she asked the girls.

Stella nodded her head vigorously. Amelia Louise was more vocal in her appreciation.

"Mila sum good," she said.

"I think the Mila thing is going to stick," said Windflower.

"Everybody at daycare who can speak calls her Mila. So do the workers," said Sheila. "I think we're done on that one. We'll still call her what we like at home, but it will be Mila everywhere else, until she changes it."

"Why would she change it?"

"Wait 'til she hits puberty and then her teenage years. Girls go a little crazy then. The good news is they grow up quickly. One day they're boy crazy, and all they want to do is paint their toenails. Then another day they declare they're a young woman and start acting like it."

"Sounds like a scary time."

"I can remember it being nerve-wracking for me, and I suppose it was for my parents too. But at least they're not boys."

"Why do you say that?"

"Boys never grow up."

"Are you talking about me?" asked Windflower.

"I saw a quote the other day. I'm not sure who said it," said Sheila. "Boys never actually grow up; their toys just get bigger and more expensive."

Windflower started to protest, but Sheila cut him off. "I'll clean up. You go relax in the living room with the girls."

Windflower and the girls played Jenga until Sheila came out with a plate of cookies and a pot of tea for her and Windflower. She joined in the game, which went quite well until Amelia Louise decided it would be more fun to just knock the whole stack over and laugh. Or when Lady figured that she should be in on the game and knocked it over with her sizable rear end.

But everyone laughed and was in good spirits. They watched a little TV until the girls started to tire out, and Sheila took them up for their bath. Windflower and Lady went outside. The snow was really coming down now, and big, beautiful swirling flakes landed all over their faces. Lady loved new snow and tried to eat as much as she could before it hit the ground. It was a pleasant walk, and a great way to end that part of the evening.

Back home, Windflower read Stella her stories and tucked her in. When he got back downstairs, Sheila was going through the Netflix guide looking for a movie.

"Any suggestions?" asked Windflower.

"How about something mindless like the new Avengers movie?" asked Sheila.

"Perfect. I'll make the popcorn."

Windflower returned a few minutes later with a bowl of buttered popcorn and sat beside Sheila on the couch. The next couple of hours were as advertised, completely fictional and fun.

"That was great," said Windflower as the movie credits rolled on the screen.

"Just what I needed," said Sheila. "I'm going to have a long bath and read my book."

"I'll let Lady out and then go to bed," said Windflower. "It's my turn to get up in the morning."

"I know," said Sheila with an impish laugh as she went upstairs.

Windflower didn't really mind getting up Sunday mornings with the girls. It was a special time with them, and he knew these days wouldn't last forever. He let Lady out in back and watched as the snow continued to fall. Once Lady was done, she came back to the door, and Windflower dried her off and went up to bed. He started to read, but his eyes were closing faster than he could turn the pages.

He didn't hear anything else until Amelia Louise's voice came over the monitor. He got out of bed as quickly as he could and got Amelia Louise. Stella must have heard them because she was waiting for them at the top of the stairs just outside Amelia Louise's room.

40

Windflower put on the coffee and let Lady out. It was still snowing, and there was quite a bit down on the ground. He turned on cartoons for the girls and checked the weather on his phone. The snow was expected to taper off later in the morning and end by noon. And even better, when he took a look at the long-range forecast, it said it would get cold overnight and stay that way. The high the following day was only going to be minus five.

All across St. John's people were already shivering as they thought about how cold it would be, but Windflower was dancing in his kitchen. Soon he was joined by Stella and Amelia Louise and Lady when she was let back in.

Windflower looked in the cupboard for his Sunday morning special treats, and two wide-eyed little girls waited patiently for their Pop Tarts. But as frantically as he looked, he could not find them anywhere. This was not good, he thought to himself. Time to think of a new plan and fast. He looked around the fridge and could only see healthy foods like fruit and vegetables. That certainly wouldn't do.

In desperation, he opened the freezer. "Eureka," he said.

"Reeka," said Amelia Louise, clearly hoping that would mean good news on the food front. Stella looked unconvinced.

Windflower took a frozen pizza out of the freezer and turned on the oven.

"Pizza for breakfast," he said.

Amelia Louise knew that was good news and started dancing around the kitchen singing, "Pizza, pizza, pizza". Stella knew for sure this was good news, and she joined in the dancing. Lady was also quick to join the party even though she wasn't sure what the fuss was all about. Pretty soon it got really loud.

"What is going on down there?" asked Sheila after being woken by the noise.

"We're just getting breakfast ready, sorry," said Windflower.

"Pizza!" yelled Amelia Louise.

"Shhhhh," said Windflower, and he put his finger to his lips. Amelia Louise followed suit. So did Stella, who wasn't even speaking.

"What?" asked Sheila.

"They're just happy to hear your voice," said Windflower. "You just relax, and I'll bring you up a cup of coffee."

He got the girls half an orange each and brought Sheila up her coffee.

"Is everything okay?" she asked. "What are you making them for breakfast? I didn't get any more Pop Tarts. Those things are awful."

"Yes, they're awful," said Windflower. "They're eating an orange right now," he added, hoping she wouldn't ask any more questions. Luckily, she didn't, and he went downstairs to check on the pizza. Five more minutes and it would be done.

When it was cooked, he sliced up a piece for each of the girls and had one for himself while he was waiting for theirs to cool. He brought another piece with him when he served up their order in front of the TV. It was so good that everybody had another piece, and Windflower got rid of the evidence in the recycling bin.

When Sheila came down, Windflower made her some fruit and toast, and she seemed none the wiser. She got ready for church with Stella while Windflower and Amelia Louise got dressed for Windflower's Sunday morning run. He helped Sheila get her car out of the driveway and pulled the van in near the house. The good news was that the snow had slowed to a white trickle and would soon be over by the looks of it.

Windflower put Amelia Louise in the carrier and took off for his run. He stayed on the side streets and in the middle of the road wherever possible. It was slow going, but it felt good to be outside. By the time he came back around to Forest Road from a long loop down by the waterfront, he had a pleasant runner's high thanks to the endorphins he had released. He was also getting a little tired and slowed near Wilf Pittman's house.

Pittman was in his garage putting his snowblower away.

"Morning, Winston," he said. "Whaddya up to today?"

"Just out for a run," said Windflower. "Looks like the snow is done, at least for now."

"I'd say so," said Pittman. "Gonna turn cold tonight. I might put my rink in."

"That's exciting," said Windflower. "Mind if I come over for a look?"

"Come over anytime after supper, although there's not much to see."

"I'd still like to see how you do it. Anyway, I gotta go. Sheila's gone to church, and I've got to get things ready for lunch. We're going to Bowring Park after that."

"That was one of Lucy's favourite places. We'd go in for a walk around almost every Sunday."

"Hey, why don't you come with us?"

"I couldn't intrude on your family time."

"Don't worry about that. We have no privacy anyway," said Windflower with a laugh. "We'll come by and get you after lunch."

"Okay, but why don't we take my van? You'll want to take her, for sure," said Pittman, pointing at Lady.

"Perfect," said Windflower. "Sheila will be back from church soon. We'll get them a bite, and then we're ready to go. Come by around one."

Windflower waved goodbye to Pittman and hurried the last few steps home, arriving just before Sheila and Stella. After getting everyone into the house and undressed, Sheila made them pancakes with fruit for lunch.

Windflower told her about Wilf Pittman and that he was coming with them to Bowring Park.

"That's great," said Sheila. "He's a very nice man."

"And I'm going over after supper to see him put his skating rink in."

Sheila rolled her eyes, but Stella looked really excited.

"Maybe he'll let you try it out," said Windflower. "Then, we'll build our own too."

Stella looked like she was going to burst.

"Don't get her hopes up," said Sheila. "You haven't got a rink yet."

"Only a matter of time," said Windflower. "Speaking of time, it's almost one. We better get moving."

41

A few minutes later Wilf Pittman's van pulled up in front of their house, and the Windflower clan got on board with Lady bringing up the rear in the back with the girls' wagon. She looked a little cramped but was happy not to be left behind. Pittman drove across town and parked at the west entrance to the park. Everyone got out, and Windflower put the girls in the wagon and Lady on the leash.

It was a beautiful day now that the snow had stopped, and many families were out enjoying themselves. The paths had been cleared so everyone could walk or run at their leisure.

As they walked along, Wilf Pittman was very quiet. Windflower let the girls out of the wagon, and they ran on ahead with Lady on the leash while he and Sheila stayed back with their new friend.

"It must be hard without your wife," said Sheila. "How long were you together?"

"Forty-two years," said Pittman. "I do miss her, but coming here helps. Apart from Grates Cove where she was born, this was her favourite place on earth."

"We like it too," said Windflower. "It feels like this park has been here forever."

Pittman laughed. "The land has been here forever. It was once a farm that was bought up by the Bowrings on the 100th anniversary of being in business in Newfoundland. They donated it to the city in 1911, and the park was officially opened in 1914, just before the war."

"You know a lot about the history of this place," said Sheila.

'We spent a lot of time here, and I started looking up the story of the park," said Pittman. "They really expanded the place during the 1970s, buying up another 150 acres of land that once belonged to Sir Richard Squires. But the magic of the place to me and Lucy was always the duck pond and Peter Pan."

"I love that statue," said Sheila. "I remember the times we'd come to St. John's, and my cousins and I would go swimming in the pool, get custard cones at The Bungalow and go see the ducks and Peter Pan."

They were entering the area where the duck pond was, and Windflower called the girls back to join them. Together they walked down by the water where even in winter people came to feed the ducks. Windflower didn't have any food for them, a great disappointment for both ducks and girls. But he promised to bring some next time.

Stella and Amelia Louise both loved the Peter Pan statue at first sight.

"All my children loved Peter Pan," said Pittman. "My grandkids too."

"It is pretty magical," said Sheila, "with Peter Pan playing the flute, and it looks like all the fairies and animals are climbing up towards him."

"Do you know the story of the statue?" asked Pittman.

"Wasn't there something about one of the Bowring children?" asked Windflower.

"Correct," said Pittman. "The statue was erected in memory of Sir Edgar Bowring's grandchild Betty Munn. She drowned along with her father when the passenger ship, the Florizel, sank off the Southern Shore in 1918.

"I love the inscription," said Sheila. "In memory of a little girl who loved the park."

They walked back up to the parking lot, piled back into the van and drove down towards the eastern part of the park.

"Anybody for ice cream?" asked Pittman. "There's a place not too far away."

"Ice cream," yelled Amelia Louise.

"Ice cream," said Stella much more quietly. But Sheila and Windflower noticed.

"I think it's unanimous," said Sheila.

"Great," said Pittman, and he started to turn right just past the park.

"Wait," said Windflower as they rounded the corner. Pittman slowed the car and parked.

"Is everything okay?" he asked. "You don't want ice cream?"

"It's not that," said Windflower as he got out of the car. On his left was a large white church and up ahead was a bridge over a fast running river.

"What's that river called?" asked Windflower

"It's the Waterford River," said Pittman. "Some people call it the singing river. There's an old story about a woman who supposedly lived near here but got washed away in a flood. Her body was missing and never found. It's said that she comes back every night to sing by the river."

Windflower got back in the van.

"Are you all right?" asked Sheila.

"I am," said Windflower. "Let's go for ice cream."

Everybody cheered at that news. Windflower smiled along with the fun, but inside he was churning. There's something going on—I just have to figure out what, he thought. But that would have to wait until he got back home and found a quiet place to think.

Pittman drove over the bridge, and a short while later they were on the highway out to the Town of Conception Bay South. He took the Manuels exit and pulled up to a very busy ice cream shop. Everyone quickly got out and into the lineup.

Windflower and his crew got a chance to look at the menu with its dozens of flavours of ice cream, frozen yogurt and milkshakes. Sheila ordered small soft-serve twists on homemade waffle cones for the girls and took a lemon-blueberry yogurt in a cup for herself. Windflower had the chocolate peanut butter parfait and Wilf Pittman had a medium vanilla cone. He tried to pay when they got to the cash, but Windflower beat him to it.

With plenty of napkins in hand for the girls, they all went to the van to eat their ice cream. After their treats were gone, Pittman suggested they drive out towards Topsail and then make their way back through St. Philip's. Windflower had done this drive many times, and he and Sheila happily agreed.

Amelia Louise started to drop off a few minutes into their journey, and by the time they reached Topsail, Stella was nodding off too. Windflower was sitting in the front with the older man and enjoying the scenery as Conception Bay came into view. Then they skirted along the shoreline and wound their way back towards St. John's. Before they knew it, they were coming up by Bell Island and heading towards the airport. Soon after that Pittman pulled up in front of their door.

"Thank you for a grand day," said Pittman as Windflower started unloading a sleepy-eyed Stella.

"Thank you for the ride," said Sheila. She took Amelia Louise in her arms and went inside.

Once Stella was inside too, Windflower went back to the van for Lady and the wagon. "I'll see you after supper," he said to Pittman.

Sheila let the girls watch TV while they came back to life. "I can organize supper if you give these guys a bath," she said.

"That's a pretty good deal," said Windflower. "Bath time," he announced.

"Baff time," said Amelia Louise.

"It's bath time, Mila," said Stella.

Windflower and Sheila looked at each other as if to say, "What gives?"

"Okay," said Windflower. "Last one up is a rotten egg," and he took off up the stairs. Stella and Amelia Louise came running after him.

"It's a tie," he declared as he waited at the top of the stairs. "Two rotten eggs going in the bath." He ran the water and added some bubbles while the girls started tossing toys into the tub. Windflower slowed them down on that activity and got them undressed before the girls joined up with the toys.

He sat and watched them play. It was a very relaxing time for all of them, and after they got out, he made sure they were dried off and wrapped each of them in a towel. Then he went to their bedrooms and laid out their pajamas. Stella sat and took her time putting hers on. Once Windflower caught Amelia Louise, he saw to it that she got into hers as well.

42

Windflower carried the girls downstairs to join Sheila as she finished making the salad.

"Something smells pretty good," he said.

"It's my last casserole," said Sheila. "I'll have to find some time next weekend to make more. They're lifesavers. Can you put on a can of corn to go along with this salad and the casserole?"

Windflower laid the girls down, opened the corn and put it in a pot. "Are you ready for this?" he asked.

"Casserole is just about done," said Sheila after she had opened the oven door for a peek. Minutes later Windflower put some salad and corn on the girls' plates, and Sheila took the casserole dish out of the oven and laid it on a trivet.

"It looks fabulous," said Windflower. "What is it?"

"It's a Cajun shrimp casserole. I didn't make it as spicy as we would like because I wanted to make sure the girls would eat some," said Sheila. She gave Windflower a helping, scooped a large portion on an extra plate to let it cool and sat to eat her salad and corn.

"What's in it?" asked Windflower.

"Shrimp and a special alfredo sauce with parmesan cheese, along with garlic rice and spices. So how is it?"

"Oh, my goodness. This is divine. Another hit, Sheila Hillier."

Sheila took a taste and had to agree. "Mmmm. This is really good," she said. "We'll have to repeat this one for sure."

After dinner they shared a can of peaches with whipped cream and took a plate of cookies to the living room to watch a bit of TV before the girls went to bed.

Windflower had a quick cup of tea and then got up. "I've got to go see a man about a skating rink," he said.

Lady was already at the door. "Might as well take her with you," said Sheila. "But don't let her get wet. It's too cold."

Windflower waved his hands as if to say don't worry about it and took Lady with him to see Wilf Pittman.

Pittman had a big spotlight over his back door and had cleared the empty rink of snow, except for a packed layer that covered the ground. He was laying out the hose when Windflower came to his back gate.

"Just in time," he said to Windflower as he sprayed water gently all over the snowy surface. "Leave a packed layer of snow on the bottom to protect the ground and give you a solid base. Then spray the water on lightly. You don't want to melt the snow."

"That's interesting," said Windflower. "So, you actually try and get the water to meld onto the snow."

"That gives you the best base," said Pittman. "I'll come out in an hour or so and spray another layer. It's good and cold for it tonight. Then one more spray later on, and if all goes well, I'll flood it and let it set."

"Excellent. I'll come back tomorrow and see how well you've done."

"Absolutely," said Pittman. "See you tomorrow."

Windflower took Lady home. He heard Sheila upstairs bustling around with the girls. He went upstairs and then took Stella and Amelia Louise downstairs and let them play with their dollies, freeing Sheila up to finish the housework upstairs. She came down a few minutes later with a load of laundry.

Windflower made them a pot of tea, and when she came back, Sheila joined him in a cup.

"How was Wilf tonight?" she asked.

"He was great, his usual self," said Windflower. "Aren't you going to ask me the important question?"

"What's that, Winston?"

"How's the skating rink coming along?"

"Oh yeah, and I guess you want to tell me your plans too. Okay, shoot."

"Thank you for your interest," said Windflower. "Wilf's rink is coming along very well. It might be ready in a couple of nights.

Maybe, if you have time, you could go skating."

Instantly, Stella was at Sheila's feet with begging eyes hoping for a positive response.

"Well, if everyone behaves at school, and it's okay with Mr. Pittman, I think we might be able to do that," said Sheila.

With the widest grin possible, Stella was soon jumping and dancing all over the place. Amelia Louise didn't know what her sister was celebrating, but she was very happy to join in the fun. That burst of energy lasted quite a while, but eventually both girls were tired enough to go to bed. As Windflower tucked Stella in, he noticed she still had a big grin plastered on her face. In no time the two little ones were asleep.

"She probably fell asleep thinking about skating," said Windflower as he came back downstairs to join Sheila, who was now folding laundry. He picked up a pile and started folding too.

"Probably," said Sheila. "She's sure looking forward to it."

"It will be great when we get our own rink," said Windflower.

"You might have to wait for it. Forecast is calling for more snow later in the week."

"It's a long winter, and you can't keep a good rink down." Windflower passed over his folded laundry.

"'The very substance of the ambitious is merely the shadow of a dream,'" said Sheila.

Windflower was trying to think up a good quote in response when his cell phone rang. He picked it up and walked into the kitchen.

"Evening, Sarge, hope I'm not disturbing you," said Tizzard.

"No problem, Eddie. What's up?"

"I've got three reports from neighbours now who say that there've been people inside that house across the brook. They think they were doing drugs in there."

"Have you been inside? What's it like?"

"Not yet. I have to report my activities to Lundquist, and when he heard about this, he said we had to get a warrant. I told him the door was open and there was likely illegal entry, but he said to get a warrant before we went in. I have to wait until Judge Wareham comes back tomorrow morning."

"I'll call Quigley," said Windflower. He hung up right away and called the inspector. No answer. That usually meant that Quigley was with his girlfriend. Her conditions were that he left his phone and his service weapon outside her home. She didn't want to be exposed to either. Windflower left a message in as calm a voice as he could muster. But he was pretty sure Ron Quigley would know he was pretty peeved with Lundquist.

When he came back to the living room, Sheila had gone upstairs. He let Lady out one more time and looked up at the moon, which was still nearly full. He said another prayer to Grandmother Moon and a special one for his Auntie Marie, who he was sure was up there too. He asked Auntie Marie for her blessings and guidance, and as he opened the door to let Lady in, he also asked his Auntie to help him be kind and gentle, especially to those he didn't particularly like.

The cold meant Lady didn't need much coaxing to come inside. Windflower said goodnight to her and Molly before heading upstairs.

"'Our doubts are traitors and make us lose the good we oft might win by fearing to attempt,'" he said to Sheila, finally coming up with the quote he was looking for as he entered the room.

"Go to bed, Winston. Maybe you can think about your rink of dreams," said Sheila.

"That's a good idea," said Windflower as he made himself comfortable. The night was calm and clear outside, and he felt himself easily falling asleep as he thought about his skating rink, smiling as much as Stella had earlier. There were no dreams, only a gentle sleep that left Windflower well rested and ready for another week.

43

The Monday morning routine was as frantic and hectic as ever, but Windflower managed to get downstairs and make some coffee for the adults and scrambled eggs for everybody. Stella and Amelia Louise came down looking for him when he was making their toast and slicing an orange to go along with their eggs. The girls were contented to sit quietly with their breakfast.

"Coffee?" asked Windflower when Sheila came down.

She smiled and took a cup while he made her toast and placed it on her plate of eggs.

"Thank you, I like the service," said Sheila

"'No man can sincerely try to help another without helping himself,'" said Windflower as he sat down to his own eggs. Then he remembered that he had forgotten to tell Sheila that Herb Stoodley was coming to town.

"Herb is expected today to run his errands for the café. We're going to meet up and were wondering if you can join us?"

"I don't think I can. I've got a meeting with my advisor," said Sheila.

"Oh, too bad. I'm sure he would've been happy to see you."

"I've got to get my advisor to help me get some more credits transferred over. Otherwise, I'll have another full term to do at the end of my program."

"That wouldn't be good. I'd be surprised if we were still in St. John's then."

"What do you mean? Not that I mind going back to Grand Bank, but we just got here."

"I dunno, but I don't think I'm a desk guy. I much prefer to be on a case or at a detachment."

"Well, you're on a case now."

"True. I'm not unhappy, Sheila. Just thinking ahead."

"That's not like you. Usually you try to stay in the moment like some Zen master."

The girls giggled at that last remark as if they knew Sheila was teasing Windflower.

"Sen masta," said Amelia Louise, and both girls laughed again. So, she did it again and again and again.

"Thanks a lot, Sheila. Despite your morning antics I'll clean up and make lunches if you get them ready. Do you want a scoop of that casserole from last night? I'm going to take some."

"Sounds great," said Sheila.

Windflower cleaned up and made lunches for everybody. He helped Sheila get the girls out the door when they came down and grabbed Lady and her leash in time to wave goodbye.

It was still cold, and the breath from the mouths of Windflower and Lady looked like two trails of smoke coming up the rear. Windflower opted to take a quick walk to the bottom of Signal Hill and slowly navigate his way back up. Even on this wintry morning, there were a few people who had decided to run up the steep hill. Windflower had done that a couple of times in the past. Nearly killed him. But he thought it might be something he could try again, sometime, perhaps when the weather got better.

After the trek up the hill, he decided he still had lots of energy, so he took a detour to Wilf Pittman's. He snuck down the laneway and peeked over the fence. The skating rink looked pristine and glorious.

"Came out pretty good, didn't it?" said Pittman, who must have seen him from the window.

"Yes, I was just admiring it," said Windflower.

"Now, all I need are some skaters," said Pittman. "My grandkids won't be over 'til next weekend, and the way the weather is around here, it might be gone by then."

"I might have somebody who'd try it out for you. Stella loves skating. Could she and Sheila come over some night?"

"Any night you please." Pittman's eyes became wide, and a broad grin appeared on his face.

"Thank you," said Windflower. "Have a great day, Wilf."

"You too, Winston."

Back home Windflower realized he hadn't left enough time to smudge. He was running late. So instead he took out his Richard Wagamese book and read a few short paragraphs. What stuck with him this morning was a section where Wagamese wrote about intentions and how they impact not just those who have them but everyone else around them. He described it by saying that whatever word or intentions are thrown out into the world, they always come back. So, Windflower decided, this meant if he threw out something like "I'm unhappy" or "I'm mad" or "I'm sad", he would attract more of the same. And if he said out loud that he was happy or grateful to be alive, that energy would surround him.

Windflower took a deep breath and yelled out, "This is the best day of my life." Lady came running towards him to see if he was okay.

"I'm okay, girl. Just practicing my gratitude," he said. "I'm grateful for you too." Windflower patted Lady on the head, and when Molly finally roused herself to see what the ruckus was about, he petted her as well. "I'm not afraid of you," he said out loud. Molly looked like she was cat-laughing at him. "Meow" was all she had to say.

"Enough of this sitting around," said Windflower mostly to himself. He grabbed his briefcase and his lunch and went to the van to go to work. The drive was a little slow, which was fine for Windflower. He took his time and waved to everybody along the way until he came to the RCMP regional HQ building.

When he got to his office, there were messages on his phone. One was from Smithson talking about the school counsellor and something about a man with a beard, and the other was from Scott Robbins in Ottawa. But before he could return any of those calls, his cell phone rang.

"Good morning, Sergeant," said Quigley. "How is life in the service of the Crown?"

"I'm doing my best," said Windflower. "'If to do were as easy as to know what were good to do, chapels had been churches and poor men's cottages princes' palaces.'"

"Ah, my dear Winston, 'things won are done; joy's soul lies in the doing,'" said Quigley.

"I am happy, Ron, but Lundquist is driving me crazy. He's interfering in the investigation again. Tizzard's found a house that we think might be connected, and Lundquist is making him wait for a warrant. We need to move."

"Okay. What's the story on the house? And how did you find out about it?"

Windflower paused. He didn't really want to tell Quigley that he saw the house in a dream, so he ignored that question. But he answered the other one. "It's an empty house in Grand Bank. Been for sale for years. But there's clearly been some people in there, and the neighbours told Tizzard that they think there's drug activity going on. Lots of reason to just go in, even if it's to protect the property."

"I'll talk to Lundquist. Anything else?"

"By the time you talk to him, we'll have the search warrant," said Windflower. "I don't want him slowing us down."

"Or maybe you still want to run Grand Bank," said Quigley.

Windflower didn't say anything. He had a pang that told him Quigley might be right. But he wasn't going to acknowledge that, at least not yet. He stayed silent for a moment longer.

"Lundquist is not a bad cop. You dealt with him before," said Quigley. "He's like all of us when we first start out. Half of him is desperate to please, and the other half is terrified of making a mistake. You've been there. If you can, cut him a little slack."

"Okay. But no more delays," said Windflower, seeking to withdraw gracefully but still get a concession.

"Absolutely. I'll talk to him. Enjoy your day, unless you have other plans."

Windflower didn't get a chance to respond. He was okay with that because Terry Robbins was standing in his office doorway.

"Buy you a coffee?" asked Robbins.

44

Windflower and Robbins walked to the cafeteria, got their coffees and sat by the window looking out over Quidi Vidi Lake.

"How was your weekend?" asked Windflower.

"It was good," said Robbins. "Went down to George Street on Friday night with some friends and then went skiing at White Hills yesterday. You?"

"Family time," said Windflower. "We went to Bowring Park yesterday. That was nice."

"Cool," said Robbins. "I love that park. Did you talk to my brother?"

"Not yet," said Windflower. "He's on my list. What's up?"

"They've made some connections between the Angels in Ottawa and girls, human trafficking. Not your girls, though, our girls, some from New Brunswick. They found one, or she found them, and they're tracking that down."

"Excellent. If we can find the pattern, we just follow it. We think criminals are some kind of masterminds, but really they are looking for the fastest and simplest way to make money without having to follow rules."

"Anyway, talk to Scottie. He's got more details. And by the way, Morecombe won't be in today."

"Is she sick or something?"

"You don't know? Her husband is dying. Stage four liver cancer. The last I heard they're moving him to palliative care soon."

"That's awful," said Windflower as they gathered their cups and went back to work. He was still thinking about Morecombe and why some of her bad behaviours started to make sense when his phone rang again.

"Good morning, Sergeant, how are you this fine morning?" asked Herb Stoodley.

"I'm great," said Windflower. "Where are you now?"

"Just pulled into Goobies. I'm going to sit and have my breakfast before I head into town. I don't want any part of the Monday morning traffic rush."

"Good stuff. We're still on after lunch? Sheila can't come unfortunately. She's got a meeting at school."

"That's too bad. But I can meet you around one o'clock if that's good for you."

"Perfect," said Windflower. "I'll see you then at the Tim Hortons."

Windflower then put a call in to Scott Robbins in Ottawa.

"Good morning, Scott. I hear you've got some news," said Windflower.

"Yeah, we found another girl in the market," said Scott Robbins. "She was hanging around outside a strip club when a cruiser went by. He thought she looked young so called it in. Our unit went by, and a female member talked to her, convinced her to come in."

"Where's she from?" asked Windflower.

"From Bathurst, New Brunswick. I don't know much more except our officer said she was very scared of the guys she was working for. Hells Angels. She's getting a medical exam this morning, and then we're going to talk to her this afternoon. I've managed to get in on the interview."

"Can you see if she knew any of our girls, or if she saw or heard about any girls from Newfoundland?"

"Absolutely. I'll let you know what she says."

"Thanks, Scott. Appreciate your help," said Windflower.

He then called Langmead at the RNC to give him an update. He was wondering how he could get around to asking about the location out in the west end that he'd seen in his dream. He didn't have to worry since he got Langmead's voice mail. He left a message and called Smithson in Marystown.

"Morning, Sarge, glad you called," said Smithson. "So, I talked to the counsellor at the school. He's talked to the girl's family, and we're all going to meet at their house this afternoon. Evanchuk is coming over too."

"That's great," said Windflower.

"And the counsellor told me that he'd seen the girl with an older guy outside the school property one day. A guy with a beard. He was riding a motorcycle."

"Another piece of the puzzle."

"The only question the counsellor had was why it took us so long to start looking into the biker activity around the school."

"Fair enough, I suppose, but we don't have the resources to do anything more than basic policing and sometimes not even that. Stay with it, Smithson, and let me know how it goes."

"Will do, boss."

Windflower stood to stretch his legs and thought about getting another coffee. But he wasn't fast enough. His phone rang again. It was Tizzard.

"Hey, Sarge. We got the warrant, and I'm at the house. It's quite a mess."

"What's in there?"

"Well, there's certainly been a party," said Tizzard. "Roaches and empty beer bottles and even a few used syringes and a sleeping bag that I wouldn't touch from Marystown."

"That's good," said Windflower. "Get as many prints as you can from the place, safely, of course, and run them through the system. Also, can you keep any that you can't identify separate?"

"Sure," said Tizzard. "What are you looking for? The girls?"

"Yes, but maybe there might be some prints from a boy or two in there as well."

"Gotcha. I'll start in right away. The good news is that Corporal Lundquist told me to take as long as I needed. Even said he would pull my overnighter if needed."

"That's good too," said Windflower. "Thanks, Eddie."

After he hung up this time, he did manage to get out of his office and down to the cafeteria. He took his casserole with him to heat up in the microwave. It was a little early, but he'd learned that he should eat when he could because he might not get a chance later. Maybe it was Eddie Tizzard who had taught him that. Windflower got his coffee and sipped on it while the casserole spun around in the microwave.

The shrimp dish was just as good warmed up as it was the day before, and Windflower savoured every bite. He washed his container and took the remainder of his coffee back to his office with him. There was a message on his phone from Carl Langmead asking Windflower to come over and meet at two o'clock. He called back, but Langmead was gone. He left a message saying he would be there.

The timing was perfect. He could have an hour with Herb Stoodley and then pop in to see Langmead. He might even have a donut. He'd been thinking about a Boston Cream donut for weeks now but had resisted the temptation. Today might be his lucky day.

Indeed it was, and he didn't even have to order it. Herb Stoodley was sitting in the corner of the coffee shop with two large coffees and two of Windflower's favourite donuts in front of him.

"I got you black," said Stoodley. "If you want, you can get sugar or milk at the counter."

"No, no this is perfect," said Windflower as Stoodley passed him his coffee and a donut.

The two men enjoyed their beverages and snacks and passed away nearly an hour just talking about eating, fishing and their families. The time flew by, and before he knew it, Windflower had to beg off to go to his meeting.

"No worries," said Stoodley. "I have to get back anyway. Somebody said there might be snow in the forecast. But come to my van with me. I'll get your CDs."

Windflower followed him out.

"I know I've shared a lot of Beethoven with you, but this Symphony No. 3 by the Pittsburgh Symphony Orchestra is just outstanding," said Stoodley. "It's traditional, but it almost sounds brand new with the twists that the conductor has introduced."

"Thanks," said Windflower. "I'll listen to it on my Sunday morning run."

"And I've been looking for this one forever. I had a copy years ago and lent it out," said Herb as he handed over the other CD.

Windflower read the cover. "Wow," he said. "The 50 Greatest

Pieces of Classical Music, recorded by the London Philharmonic Orchestra. This is amazing."

"It's got everything from Grieg to Verdi to Mahler and everything in between," said Stoodley. "Every lover of classical music should have this in their collection."

"Thank you, Herb. I'll bring them back."

"No, you keep them. My gift. Give my love to Sheila, and kiss both those girls for me."

"We'll see you soon in Grand Bank," said Windflower, and he watched Herb drive away.

45

Windflower took the remains of his coffee and walked up to the RNC building. He had Langmead paged and then followed him up to a small boardroom where Hayes and Foote were waiting.

"Hayes, you go first," said Langmead.

"They've got troops marshalled on both sides," said Hayes. "The Angels and their locals have brought in four or five heavy hitters we know about from New Brunswick and Nova Scotia. Full-patch members, all with lengthy and violent backgrounds. They've already had a war council and are waiting for an attack. They've fortified their club house and have set up a couple of safe houses around the area."

"Show them the pictures," said Langmead.

Hayes opened his folder and passed them around.

In the pictures, Windflower saw bikers hanging around outside a low concrete building. A construction company was putting a new steel door on the front. He thought he could see a river running behind what was obviously their clubhouse. "Where is this?" he asked.

"It's on the Old Waterford Bridge Road," said Hayes, referring to a winding narrow road that was poorly maintained and infrequently used. "It's an ancient foundry or something hidden away from the residential neighbourhoods on Waterford Bridge Road. Building has been there forever. The Angels bought the property a few years back and have been letting their puppets use it."

"Can we get inside?" asked Windflower.

"If we have a warrant, we can," said Langmead. "Why not? Hayes, why don't you get working on that when we're done? And what about the other guys?"

"Yeah, so the Outlaws have moved almost all their guys in from Grand Falls," said Hayes. "Together with their locals they would have about twenty riders and a few more hang-arounds. The Mounties out there say they have more than enough weaponry on hand to make a big splash."

"When I was out there a few years ago, we found a stash that included everything from stun grenades to fully automatic rifles," said Windflower.

"If there's going to be a firefight, we're hopelessly out-gunned," said Langmead. "Plus, we really don't want to be into that at all if we can help it. We have to head it off. That's why a raid is a good idea."

"Where are the Outlaws set up?" asked Windflower.

"They don't really have one location," said Hayes. "Because they're newer and because they're afraid that the Angels would blow them up, they have a few safe houses, but no real clubhouse. There're some bars that they run out in the west end though. That's where we could find most of them if we were looking for them."

"We might have to do both," said Langmead. "Do you think your tactical guys could help us out with a few bodies?" he asked Windflower.

"I can ask," replied Windflower.

"Okay, let's hold off any action until we know if the Mounties can help," said Langmead. "Foote, you're next. What about the new girls?"

"Same pattern," said Foote. "Girls go a little wild, especially the ones from out of town, and come into the bikers' radar. They scoop them up for a party, and then they're gone. We're no further ahead than we were before, only now we've got more missing girls."

"Why don't you tell us what's going on in Ottawa?" Langmead asked Windflower.

"Well, first of all we're trying to track down some connections on the south coast," said Windflower. "We're talking to a girl and her family this afternoon in Marystown. She says she was approached but turned the bikers down. And we're still trying to find a boy who may have served as a go-between in Grand Bank."

"That's really good," said Foote. "The only real success we've had on these cases is when we've had a girl talk to us, and if you can get the boy, that would be great."

"We're working on it," said Windflower. "As far as Ottawa goes, nothing new on the Murphy girl, but they picked up another girl. This time from New Brunswick. She agreed to go with them, and they're interviewing her this afternoon. I'm getting a report from my contact."

"Okay, so some progress, but nothing substantial yet. I guess we keep plugging. We'll get the warrant going if you'll check on the help from your side," Langmead said to Windflower.

"Will do," said Windflower, and he shook hands with everybody before Langmead walked him to the front.

"Seems like we keep getting pulled further into the hole without any light at the end of the tunnel," said Langmead as they shook hands at the entrance.

"It's getting murkier," agreed Windflower. "But sometimes it is darkest just before the dawn."

"Let's hope so."

Windflower hoped that, too, as he drove back across town to his office. He phoned Ron Quigley when he got there.

"Sergeant, what can I do for you today?" asked Quigley.

"I guess I owe you a thank you," said Windflower. "Looks like Lundquist has given Tizzard some rope to deal with our case. I appreciate that."

"I'd like to take credit," said Quigley. "But I haven't talked to him yet. Maybe he's figuring some things out on his own."

That surprised Windflower so much, it took him a second to recover. "Anyway, Tizzard is checking the house in Grand Bank, and Smithson and Evanchuk are meeting the other girl and her family this afternoon."

"I knew about Smithson, but I haven't seen him come back yet," said Quigley. "I'll get him to call you. Anything else?"

"The Ottawa police found another missing girl, not one of ours, from New Brunswick. I think she may talk about what happened to her. I'm getting a report on that from Robbins's brother. And the biker war looks like it's ready to blow."

"I heard some things about that. A few of the locals were asked to go to St. John's to get ready."

"I guess they're coming from all over. That's one of the reasons for my call. They need back up. Can we get some help from our Emergency Response Unit?"

"What do you think they need?"

"I don't know exactly, but they're going to be outmatched in weaponry, that's for sure. Maybe you can talk to Langmead and then make the request. They're working on a warrant for the Angels clubhouse right now."

"I'll call him," said Quigley. "You know, 'great things can happen when you don't care who gets the credit.'"

"That's not Shakespeare," said Windflower. "Is it?"

"Mark Twain," said Quigley, and once again he was gone before Windflower could respond.

Windflower smiled to himself and was still smiling a little while later as he packed up his stuff to go home.

46

Sheila and the girls were making supper together when Windflower got home, and he was pressed into service as a dog walker. He didn't mind at all, and he and Lady had a very pleasant stroll down to the edge of the lake again. On the way back he took another quick look at Wilf Pittman's rink, this time without getting caught. It looked perfect.

When he got home, Sheila had put the macaroni and cheese in the oven, and Windflower helped clean up both the kitchen and the girls. When that was done, he got changed, sat in the living room with them and watched TV until supper was ready.

Sheila called him in to the kitchen so she could find out about his visit with Herb Stoodley. He told her all the happenings in Grand Bank and then his big news.

"Wilf Pittman's rink is ready, and he said that it would be okay if you and Stella went over to try it out," he announced. "I didn't want to say anything in case you didn't want to do it. But you could go over tonight if you were up to it."

"I think it would be great. But I don't want Amelia Louise going. I think she's coming down with something. But Stella and I could go. She'd love that."

"Great. I'll just pop down and let him know."

He walked down to Pittman's house, and of course it was okay with Wilf. "Tell them to come over any time," he said. "I'll put on the spotlight right after I have my supper."

When Windflower got back, Sheila was scooping broccoli and carrots into a bowl and had taken the mac and cheese out of the oven.

"That smells wonderful," he said.

"Everything edible smells wonderful to you," she quipped back.

"Only what you make me," he said. They both knew that wasn't true.

Windflower got the girls and settled them in for their meals. After supper he and Sheila cleaned up. He then took Amelia Louise upstairs so she wouldn't kick up a fuss when Sheila left with Stella. Sheila was right, thought Windflower. Amelia Louise had a bit of a fever, and she hadn't eaten much for dinner. Maybe she did have a bug. He made her a bath, and she sat in it without even moving around very much. Definitely not okay, he thought.

A few minutes later he heard Sheila and Stella leave. He read Amelia Louise her Goodnight Moon book, but she didn't seem to have the energy to find the mouse tonight. He laid her in her crib and covered her up. He turned on the monitor and went downstairs. He thought he could hear her cough a few times and then nothing. When he checked in on her, she was sleeping.

He turned on the TV but didn't really pay attention to it. Lady came and sat at his feet to keep him company while Molly saw an opportunity to get rubbed. He was still absent-mindedly rubbing the cat when Sheila and Stella got home.

"So how was it?" he asked Sheila. He didn't have to ask Stella. She was grinning from ear to ear.

"It was wonderful," said Sheila. "She could have stayed out all night."

"So, a backyard rink is a good idea?"

"I agree completely. I'll even help. How's Amelia Louise?"

"She wasn't well. She went to bed pretty much right after her bath. I thought I heard her coughing too."

"I'll check on her if you make Stella's bath," said Sheila.

Windflower took the still-smiling Stella in his arms and carried her upstairs. He started to run the water. Soon Sheila came into the bathroom and looked in the medicine cabinet. "Shoot," she said. "We're out of children's Tylenol, and Amelia Louise's got a fever."

"I can go get some," said Windflower. "I think the drug store on Topsail Road is open until ten."

"I think we should. I'll take over in here."

Windflower went outside and got into his van. The sky had

clouded over, and he couldn't see even one star in the sky. That wasn't a good sign, he thought. Maybe the snow is coming after all. He drove across town and got the medicine at the drug store. On his way back he took the long route, down by the waterfront and then up Prescott Street towards home.

He was driving past the War Memorial when he saw a young woman in a miniskirt standing on the sidewalk. He waved to her, but she ignored him. She looked a bit too young to be out there this time of night, thought Windflower, and he was pretty sure what she was up to. He circled the block and came around again. To his surprise the girl came up to the van. Didn't she know this was a police vehicle? It was marked pretty clearly.

Windflower soon found out she did indeed know it was a cop vehicle. She came to the driver's window, and he lowered it.

"I need help," she said.

Windflower didn't hesitate. "Get in," he said.

He drove away quickly. He wasn't sure exactly what he was going to do, but he knew he had to drive away from where he had stopped. Somebody would be looking for her, whoever she was.

"How old are you?" he asked.

"Eighteen," she said. When he looked suspicious, she added, "I have ID."

"Okay," said Windflower. "I'm Winston Windflower, but everybody calls me Windflower."

"I'm Cassie," said the girl. "Where are we going?"

"I'm going to take you somewhere safe."

Windflower drove up Military Road past the Basilica. Then he turned into the police compound at Fort Townshend.

"You're arresting me?" asked the girl.

"No, no," said Windflower. "There's a female cop who knows where you can go. I want to find her. Don't worry. It's going to be okay."

He parked the van in front of the building and started to get out. The girl bolted, and she was halfway across the parking lot before she realized she had run straight into the arms of an RNC officer coming from the storage area.

Windflower caught up, breathless. "Windflower, RCMP," he

said, taking out his badge to show the officer. "I'm taking her in to see Constable Anne Marie Foote."

The officer let go of the girl, introduced himself as Constable French and watched as Windflower guided her as gently as he could, while she resisted as strongly as she could, into the building. "Can we find a safe place for her until I get this sorted out?" he asked the RNC officer, who had followed them in.

"No problem," said the other cop.

"Not a cell," said Windflower. "An interview room?"

"Sure," said the officer. "Do you want a drink? Coke, maybe?"

Cassie shook her head and sneered at Windflower.

He smiled back. "I'll see you in a few minutes."

47

Windflower sat on the bench outside the reception area and watched as Cassie was moved along by the RNC guy. He phoned Langmead's cell phone. Luckily, he answered and said he would phone Foote.

"She lives close to the building," said Langmead. "Just up on Merrymeeting Road. If I can find her, she'll be there really soon."

There was some good luck again for Windflower because Constable Foote showed up 10 minutes later.

"Sorry, I would have been here faster, but it's my bowling night," said Foote. "I hear you brought in a girl."

"She kind of found me," said Windflower. "I was going by the war memorial, and she came up to my van and said she wanted help. She wasn't so sure that she would find it here, though."

The other officer came back to the reception area. "She's in interview room three," he said.

"Thanks, Frenchie," said Foote. "Do we know her?"

"I haven't seen her here before, but I'm not usually downtown anymore," said French. "I'm in logistics now."

"Okay. Let's go take a look," said Foote. Windflower followed her to the back of the interview room and took a look through the mirror. The girl was eating a bag of chips with a diet Coke and playing with her phone.

"I guess I should have taken that away," said Windflower, pointing to the phone.

"Yeah, I'll search her after you talk to her. She might have other stuff too," said Foote.

"She looks so young in there," said Windflower. "She said she's 18, but she looks like a little kid."

"She probably is," said Foote. "They don't normally let them out on the street until they're old enough. We usually pick them up too quickly when they're underage. This girl is new, though. I haven't seen her before. I usually know all the regulars. Are you ready to talk to her?"

"Just let me make one quick call," said Windflower, and he stepped to one side.

"Sheila, I've been delayed. No, everything is okay. I'll be about half an hour or so. See you soon." He hung up the phone and walked back to Foote. "Had to check in at home. I only went out for some Tylenol for our daughter."

"Sorry about that," said Foote. "I hate it when kids get sick. You always feel so helpless."

"She'll be fine," said Windflower. "Let's go see Cassie."

Windflower and Foote walked into the interview room. The girl sat up straight in her chair in a defensive position. Foote spoke first.

"Can I see your ID, please?" she asked.

The girl pulled her ID out of the back of her phone case and handed it over. It was a driver's licence issued to Cassandra Fudge, West Street, Corner Brook.

"Can I call you Cassie?" asked Foote.

The girl nodded.

"You told Sergeant Windflower you needed help. What's going on Cassie?"

The girl tried to look tough, but as Windflower and Foote waited for her to respond, her resolve crumbled, and she looked like she was going to cry. Then a tumble of mostly unintelligible words came out, and finally Cassie started sobbing. Foote went to her and held her until she settled into a softer but steady cry. She motioned to Windflower to go outside, and he waited for Foote on the other side of the door.

"She won't likely to be able to talk much tonight," said Foote once she joined him. "I'll find her a safe place and talk to her in the morning."

"Aren't you worried about her running off?" asked Windflower.

"Not really," said Foote. "She's afraid of us, but she's scared to death of whomever she's trying to get away from. Plus, we don't really have anything to hold her on, unless she's got outstanding charges. I'll run her through the system on that."

"Okay then, I'll leave it with you," said Windflower.

Foote turned to go back inside. She paused at the doorway. "I'll call you tomorrow."

Windflower nodded and made his way back to the van. It was snowing when he got outside, but he raised his eyes to the sky and said a silent prayer of thanks to Grandmother Moon for sending Cassie to him. He prayed that she would keep her safe, and then he drove home.

He let Lady out back and went to see Sheila to give her the Tylenol, but she was sleeping. He went back downstairs to let Lady in, and then he, too, went to bed. Sometime in the middle of the night he heard Amelia Louise coughing and Sheila getting up to see her.

"She's got a fever and a cough," said Sheila. "I gave her some medicine, and I think she'll be okay tonight. I'll keep her home tomorrow. I can skip my class. Can you take Stella to school?"

Windflower nodded yes, and Sheila snuggled back into him. The next thing he heard was Amelia Louise coughing again in the morning.

Windflower got Amelia Louise some water and held her while she whimpered a little in his arms. Eventually, he got her changed into fresh pajamas and carried her downstairs where he wrapped her in a blanket on the couch. This might be a stay-in-your-PJs-and-watch-TV kind of day, he thought as he switched on the cartoons. Stella followed soon after, and Windflower wrapped her up in another blanket and went to put on the coffee.

Sheila came down and got Amelia Louise to take some more medicine and then sat and had a coffee with Windflower. Lady was waiting not too patiently beside them, so he got up to take her out while Sheila went to make breakfast.

It was really snowing, and there was already a significant amount on the ground. Windflower and Lady trudged on, and he was happy to get back to the house.

"That was quite a workout," he said.

"You get your shower, and I'll give the girls their oatmeal," said Sheila.

When he came back down, he had a bowl of oatmeal and sat with Amelia Louise while Stella got dressed. A few minutes later Windflower was putting Stella in the car and waving goodbye to Sheila and Amelia Louise, who were watching from the window. He drove across Elizabeth Avenue and stopped in the school drop-off zone to let Stella out. She was led inside by a teacher but turned to smile and wave at him before she went inside.

Windflower smiled and waved, too, and then drove back across town to his office. When he got there, he found another sign on his door. This one was written much more politely than the last, but the message was the same. Go see Morecombe.

48

Windflower decided to fill his coffee cup before he followed the direction on the note. He was standing in line at the cafeteria when his phone rang. It was Ron Quigley.

"Good morning, Sergeant. I come bearing gifts."

"Good morning to you, Inspector," said Windflower. "I'm sure I read somewhere to be cautious with those who are bearing gifts. Maybe Julius Caesar."

"Not to worry, my friend. I have secured a full tactical team to be deployed at the service of Langmead and the Royal Newfoundland Constabulary. Full squad. Full gear. They've been doing training exercises, and their sergeant said they'd love a real scenario."

"Well, I think they'll get it. The place we're going to looks like a fortress. And thank you for your intervention. The RNC guys need it and will appreciate it."

"Also, I bring good news from Smithson. He's picked up the biker guy, the one with the beard. Marco somebody. He's questioning him now. He'll call you later with a report."

"Thank you again. On another but quite possibly related matter, I had an interesting experience last night. A girl approached me on the street, said she needed help. I took her to the RNC."

"Must be your charm," said Quigley.

"It's more about the van," said Windflower. "I'm a mobile ad for the RCMP."

"'Men at some time are masters of their fates,'" said Quigley.

"'Fortune brings in some boats that are not steered,' too," said Windflower, but Quigley had managed to escape again. He put his phone in his pocket, paid for his coffee and went to see Morecombe.

He said good morning to Muriel and was ushered in to see

Morecombe sitting behind her desk.

"Come in," she said. "A couple of things, Windflower. First of all, whenever you have an interaction with a civilian, you are required to submit a report. Muriel will give you the form." She waited for a reaction from Windflower. "How did I know?" she continued. "The RNC comms section provides me with a report of any interaction between my section and civilians that come into contact with them."

"Okay," said Windflower. "I didn't know. It only happened last night."

"It's in the manual," said Morecombe. She again paused and waited for Windflower's reaction. Then for the first time since he had met her, she smiled. "I'm not looking to bust you," she said. "I'm actually trying to show you the ropes, something I should have done all along."

"Thank you," said Windflower. "I appreciate that."

Morecombe nodded. "Let's start again, shall we?"

"That would be great. You should know that I also have asked Inspector Quigley to intervene and get some backup for the RNC."

"I know about that too. They asked my opinion. I said if you were recommending it, they must need it."

Windflower left Morecombe's office with a little extra bounce in his step. He stopped and chatted with Muriel, who offered him a much-appreciated homemade muffin along with the form. Back in his office he enjoyed the blueberry muffin and the rest of his coffee. Looking out the window he could see that the snow was really coming down now. In a few more hours they would have to close the office. So, he decided he had better make the best use of the time available. He called Scott Robbins in Ottawa.

"Morning, Sergeant," said Robbins. "I'm glad you called. The whereabouts of Larissa Murphy are unknown again. There's a report from the street that she was picked up by three guys in a black panel van. The witness said he thought they were bikers."

"That's not good," said Windflower.

"No," said Robbins. "They often like to make examples of the girls who get out of their clutches. As a message to the others. But I do have some good news too."

"I could use that."

"The New Brunswick girl said she was held out in a building in Carlsbad Springs, just outside of Ottawa. That's the Angels clubhouse. And she said there were other girls there too. She didn't know their names, but she said they were from Newfoundland."

"They may be still there."

"Exactly," said Robbins. "Right now we're having a discussion about going in there. We've wanted to for a while, but this gives us what we need for a warrant. These are dangerous guys, so we'll get our SWAT guys lined up first and then go in as soon after that as possible."

"Understood," said Windflower. "The RNC is looking at a similar operation here. Let me know how it goes up there. Thanks for the update."

That is all very interesting, Windflower thought after he ended the call. It wasn't so good for Larissa Murphy, but maybe there was a light at the end of the tunnel. He was still thinking about that when his cell phone rang again. It was Foote from the RNC.

"Good morning," said Windflower. "I have some news from Ottawa. It looks like Larissa Murphy may be back with the bad guys."

"Oh no," said Foote, clearly upset.

"But they may have a lead on where the bikers are holding some of the girls. They have a clubhouse outside Ottawa."

"A mixed blessing. But that's often how this work goes. Cassie Fudge is safe and a little calmer this morning. I talked to her briefly. She definitely wants out, and I'm setting her up with the social workers."

"That's good. Will they make a transition plan for her?"

"Yes," said Foote. "They'll try to move her closer to home, then get her housing and then a training plan. I suspect she'll have to go back to school to get her high school as a start. But she'll be on a good path, if she wants it."

"I guess they slip back sometimes," said Windflower.

"It's all they've known. Many of them have abuse issues, and all of them have trust issues. Luckily, Cassie doesn't have a criminal record, not yet anyway."

"Did she say anything yet about how she got into this and how it works?"

"We're not there yet. But I'll talk to her later today, and I'll try to get what I can."

"Okay, thanks."

His next call came from Eddie Tizzard in Grand Bank.

"Good morning, Eddie. How are you today? Is it snowing there yet?"

"Yes b'y, she's coming down pretty good," said Tizzard. "I thought you'd want to know I'm making progress on the prints. We've identified two of the local biker hang-arounds, but some we've not been able to identify."

"That might be the girls," said Windflower.

"Maybe. But there is another interesting print that showed up, Robbie Bennett."

"Who's Robbie Bennett?"

"He's a high school student, one of the boys we brought in the other day. Now we've got a solid reason to interview him."

"That is good news," said Windflower. "He might be the boy we're looking for. How did we have his prints?"

"Impaired driving. He picked it up in St. John's."

"Good work, Eddie. Let me know what Robbie has to say."

"Will do," said Tizzard.

"Oh, and before you pick him up, give Corporal Lundquist a heads-up, will you?"

It doesn't hurt to make an effort, thought Windflower as he ended the call.

49

The snow was heavier than ever now as Windflower looked out the window. He didn't have time for much more looking because Sheila called.

"They're closing the school at lunch," she said. "Can you pick up Stella?"

"Sure, is she ready now?" asked Windflower.

"You can go by anytime. I'll let them know you're coming."

Windflower left his office a few minutes later, and despite the raging snowstorm, traffic was still pretty heavy on the way to Stella's school. The biggest tie-ups were near the liquor store and the supermarket. People were stocking up on their way home from work. That's a good idea, thought Windflower.

He phoned Sheila back and got her order for a roasted chicken and a few odds and ends that they needed. He managed to get in and out of the supermarket parking lot fairly easily, another benefit of driving a bright RCMP van. People thought he was on official business when he was really picking up dinner and an extra bag of potato chips as storm snacks.

That mission complete, he stopped near the school and ran into the office to ask for Stella. She came out soon with her knapsack, happy to see him and ready to go. A few minutes later they were safely at home. Windflower managed to rev up his van over the first bump the snowplow had made during this storm. He helped Stella negotiate the drifts and got both of them inside.

"We're home and in for the rest of the day," said Windflower. "I barely got in the driveway."

Sheila was sitting with Amelia Louise lying across her lap. She put her finger to her lips and shushed him. Slowly, she extricated herself from the couch and repositioned Amelia Louise so she could lay with a pillow under her head.

She followed Windflower and Stella into the kitchen.

"Did you have a nice day at school?" she asked Stella. Stella nodded. "Do you want some lunch?" Another nod.

"I can make us a grilled cheese sandwich if you want. I got some chips at the supermarket to go with it," said Windflower.

"A perfect storm lunch," said Sheila. "Although the snow is supposed to let up later."

"Is it going to get cold again?" Windflower asked as he got the grilled cheese sandwiches ready.

Sheila checked her phone. "It's your lucky weekend coming up. Going down to minus ten on Friday night, cold all weekend. Seems like the polar vortex is heading all the way to Newfoundland this year."

"Great. I can put up the boards on Saturday and start the rink overnight. Might even be able to skate on it by Sunday afternoon."

"Somebody will be very happy if that happens."

Stella's eyes gleamed at that news.

"We'll do our best," said Windflower, and Stella started dancing around the room.

"How is the other little one?" he asked as he put the sandwiches on the frying pan.

"I'm sure it's just a bug," said Sheila. "Daycares are like incubators for disease. Once one kid gets sick, it goes around like the Spanish flu. I just hope that she doesn't get it too," she added, pointing to Stella.

Windflower, Sheila and Stella had their lunch in the kitchen. Afterward, Sheila got a puzzle out that all three of them played with. At least Windflower did until his phone rang.

"Hey, Smithson," said Windflower as he stepped out on the back porch to take the call. The snow was pretty thick on the ground now, and the wind had picked up a bit to create several sizable drifts in the backyard. They were proving to be severe obstacles to Lady, who had followed him out and was trying to traverse the backyard in search of just the right spot.

"Sarge, just wanted to give you the latest," said Smithson. "I finished interviewing Marco Hoddinot."

"The guy with the beard?" said Windflower.

"The same," said Smithson. "We're holding him on a weapons charge right now, but unless we can come up with something else, his lawyer might get him out sooner than we'd like."

"I'm assuming he's denying everything."

"The only thing he admitted to was his nickname."

"What's his nickname?"

"You couldn't guess?" said Smithson. "Marco Polo."

"Yeah, I guess I should've known," said Windflower. "Hold him as long as you can. What did the girl say when you met with her family?"

"She named him. That's why we picked him up. But it's only an allegation that he might have tried to get her to be part of a human trafficking ring. Not exactly easy to prove in court, assuming we could even get the Crown to charge him."

"So, we've got a witness saying she saw him near Freddy's house the night he was shot, and we've got the girl saying he was trying to recruit her into a sex ring. But we can't charge him?"

"Not yet, boss. But we'll keep working on it. If we have to let him go, we'll get an order keeping him away from the high school. But that's it for now."

"Thanks," said Windflower and he hung up. Before he put his phone away, he noticed he had a voice mail. He checked, and it was from Langmead telling him the raid was on tomorrow at the property on the Old Waterford Bridge Road. Windflower called him back.

"Thanks for calling," said Langmead. "We're on tomorrow. Two o'clock. Do you want to come as an observer? If you meet me here, you can gear up with us. I won't have a weapon for you, but I can loan you a vest."

"That would be great," said Windflower. "I suspect the emergency response guys will bring enough firepower for everybody. Did you hear about the girl, Cassie, from last night?"

"Yeah. That's one of the reasons we're moving so quickly. She told Foote that's where they keep the girls when they first bring them into their operations. She said there's always girls there."

"Okay, I'll see you tomorrow," said Windflower.

He hung up the phone, called Lady and started to go inside to settle in. But he changed his mind and went to tell Sheila he was taking Lady for a walk.

"Might as well take her now," he said. "She's already wet."

Sheila waved at him as she and Stella continued to work on the puzzle.

50

Windflower went out the back way and trudged through the snow to get to the front. He and Lady walked down the middle of Forest Road and up around the hotel. There was very little traffic, as most people had made it home already. The few stragglers spun their wheels and got a little stuck every time they stopped but seemed to make it through okay. The snow had now eased up quite a bit. By the time they made the turn back down their street, it was almost completely stopped.

They went inside, and Windflower cleaned Lady as best he could and left her to dry in the mud porch at the front. Sheila and Stella had moved to the living room, and Amelia Louise was now propped up eating some grapes and a small bowl of chips.

"Not the best menu, but she's eating," said Sheila.

"Are we having the chicken?" asked Windflower. "I can put on some veggies to go with it."

"That would be great," said Sheila.

Supper was simple and fast that evening. Afterward the whole family lounged around the living room until it was bath and story time for the girls. Amelia Louise had livened up enough to play a little in her bath, and Windflower had to read her story twice before she would settle down. Stella followed soon afterward, and Windflower and Sheila managed to have a bit of adult time before they, too, succumbed to the day and went to bed.

Windflower was tired and fell to sleep easily. But not long after he woke up in a dream.

It was very quiet in his dream. He could not hear a sound except when he started to walk, he could feel and hear the ground crunch beneath his feet. It was winter, and that was clearly snow he was walking in. He was near the lake that he'd seen in a previous dream, but there were no signs of life and certainly no beavers.

But far out on the ice, he could see what looked like a hut. Maybe a fishing hut, he thought. He walked out onto the ice. It was steady underneath him, frozen solid. As he neared the hut, he faintly saw smoke coming from its chimney. He kept going right up to the door, and then he heard someone singing. Not very well, he thought. Then, he recognized the voice.

Windflower pushed open the door of the hut. Sure enough, sitting inside around a camp stove was Uncle Frank.

"Close the door," said his uncle. "I just got the place nice and warm in here."

"Uncle Frank," said Windflower. "What are you doing here?"

"You know better than that, Winston," said Uncle Frank. "It's easy to see what I'm doing. I'm ice fishing. The real question is what are you doing?"

"What do you mean?" asked Windflower. "I was just sleeping, minding my own business."

Uncle Frank laughed. "You're getting good at this, Nephew. But why are you alone here? Where are all your friends?"

Windflower thought for a moment and then realized his uncle was right. Usually some ally would come visit him in his dreams; sometimes many of them came. Today, apart from his uncle, he was alone.

"So, tell me Uncle, why am I alone?"

"Now you might be getting somewhere, my boy," said his uncle with a cackle. "Hold my line while I make tea."

He passed Windflower his fishing pole and got up to put the kettle on the stove. As the kettle warmed and started to boil, Uncle Frank sat by Windflower and started to talk. "Why are you looking for missing girls?" he asked.

Windflower was a little bewildered. "That's my job. That's what I do. I'm a police officer," he said.

"Okay," said Uncle Frank as the kettle started to steam. He poured the hot water into a tea pot and added some fresh tea. The aroma of lavender enveloped Windflower and the fishing hut.

"What is that smell?" asked Windflower when Uncle Frank

handed him a cup of tea.

"Oh yeah, they make the best tea over here. But back to you." Uncle Frank took a seat again. "Why are you surrounded by women and girls, and yet you never ask them for help or advice?"

Uncle Frank sipped his tea and waited for Windflower's response. Windflower sat there holding his cup, a little mesmerized. Then he felt the fishing pole twinge. Well, it was more than a twinge. It was almost pulled out of his hands.

"I think you got a big one," said his uncle.

Now Windflower was holding on with two hands and barely keeping upright as the pole dipped in half. He could feel something really big pulling on his line.

"Just relax," said Uncle Frank. "Let it be what it will be."

Windflower did just that. He loosened his grip and the line slackened. The more he let go, the more tension was released. When he finally laid down the pole and picked up his tea, a fish jumped up through the hole and started flopping around on the floor.

It was a salmon, and maybe not surprisingly, since it was a dream, the salmon spoke.

"I'm here. Let's get this thing going because, as you can see, I can't really breathe out here," said the salmon. With that, the salmon turned grey, rolled over on the floor of the hut and remained perfectly still.

"Is it dead?" asked Windflower.

The salmon jumped up and started laughing. Uncle Frank joined in.

"That was a good one," said Uncle Frank.

"Thank you," said the salmon. "It was nothing. So, where were we? And I'm a she by the way, not an it."

"Okay," said Windflower, still in a little shock after seeing the salmon supposedly die and then miraculously come back to life. "I'm confused. I thought I was the one looking for the missing girls, but my uncle is suggesting something else. What's going on?"

"That at least is a good question. If you admit you have a problem, and you ask for help, then why not follow the advice you've been given and then show your gratitude?" asked the salmon. "Maybe as you grow up, you will learn to give thanks first because help is already on its way."

Then the salmon writhed around on the floor and squiggled her way back down the hole with a very large plop that splashed water all over Windflower and Uncle Frank. Windflower started to wipe the water off his face when he woke up in bed with Sheila. His face was cold and wet. Sheila didn't stir, so at least he didn't have to answer her questions tonight. But as was true after all his dreams, he had a lot of questions to ponder himself. He was doing just that when sleep took over, and he didn't ponder anything until he heard Amelia Louise coughing in the other room. Then he heard Stella doing the same thing.

51

Once again Windflower had a lot on his mind and things to figure out. But that would all have to wait while he and Sheila dealt with not one, but two, sick little girls.

"I'm going to stay home today," said Sheila.

"I'm sorry, but I have to go in," said Windflower. He didn't bother telling her exactly why. The girls were more important right now. Amelia Louise was at least mobile this morning, so he took her downstairs with him. He put on coffee and let Lady out while she took up her familiar perch on the couch. Windflower got her some orange pieces, and she seemed fairly content to suck on them and watch TV.

Sheila came down soon after with a report on Stella.

"Cough and a fever," she said. "I gave her some Tylenol. Maybe she'll sleep for a while."

"That would be good," said Windflower. He handed her a cup of coffee and took one for himself. "The snow's stopped, but we got a pretty good hit."

"Too bad they're all sick, or we could have had some fun outside today," said Sheila.

"Want some oatmeal?" he asked.

Sheila nodded wearily and went out to join Amelia Louise on the couch.

Windflower let Lady back in and dried her off, but there was still snow all over the floor. He wiped that up and made the oatmeal. He delivered three bowls to the living room and had his breakfast with Sheila and Amelia Louise.

After breakfast he got showered and changed before taking Lady around the block. As usual, she wanted more, but Windflower didn't have that kind of time today. He went to see Stella before he left. She was damp and sticky but still sleeping. He left her and said goodbye to Amelia Louise and Sheila.

"I have to go," he said. "But I'll try and come home early. I wasn't going to tell you, but there's a special operation with the Constabulary and our Emergency Response Unit today."

"The guys with the tank?" asked Sheila.

"They don't have a tank, armoured vehicle, here. But yes, they will be heavily armed. I am only a spectator, though."

"Be careful. I'm glad you told me. I might have had to kill you if you didn't."

He kissed her and Amelia Louise and went outside. It took him a few runs with the van to get out over the mini snowbank left by the plow, but finally he was off to work.

Traffic was light, and Windflower was at work in no time. He had just opened his computer when Terry Robbins came into his office.

"They found Larissa Murphy," he said.

"What? In Ottawa?" asked Windflower.

"Scott just sent me a text. He said to tell you they found Larissa Murphy at the house in Carlsbad Springs. She's now in OPS custody. Said they found large quantities of drugs and three other girls. No others from Newfoundland."

"That is great news. Anything else?"

"He said he'd call later. They are processing everybody now."

"Excellent. Can you thank him and the Ottawa police for me? And ask him to make sure they hold Larissa Murphy, at least until we can get in touch with her parents. I'm sure they want to talk to her."

"Will do," said Robbins.

"Thanks. Hang on a second. I'm going to phone the RNC."

Windflower picked up the phone and called Langmead's number, but there was no answer. Instead of leaving a message, he tried Foote. She answered on the first ring.

"I've got good news," said Windflower. "They've got Larissa Murphy in Ottawa. She was with some other girls at a clubhouse. I've asked that they hold her until we make contact with her family."

"I'll call her mother right away," said Foote.

"Great," said Windflower. "Our contact in Ottawa is Scott Robbins. You met his brother, Terry, at the press conference. He can be the contact back and forth." He looked at Robbins just to make sure he was okay with that, and Robbins nodded his head affirmatively.

"Yeah, we're good on our end," said Windflower. "You good?"

"I'm good," said Foote. "I'm hoping for more good news today."

"Me too," said Windflower, and he hung up the phone. Robbins invited him for a coffee, but he begged off and closed the door to his office. He needed a few moments to think and process everything that was happening to him.

52

Windflower closed his eyes and let himself sink into the pool behind them. It was an old meditation technique he had learned years ago but hadn't practiced in a while. As he found himself in that pool, he could feel the anxiety and mental strain slowly being released until he felt almost light with nothing on his mind.

That was the state he wanted to get to. He opened his eyes and started thinking about what was happening in his life right now. It was true what his Uncle Frank had said to him in his dream. He had women, girls and female energy all around him, and he had no idea how to access that power to help him. What was he going to do about that? He needed a plan. He took out his pen and started to write.

First, he would actively seek out advice from the women in his lives. That included Sheila at home and Morecombe at work. He'd never even thought of Morecombe as an ally before. Maybe he'd include Foote too. She knew way more about human trafficking and girls on the street than he did. And Cassie, the young girl that he met last night, she would know exactly how that life worked because she had lived it.

Then he thought about his own daughters. He realized that he didn't consider just Amelia Louise his daughter but Stella as well. They were equally his daughters in his heart for sure. But how would he listen to them when they couldn't even speak? That was a challenge, but he knew what Amelia Louise wanted almost by instinct. So, he needed to trust his instincts. Stella could speak but usually chose not to. Maybe with her he was supposed to learn how to listen better.

Finally, he thought about the wisest woman that he'd known in his life, Auntie Marie. He had loved his mother fiercely, and she had given him great gifts. But his aunt had given him more than had he been her own son. He had learned how to be a man from Grandfather, but he had learned how to be a human being from Auntie Marie. He almost cried when he thought about her and how much he missed her. Then he remembered the Richard Wagamese story about missing his mother well.

Wagamese had been really sad about the death of his mother, and he went to an old woman, an elder, for guidance. The old woman suggested that he learn to miss his mother well. When Wagamese asked how he could do that, she suggested he look for the beauty and the wonder in the world. She told him his mother lived in a beautiful sunset or a sky full of stars. Windflower looked out the window of his office and saw the old discarded Christmas tree he had seen on his first day on the new job. He thought again about the beautiful Christmas he had just had with his own family and all the magical times he'd spent with Auntie Marie over the years. And he missed her well.

He said a prayer for all the women and girls in his world and asked them, especially Auntie Marie, who he felt was watching him from the spirit world, to guide him on his journey. Then, feeling at peace, he opened his office door and went to see Morecombe.

He said good morning to Muriel and went into Morecombe's office.

"I want to apologize," he said to a somewhat startled Morecombe. "I realize that I should have been asking you for help with my investigation. It is certainly a public relations exercise as much as anything, and you are the expert in that."

Morecombe was still looking a little shocked, so he continued. He gave her an update on where they were and the fact that they'd found Larissa Murphy.

"Good," she said. "Now claim victory. Once you can establish that the girl is safe, go back to the family and ask them for a statement. We can write that for them. Then get that out to the public. This is a beacon, a sign of hope to any other girls who've got themselves in situations they don't like anymore. It shows them there's a way out."

"That's really good. We have the operation this afternoon, but that's just going to scare any girl who's already terrified. I love your approach. I'm going to suggest it to the RNC," said Windflower.

"No problem, Sergeant," she said. "Happy to help."

"I also want to say I'm sorry about your husband. Robbins told me."

"It's hard, but we have to go through it. People ask me why I just don't leave work and stay with him, but this is his wish. He said if I left, it would be like both of us losing, and he didn't want me to have nothing when he was gone."

She started to tear up but stopped herself and smiled at Windflower. "Thank you for your concern. I'll be okay."

Windflower took that as his cue to leave. "Thank you for your advice. I'll give you an update when I have some news."

He left and stopped to chat with Muriel as she wanted to show him pictures of her granddaughters. He was happy to oblige and was offered a fresh partridgeberry muffin, his favourite, in return. Fair exchange, he thought to himself after he got back to his office and enjoyed his treat.

He was feeling pretty pleased with himself when the phone rang. It was from Grand Bank, and to Windflower's surprise, it was Corporal Lars Lundquist.

"Good morning, Sergeant," said Lundquist. "I'm here with Constable Tizzard, and we need your help."

53

Now it was Windflower's turn to be surprised.

"How can I help?" he asked.

"Well, we're wondering if you could come to Grand Bank. The boy, Robbie Bennett, knows something. We're sure of that. But neither I nor Constable Tizzard can get anything out of him," said Lundquist. "We'll have to let him go soon. Other than illegally being in somebody else's property, we don't have enough to charge him."

"What do you think I can do?" asked Windflower.

"Excuse me, Corporal, can I say something?" asked Tizzard.

"Go ahead," said Lundquist.

"We've tried all our tricks, but nothing works on this kid," said Tizzard. "We thought a fresh face might help. I've seen you do it before."

"Me too," said Lundquist in another surprise to Windflower. "When you interviewed that hard-case biker in Grand Falls, you actually got something out of him."

Windflower thought about it for a moment. "Have you talked to his parents?" he asked.

"His dad wanted to be in the interview, but we told him no," said Lundquist. "Bennett is eighteen and old enough to be interviewed on his own. We thought the father would just interfere."

"Maybe," said Windflower. "But he also might be able to talk some sense into his kid."

"That's a good idea," said Lundquist. "We'll try the father. Thanks again, for your help."

"No worries," said Windflower as he hung up. That was strange, he thought to himself, but after his visit to Morecombe, maybe shaking things up might not be a bad idea.

Terry Robbins came into his office a few minutes later.

"What the heck did you do to Morecombe?" he asked. "She's all smiling and helpful, asked me if I needed anything. Muriel said you were in to see her. What did you say?"

"I asked her for help," said Windflower. "We're supposed to ask the female elders in our lives for their advice and guidance. Didn't you know that?"

Robbins looked at him like he had three heads. "I just came to see if you wanted coffee."

"I do," said Windflower. "Let's go."

Windflower grabbed a sandwich to go with his coffee. The muffin was clearly not going to be enough. He ate his sandwich and chatted with Robbins for a few minutes until his cell phone buzzed. He left Robbins and started to walk back to his office as he took the call. It was Lundquist again.

"Sorry to bother you, but we've talked to the father," said Lundquist. "You were right. He's worried that his kid might be on the wrong track. He wants to be involved."

"That's great news," said Windflower.

"But there's a catch," said Lundquist. "He only wants to talk to you. He said he trusts you, somehow. Do you know him? Harold Bennett."

"Name rings a bell," said Windflower. "But I've been in Grand Bank a long time. I can talk to him if you want, but only if you're there."

"Can you come to Grand Bank?"

"Not today, that's for sure. We have a big operation here this afternoon. How about doing it by video conference?"

"How would we do that?"

"Talk to Smithson. He can set it up."

"Good idea. I forgot about Smithson. He's a whiz with technology. I'll talk to the father and then get Smithson to set it up. Can we do it tonight?"

"How about tomorrow morning?" asked Windflower. "I don't know what this afternoon will bring yet."

"Perfect. I'll get back to you," said Lundquist.

Maybe that was just another piece to the puzzle falling into place, wondered Windflower as he finished his lunch. He decided it was time to head over to the RNC to meet Langmead and on the way phoned Sheila.

"Well, there's one on the mend and one down for the count," said Sheila. "And Stella's worker is coming by this afternoon."

"What's that about?" asked Windflower.

"They want to see how Stella is doing in St. John's and with us," said Sheila. "I think it's just a routine visit."

"Okay. I was asked to go to Grand Bank today. By Lundquist."

"Oh. It's not great timing. Looks like Stella will have to be home at least for tomorrow."

"Don't worry. I'm going to do the interview by video conference. I wouldn't leave you in the lurch like that."

"Good," said Sheila. "I was planning to ship Amelia Louise back to daycare tomorrow if you'll drop her off. I can manage one, but two is full-time work."

"Good luck with today," said Windflower. "I'll call later."

"Winston, be careful today, okay?"

"I will. Love you."

54

The drive across town was quiet and uneventful. Windflower did his public relations wave at every opportunity. He was starting to even like it. It seemed these were the few times that people were actually grateful to see the police. His last wave was right in front of the cop shop to a little old lady who took forever to cross. Windflower waited patiently and waved goodbye to her as he pulled into the visitor parking section at the Royal Newfoundland Constabulary.

Inside he was directed to the mobilizing area in the bowels of the building. He met Langmead, who gave him his vest and asked him to wait until their tactical unit head showed up to give them their orders. He noticed Foote standing with some other RNC officers and waved. She came over to see him.

"You observing too?" asked Windflower.

"I'm here in case there are any girls in the clubhouse," she said.

"Did you talk to Larissa's parents?" asked Windflower.

"They are over the moon and can't wait to talk to her. It's a good news story."

"It is indeed. My boss, Morecombe, had an idea. Once Mr. and Mrs. Murphy talk to Larissa and make sure she's safe, do you think they'd be willing to make a video that we could send out?"

"I'm sure they would," said Foote. "That's a great idea. It sends a message to the other girls out there that they could have a chance too. I love it."

The commander of the RNC tactical unit came out wearing an RNC hat and a windbreaker with TRU on it.

"What's TRU?" asked Windflower.

"Tactics and Rescue Unit," said Foote. "This is Lieutenant Bannister."

Windflower watched as the commander outlined everyone's mission, how they would proceed and who would go first. He said he had talked to the head of the RCMP tactical team, and they would take the lead. They would all meet at an abandoned school not far from the clubhouse and go from there.

That makes sense, thought Windflower. The RNC guys looked fierce enough all geared up, but they didn't have the raw power the Mounties could bring. As the team was heading out, Langmead came to speak with him and Foote.

"I'm going with the TRU guys," said Langmead. "Windflower, you can get a ride with Foote. I'll see you at the staging area."

There were three TRU vehicles, and they left about five minutes apart, taking different routes so not to arouse too much suspicion. After the last vehicle pulled out, Foote and Windflower drove out of the underground parking lot and headed west towards the school. When they arrived, the RCMP guys were already there, and Windflower went to say hello.

"Winston Windflower," he said to the sergeant standing near the RCMP vehicles.

"Hey, Windflower," said the sergeant. "Phil Geraldton. So, you're the guy who got us into this mess."

Windflower laughed at what was clearly a joke by Geraldton. If he knew anything about these tactical unit guys, Windflower knew they loved action. "I heard you were bored," he quipped.

"That's true," said Geraldton. "Anyway, nice to meet you. I gotta go see their guys."

Geraldton walked over to Bannister, and the two chatted for a moment until they both went back to their crews. Langmead came to Windflower and Foote again.

"There's a vantage point near the bridge," he said. "Traffic will be shut down in the zone, so you can set up there whenever you are ready."

Foote nodded to Langmead, and Windflower waved to Geraldton. Then they drove to the bridge across from the park and waited for the action to begin.

"Perfect view," said Windflower. Foote was intently watching the scene for any signs of activity.

It didn't take long. The RCMP vehicles came around the corner quickly and took up a position in front of the building. The RNC vehicles came in close behind.

Windflower could hear a loud voice booming from a megaphone or speaker. Geraldton, he guessed. The words were muffled, but he was pretty sure they were demanding whoever was inside to come out. There must not have been the required response because the next thing he heard sounded almost like an earthquake.

"That's the battering ram," said Windflower. "If that doesn't work, they have some explosives." But based on the next sound—a large crashing noise—they concluded the battering ram had proven effective.

All this time there had been relative radio silence. That all changed when the RCMP officers charged into the building. There was a lot of shouting and yelling, but once again it was hard to make out what exactly was being said. As Windflower was trying to figure that out, Foote swung the car around, siren blaring, and started racing down Waterford Bridge Road, where people were starting to emerge from their homes to check things out. "Call it in," Foote told Windflower. "There's a car coming out of the back, and it's heading east towards downtown."

Windflower grabbed the radio. "Windflower and Foote in pursuit of a vehicle heading east on Waterford Bridge Road."

Foote sped around the narrow corner, and before they knew it, a dark blue vehicle was right in front of them, rushing down the tree-lined road. The car took the next corner, and before they could catch up, they heard the crash. When they got there, the dark blue vehicle was on its roof and another RNC cruiser was moving towards it.

Windflower and Foote ran to the vehicle and arrived at the same time as the RNC officer. All three peered into the car. The driver was pretty smashed up against the steering wheel, with the air bag pushing in on his bleeding head. There were two other people in the back seat. Two girls.

It was hard to tell how hurt they were. Windflower pulled on the door, and the RNC guy went around to the other. But nothing budged. The girls were moving a little. That was a good sign. So too was the next noise they heard—sirens, followed rapidly by both paramedics and the fire department.

Windflower, Foote and the RNC officer all moved back to let the experts take control of the situation.

55

The firefighters moved quickly to assess the situation and the danger to themselves and the occupants of the vehicle. Gasoline was pouring over the ground, and several of the firefighters were assigned to spraying foam all over the flammable liquid. Two others were working on the doors, trying to pry them open. With great effort they managed to get one side open and take out first one and then the other girl. They laid them on the ground, where the paramedics examined them.

All of this took place in what seemed like the blink of an eye to Windflower as he watched the paramedics load the girls onto stretchers and take off. Foote grabbed him by the arm. "Let's go."

Windflower ran back to her car. Soon they were speeding across town behind two racing ambulances to the Health Sciences complex. Foote called in to let Langmead know they were behind the ambulance with the girls. He replied back that they had a lot of people on their end of the operation. Windflower would have liked to have heard more about that, but they were at the hospital, and he once again ran after Foote as she chased the paramedics into the emergency department.

Windflower stood back just inside the door and watched the frantic activity as the emergency doctors and nurses swooped in on the new arrivals. As fast as they could, they examined and triaged and then whisked the new patients off to their pods inside the emergency area. Foote was talking to the registering nurse, who was attempting to get details on the girls. She and Foote agreed to follow the patients and see if they had any ID on them.

A few minutes later Foote came back. "One of them is Brittney Hodder," she told Windflower. "I recognized her from the picture.

She looked like she was in a lot of pain, but I didn't see any blood. Might be internal injuries or broken ribs. I don't know the other girl. No IDs in their pockets."

"I know the Hodder family," said Windflower. "I can contact them."

"That would be good," said Foote.

Both of them stopped in their tracks as they heard the ambulance pull up outside the door. The noise was deafening as the sirens continued to scream while the paramedics brought in another patient.

"I think it's the driver," said Foote.

Windflower watched as the paramedics rolled by them. Their patient looked bruised and bloodied and was not moving. One of them looked at Windflower and shook his head. They continued on in through the screening area.

"That doesn't look good," said Windflower.

They didn't have much more time to talk as the emergency area soon filled up with half a dozen other police officers, some still in full tactical gear. Langmead was among them.

"What's going on here?" he asked.

"Two girls inside," said Foote. "One of them is Brittney Hodder. The other unidentified. They just brought in the driver."

"He's in bad shape, may be gone," said Windflower. "I know the family of the Hodder girl."

"Call them," said Langmead. "We found two more girls at the clubhouse. I'll need you to go to Fort Townshend when you're done here," he said to Foote. "Some of our guys are there. We found some drugs, but they'll need to get back to scour the place."

"Can you stay here while I go back?" asked Foote to Windflower.

"Sure," he said. "I'll wait for an update. And I'll try and reach the Hodders."

Foote left, and Windflower went to find a quiet place to make his call.

He called the Grand Bank Volunteer Fire Department to see if he could find Chief Hodder, but there was no answer. He didn't want to leave a message about something like this. He didn't have the family's home number, but he knew someone who did.

"Hi Winston, nice to hear from you," said Sheila. "The social worker just left and…"

Windflower cut her off. "Sheila, I'm sorry to be rude. But I need the Hodder's phone number. We've found their daughter."

"Oh my God," said Sheila. "Is she okay? Hang on a second and I'll look it up." She was back in a flash. "Here it is. Barb and Martin Hodder." She gave him the number.

"Thanks, Sheila," said Windflower. "Brittney's been in an accident, and we don't know what's going on yet. I'm at the Health Sciences. I'll call when I can."

Windflower dialled the number.

"Hi, is this Barb?" he asked when a woman answered. When she said yes, he continued.

"Barb, this is Winston Windflower. I'm in St. John's now. We've found your daughter, Brittney."

"What? Is she okay?" asked the woman.

"She's been in an accident and is at the Health Sciences complex in St. John's. I'm there now, and I will stay here until we get an update," said Windflower. "Is your husband around?"

"Not right now, but I'll call him," said Barb Hodder. "Is there anything else you can tell us about Brittney?"

"Only that she was in a car accident, ma'am. But you or your husband can call me anytime. Here's my cell phone number."

"Thank you," said the woman.

After he hung up, Windflower went back into the emergency area to see if he could find out any news. He saw Langmead talking to several other RNC officers near the entrance.

"Any news on the girls?" he asked Langmead.

"We've identified both of the girls here as Brittney Hodder and Melanie Foley. Still waiting on a medical update," said Langmead.

"The Foley girl wasn't on our list, was she?" asked Windflower.

"No, but the two girls we found at the clubhouse were. Plus, I just heard that they found a pile of meth. It was in a hideaway underneath the building. That should be enough to lay charges against most of the bikers we found out there."

As they were speaking, one of the TRU guys showed up at

emergency and went to Langmead. He pulled him aside. The two men talked for a minute, and Langmead came back to Windflower.

"They hit two of the hangouts for the other gang," said Langmead. "Not as lucrative a haul as the clubhouse. But some drugs and weapons. Enough to charge some of them as well."

"Not a bad day's work," said Windflower. "Can we find out what's going on with the Hodder girl? Her parents are pretty anxious."

"Let me check," said Langmead. He went to reception and talked with the intake coordinator. He came back to Windflower.

"She said they're still being examined," said Langmead. "She'll let the doctor know you've got a family contact. Why don't you go get a cup of coffee? I'll be around here if the doc comes looking for you."

"Thanks, think I will," said Windflower.

He walked down the corridor to the cafeteria, got himself a cup of coffee and sat, looking out the window. He felt his phone vibrate in his pocket and opened it. It was Smithson.

"Smithson, what's up?" he asked quietly, not wanting to be overheard.

"Hey, Sarge," said Smithson. "Corporal Lundquist asked me to call you to tell you that the conference with Harold Bennett is set up for nine tomorrow morning. Is that okay with you?"

"Fine," said Windflower. "How do I connect to this thing?"

"I set it up on Zoom. It's really easy. You can just download the app and go from there."

"Apps are what I have when I go for beers with the guys," said Windflower.

"Okay. I'll send you an email with the link, and you just click on it from your laptop. And I'll be on the call, in case you have any difficulties."

"Okay, send me that link. I gotta go. I'm at the hospital."

His phone buzzed again. This time it was Langmead.

"The doc is here," he said.

Windflower left his coffee and raced back down the hall.

56

Langmead was standing next to a tall doctor in blue scrubs when Windflower came into emergency. Langmead saw him and introduced the men.

"Doctor Frechette, this is Sergeant Windflower from the RCMP," said Langmead. "He's been in contact with the family."

"Nice to meet you," said the doctor. "As I was telling Detective Langmead, the Hodder girl is in much better condition than the other girl. It's hard to tell you about the extent of injuries at this point, but the Foley girl has very little brain activity. Brittney Hodder on the other hand has steady vital signs and I suspect a concussion, but we'll know more following some tests."

"What's next?" asked Windflower.

"Well, the Foley girl is on life support, and I'd be very surprised if that does any good. We'll need to talk to her family about what decision to make," said Doctor Frechette.

"We're working on that," said Langmead. "But nothing yet."

"What about Brittney Hodder?" asked Windflower.

"We've induced a coma, and we'll know more in the morning. For her I'm slightly optimistic. Like I said, her vital signs are good, and unless we find out she has a lot of internal bleeding, I think she has a good chance. Anyway, I've got to go."

"Thank you, Doctor," said Langmead.

"Yes, thanks," said Windflower.

"I didn't tell the doctor, but when I called the Foley girl's family, the father said that as far as they were concerned, she was already dead," said Langmead. "I'll get Foote to talk to them again now that we have this bleak update."

"That's pretty cold," said Windflower.

"Some families are pretty screwed up," said Langmead. "And some of these girls have put their families through hell. We don't know what's gone on before all of this. It's like we're always at an accident scene."

Windflower didn't have much to say in response to that.

"We've got this under control here," said Langmead. "If you want, I can get you a ride back to your office."

"That would be great," said Windflower. While he was waiting, his phone buzzed again.

"Sergeant, it's Martin Hodder. What's going on with Brittney?"

"It's hard to say so far," said Windflower. "She's been in a car accident and is at the Health Sciences in St. John's. I just spoke with the doctor, and he said that her vital signs are good. She's in an induced coma while they wait to see about any internal injuries. They'll know more in the morning. The doctor looking after her right now is Doctor Frechette."

"Have you seen her? What does she look like? Is she going to be okay?" asked Hodder in rapid succession.

Windflower had no good answers for any of those questions. "All I know is that the doctor said her vital signs were good. He said she had a good chance to pull through."

"Okay, thank you, Sergeant. Thank you for finding Brittney."

"Well, I was just one of many people working on this case. The Constabulary did most of the work."

"No b'y. I told the missus as soon as I heard you were on the case that you would find our girl."

"I'm just happy we found her. I'm leaving the hospital now, but there are people here all the time monitoring her. She's as safe as she can be for right now."

"Okay. We're going to get ready and come in. We want to see her no matter what kind of shape she's in," said Hodder.

"I don't know anything for sure, but I have a feeling she's going to be fine," said Windflower. "If you need me, just call. I'll be back in the morning to check on Brittney."

Windflower's ride showed up just after. It was French, the logistics guy he'd met with the young girl in the RNC parking lot. French didn't say much, and Windflower was grateful for that. He needed a few minutes to decompress and process everything that had just happened.

French dropped him at the door of his building, and he went straight to his office. He picked up his stuff and closed the door. He successfully made it out of the building without having to speak to anyone and started to drive. He wasn't exactly sure where he was going. He just needed to get out.

He drove east to avoid the traffic. He wasn't in the mood for a lot of waving right now. He ended up down Marine Lab Road and stopped in the visitor's parking lot at the university's ocean sciences lab. There were no other cars. He wasn't even sure the place was open to the public this time of year. He walked around to the back of the building and down near the ocean. He found a large rock to sit on and watched the waves roll in. It was cold and getting colder, but somehow, he felt impervious to the temperature.

He thought about all the girls that had been missing. They'd found most of the ones they'd started looking for and probably some they hadn't even known were missing. There was still work to do, but it felt like they were coming near the end of this particular part of the case. There were four girls he felt he knew more about, and that made him care more. And then there was the new girl, Cassie. She had come directly to him for help. He felt a special responsibility there for sure.

But they weren't just missing girls. They were parts of families—daughters, sisters, friends. So, he thought about all the families too. He felt he knew all of the missing girls, even though he'd met just a couple. They were still just children, just starting out in life. And now one of them was in serious condition and another could die. It was heartbreaking for Windflower as a father to think about all of that, and he started to cry.

Crying wasn't a bad thing. It just meant you were human, his Auntie Marie had told him one time. "Don't worry what others may think, even your own male judge inside of you. Cry if your heart calls you to cry. Scream if it calls you to scream. And dance if it calls you to dance."

He sure didn't feel much like dancing, but he needed to find some peace in this awful place he found himself in. So, he laid down a little tobacco for each of the girls and their families in turn. For Brittney Hodder, since she and her parents were recent contacts, he said a prayer that she be given support to recover and guidance to accept the help that her parents would offer. For Mandy Pardy he prayed that she be found soon or be granted an opportunity to make a different choice with her life. For Larissa Murphy he prayed that she come to understand how much her parents loved her and wanted the best for her. For Cassie he prayed that she be given the full second chance that she had asked for when she came to his van.

Then he prayed for Melanie Foley, that she feel loved by those caring for her as she lay in the hospital. Windflower knew it wasn't up to him to pray for a miracle. That was not his job. Creator would look after all of that. He prayed that she be given the strength to carry on with her journey, wherever that might lead. Then he laid down tobacco for her and cried again.

He sat quietly for a moment and allowed all those emotions to flow through him. Then he thought about a quote from Mister Rogers that someone had shared about dealing with the difficult parts of life. How'd that go? He remembered and said it out loud.

"'There is no normal life that is free of pain. It's the very wrestling with our problems that can be the impetus for our growth.'"

He walked slowly back to his van and drove home.

57

Home was a much more pleasant, if chaotic, scene, and Windflower allowed himself to feel the love that Sheila, Amelia Louise, Stella and Lady wanted to show him. Even Molly showed up to check him out. She never did that.

"How is Brittney Hodder?" was Sheila's first question.

"She's under observation, but I think she's going to be okay," said Windflower.

"Her parents must be so relieved that she's been found."

"I talked to them both. They're coming in from Grand Bank tonight."

"I'm guessing from the look of you that everything else didn't go as well."

"Let's talk about your day," said Windflower as Amelia Louise climbed all over him. "She's obviously doing better."

"Amelia Louise is ready to go back to daycare. Stella needs another day at home, although she's doing a little better too." At the sound of her name, Stella raised her head off the couch and waved.

"How did the visit go?" asked Windflower.

"It went well, but we'll talk later," said Sheila. "I'm making chicken and dumplings for supper. Maybe you can take her out," she said, pointing at Lady. "She needs a walk."

"Let's go, girl," said Windflower. He didn't have to say that twice. Lady was at the door as fast as he could get her leash.

The evening was getting colder as they walked down towards Empire Avenue and up towards Bannerman Park. Windflower noticed the wind picking up too. It was going to be a really cold night, he thought. It would be a great night to put in his rink, but he had neither the time nor the energy for that tonight.

He and Lady swung down Military Road and took the backroads to come out at the far end of Forest Road. They were on their way home when Windflower saw the spotlight on in Wilf Pittman's backyard. He walked down the driveway and looked over the fence. Pittman had cleared the snow from his rink and was putting down a layer of water to re-set the surface.

The water steamed in the cold air as he sprayed, and he didn't even notice Windflower staring over the fence. Good job, Windflower said silently to himself as he and Lady left and turned for home.

Sheila was finishing off her dumplings and putting them in the stew, so Windflower sat and played with Amelia Louise until he heard the magic words: Supper's ready.

Amelia Louise raced to the kitchen, and Windflower helped get Stella up and carried her to her seat. Sheila had already taken up the girls' servings, which had cooled on the counter. She passed them around and then gave herself and Windflower a large bowl each.

"This is so good," said Windflower. "I like the chicken and dumplings. But the carrots and turnip and parsnip are just really delicious in this stew."

"Thank you," said Sheila. "We aim to please."

After supper Windflower played Jenga with Amelia Louise, who was now learning not to knock over the stack randomly. Lady, however, had not learned that lesson and after a couple of inadvertent knock-downs, was banished to the kitchen. After watching for a few minutes, Stella joined in the fun too."

"She's definitely on the mend," said Windflower as Sheila came into the living room.

"One more day," said Sheila.

"That's good. The weather will be cold enough to put in our rink this weekend."

Stella brightened considerably with that news.

"I think she'll be ready," said Sheila.

"I saw Wilf Pittman putting water back on his tonight. It looked perfect."

"Make sure you get him to help you," said Sheila as she picked up Stella and brought her upstairs.

"You don't trust me?" asked Windflower, sounding a little distressed.

"No. You're not handy, remember? Give me fifteen minutes in the bath with this one and then bring Amelia Louise up, okay?"

"Okay," said Windflower. "I can build a skating rink, can't I?" he asked Amelia Louise.

"Mila help Daddy," she said.

"Thank you, sweetheart. At least someone around here believes in me."

"I heard that," yelled Sheila from upstairs.

"Can't get a break," joked Windflower.

After bath and story time, Windflower and Sheila finally got time alone to talk about their days. They sat in the living room with a fresh pot of tea.

"You go first," said Windflower. "I want to hear about the visit from the social worker."

"She was very nice," said Sheila. "Both girls were napping, so we had a chance for a real chat. There are no problems on our end. She seemed very pleased."

"That's good." Somewhat relieved, Windflower picked up his tea and sipped on it.

"I told her about Stella's latest stuff at school and not speaking much. She shared that they suspect there'd been some abuse but couldn't confirm it. The worker also said that Stella had been close to her maternal grandparents and had spent a lot of time with them while her mother was in and out of rehab and trouble."

"Well, at least she had one safe place."

"Not only that, but I guess she developed a real bond with her grandfather, and he would like to come visit. I told her we would talk about it and let her know."

"I'm okay with it. You know the few times I've seen Stella really comfortable has been around older men like Bill Ford and Wilf Pittman."

"And she speaks sometimes, too, when they're around," said Sheila. "I hadn't thought about that before. So, I'll tell the worker it's okay?"

"Absolutely. I think it's a great idea. The more support she has, the better."

"Now tell me about your day," said Sheila.

Windflower wasn't sure where to begin.

"Well, I told you about Brittney Hodder," he said. "Even though she is in serious condition, that's some of the good news of the day. We also found Larissa Murphy in Ottawa and more girls out at the clubhouse. And it looks like in all locations there were drugs and guns that will help put some of the bad guys away."

"But?" asked Sheila.

"But the other girl in the accident is likely not going to make it."

"That's awful. To find your daughter and then she dies. Oh my God, I can't imagine what they're going through."

"It's almost worse. When the girl's family was contacted, they said they didn't want anything to do with her."

Sheila sat for a moment in stunned silence.

"I guess some families have their own issues," said Windflower. "As Carl Langmead said, we don't know what they've been through."

"But it is so sad," said Sheila. "To have a girl in hospital, all by herself, dying...."

Windflower went closer and held her. She clung to him and cried, and he held her even closer.

"Let's go to bed," he said. Sheila nodded and went upstairs while Windflower let Lady out. He stared up at the sky full of a thousand blinking lights. He looked for the moon but couldn't see it in his part of the sky. That didn't mean it wasn't up there. He prayed to Grandmother Moon and asked that she stay with Melanie Foley as she went through her difficult time at the hospital. He hoped that whatever happened she would find peace. He let Lady in and went to bed.

He had no thoughts as he climbed into bed with Sheila. He realized that he was becoming numb. Sometimes that happened after something horrific at work. The first couple of times it happened to him was while he was in British Columbia working on the highway, and there had been deadly car crashes. The numbness, he understood, was just another stage in his personal grieving process.

He closed his eyes, and much to his surprise, he fell asleep. And he didn't wake until the alarm went off in the morning. He turned it off and got up quickly. So far he was the only one awake. Perfect, he thought. He snuck downstairs and put on the coffee. Then he grabbed his smudging gear, pulled out his parka and went outside with Lady.

It was a bitterly cold morning, kind of like back in Pink Lake where it was so cold on January mornings that his eyeballs hurt. It wasn't quite that cold in St. John's, but it was getting there. Windflower fumbled with his medicines and managed to get a pinch of each into his smudging bowl and lit it with his wooden match. Soon a cloud of smoke was being lifted into the morning air, and Windflower used his feather to spread some of it all over him. He needed every bit of cleansing he could get this morning.

After he smudged, he let the aroma of the medicines linger around him. He thought about himself and his place in the world. He gave thanks for his many blessings and for all of his family, friends and allies that were with him on this journey. He said a special prayer for his ancestors—those he remembered, those he had heard about and those that had come so long before him that he knew nothing of them.

The only ones he could really recall were his grandfather on his father's side, his mother and father, and Auntie Marie. His mother had died when he was just a young boy, but he always smiled when he thought of her. She had been a kind and patient woman who had liked to laugh and sing. His father left soon after his mother had died. Grandfather, who became his surrogate father, and Auntie Marie had raised him after that. He had learned everything about the world and the spirit world from them, and so today he asked them for their wisdom and guidance.

There was one more prayer needed before he could move on to play his role in this morning and this life. That was a prayer for the spirit of Melanie Foley. He could feel, without having any information, that she had passed during the night, and that some part of her was still here waiting. He didn't know for what, but he felt her spirit waiting. He offered her thanks for all the good things she had brought to the world. Even though he had never met her, he knew she had brought good things even to him because every person brings gifts to their family and their community. He was not part of her family, but he had become part of her community. Then he prayed that she be given safe passage to the other world where she would again find peace.

Windflower rose and called Lady. He went inside and heard people moving around. He got himself and Sheila a cup of coffee and went upstairs to see how everybody was doing.

It was hectic, crazy and yet magical to see his two little humans wake with joy and enthusiasm for living. That's a good lesson for adults, he thought. Stella was a little bit slower than usual, but she still had a great smile and a hug for Windflower. Amelia Louise had dragged him into their doll game before he knew what was going on. Sheila came and gave him a kiss before taking her cup of coffee downstairs to make breakfast.

A few minutes later they paraded down to join her, everyone, including Windflower, wearing a blanket as a cape and carrying a doll that had been specially selected for them by Amelia Louise. Breakfast was simple, consisting of boiled eggs, toast and orange slices. After breakfast Windflower got changed and helped Sheila organize Amelia Louise. She didn't really want to go, since her sister and Sheila were staying home, but they managed to get her dressed.

Windflower carried her out to Sheila's car, the one with the car seat. He drove Amelia Louise to the daycare and brought her inside. Despite her misgivings about not having her mommy with her, Amelia Louise finally agreed to stay and took the hand of one of the daycare workers without even waving goodbye to Windflower. He waved anyway and drove back home to pick up his van.

One more goodbye to Sheila and another hug from Stella, and Windflower was on his way to work. He had a lot on his mind and had to remind himself more than once about his status as a public ambassador for the RCMP. By the time he was in the parking lot, he was happy to get out of the van and into the building.

58

Windflower was just opening his office door when his cell phone rang. It was Langmead from the RNC.

"Good morning, Carl. How are you this morning?" he asked.

"I'm okay," said Langmead. "Better than Foote. She was at the hospital most of the night."

"What's going on?" asked Windflower, knowing what was coming next.

"Melanie Foley died from her injuries in the crash," said Langmead. "Foote didn't think she should be alone."

"This is so sad. But I'm glad she was there. How's the other girl?"

"No change last I heard. Her parents came in last night. They were happy to see her but pretty worried."

"I know the family. I'm going over today to see them, if I can get away."

"I know what you mean. We're still processing the creeps from yesterday, and Foote is trying to get the girls organized. Now the chief wants to organize a press conference to show the public all the stuff we collected from the raid and the visits to the bars."

"Is there a lot?" asked Windflower.

"We're still cataloguing it. But there's everything from coke to meth to prescription pain killers. A real pharmacy. Plus, the weapons. Two sniper-quality rifles and half a dozen handguns. For us, it's a big haul. We don't get many weapons here."

"Good to have them off the street."

"Good to have some of those bikers and their friends being sent away too. Our only hope is to try and get enough on them so they get more than the two years needed to ship them out to federal prison. They already run the local jail."

"Okay, keep me posted. I've got to go. I got a call in a few minutes."

Windflower hung up with Langmead and called Smithson.

"So, what do I do?" he asked Smithson.

"I sent you an email with the Zoom link," said Smithson. "Open it and click on the link."

Windflower clicked the link, and it asked him to download the latest version of Zoom.

"Download the Zoom app," said Smithson. "When that's done, open it and your meeting should show up."

Windflower followed the directions. "Now it wants my password. What's my password?"

"It's in the email."

"Oh yeah, here it is." Windflower entered the password and found himself staring at himself in the computer. "Hey, that's me," he said.

"Click on the button that says connect with video," said Smithson.

Windflower did, and then he could see other faces on the screen. There was Smithson and Lundquist and a man that Windflower thought he recognized as Harold Bennett. He could hear them speaking, but when he said hello, none of them responded. He tried talking louder and started shouting, but nothing worked.

Then he heard Smithson's voice. "You have to unmute yourself, Sergeant. It's the little microphone icon on the bottom of your screen."

"I don't see it."

"You have to click on your screen and then you will see it."

Finally, he spoke and people seemed to react.

"Good morning, everybody," said Lundquist. "Thank you, Sergeant Windflower, for joining us. Harold Bennett is here as well. Sergeant, why don't you go first?"

"Okay," said Windflower. "Mr. Bennett, we need your help. We think your son is involved with some very bad people. His life could be in danger. We need him to cooperate with us to find a missing girl, Mandy Pardy."

"I been talking to Robbie about all this," said Bennett. "I knows he's been hanging around with the wrong people. I been after him about that. He says he's afraid to talk to you. That those guys will get him."

"He's right to be scared," said Windflower. "But he's on the edge of being caught up in something really big. We're now trying to shut those bad guys down, Mr. Bennett. If he doesn't talk to us now, we have to assume he's part of the problem. There are already serious charges being laid in St. John's in this case. You'll see it on the news tonight. Human trafficking, hard drugs and weapons."

Windflower could see Bennett processing all of this as he watched him on the screen. I think I like this Zoom thing, he thought. He let Bennett hang with it for about a minute, and then he spoke again.

"Here's the deal," he started. "You get Robbie to talk to us, and unless he's committed a murder, I'll see if we can work it so he's not charged with anything. If what he has to say to us helps us get a conviction, I'll also see about getting him protection until all trials are over. Otherwise, we move ahead and let the chips fall where they may. One thing I can guarantee you, Mr. Bennett, is that Robbie's good name will certainly be dragged through the wringer, and that's the least of his problems. Try getting a job after these types of charges. We're not talking about impaired driving here."

"Okay, okay, I get the picture," said Bennett.

"Corporal Lundquist will arrange for him to be picked up. You can be there when he questions him," said Windflower.

"I wants you to be there too," said Bennett. "People around here says that you are a man of his word. I trust that. I wants you to be the one who talks to Robbie."

"Very well, Mr. Bennett," said Lundquist. "I'll set that up right now. Sergeant, when can you be available?"

"How about around one o'clock? Smithson, will you set that up?" asked Windflower.

Smithson gave him a thumbs-up on the screen, and Lundquist ended the call.

Windflower started walking to get a cup of coffee in the cafeteria when his phone rang again.

59

Good morning, Sergeant. I hear you're in great demand," said Ron Quigley.

"You know, Inspector, 'some are born great, some achieve greatness, and some have greatness thrust upon them.'"

"Be careful. 'Uneasy lies the head that wears a crown.'"

"No crown here," said Windflower, laughing. "And I've got the bruises to prove it."

"I don't know. I keep hearing great things about you. Maybe I made a mistake in letting you go to St. John's where everybody could see you in action," said Quigley.

"Are you inviting me back?" asked Windflower. "Because I'd be happy to return. Might need a few days to convince Sheila, though. She's kind of committed to finishing her degree."

"No, I'm not inviting you back, yet. I wanted to check in on Brittney Hodder and see if there's anything on Mandy Pardy. Her parents are driving me crazy."

"I'm going over to see the Hodder girl as soon as I get off this call with you. But I think she's going to be okay. Not much on Mandy Pardy yet. Did Smithson tell you about the call this morning?"

"I haven't seen him. Is this about the father of the Bennett boy?"

"Yeah," said Windflower. "He's going to try and get the boy to cooperate. I suggested it might be in his best interest. We think he knows what happened to Mandy Pardy, may have even been involved in setting her up with the bikers."

"That's pretty creepy. I assume you are promising the kid immunity if he testifies."

"Well, I certainly suggested it might be in the cards. And

protection if he feels his life is in danger, which it may well be."

"How exactly are we going to do that?"

"I'm sure you and Corporal Lundquist will figure something out."

"Just remember," said Quigley. "'What's done cannot be undone.'"

This time Windflower was ready. "'Having nothing, nothing can he lose.'"

He heard Quigley trying to come back again but hung up the phone quickly. "Got him," Windflower said to himself. "Finally."

Just as quickly, he got out of the office and headed towards the hospital before anybody else could interrupt him.

He parked in the section reserved for police, went inside and was heading over to the emergency department when he saw Anne Marie Foote. She looked so sad that he wanted to give her a hug. But that was not professional and might even be inappropriate. So instead he smiled and asked her how she was doing.

"I'm okay," she said. "But last night was hard. I keep thinking that only if we'd found those girls a day sooner, this wouldn't have happened."

"You can't blame yourself," said Windflower. "You did the best you could. We all did. How is Brittney Hodder?"

"She's going to pull through. Her parents are in there now. The father was asking about you."

"I'm going in to see them. What about the Murphys?"

"They're over the moon. Scott Robbins in Ottawa set up a video chat for Larissa and her parents. She's flying home once she makes her statement up there. The parents are happy to do another stint with the media. Why not? It's good news."

"It is indeed. I guess that's what we have to keep in mind. We don't win them all or solve all cases, but when we do, it feels pretty good."

"Yeah, they're happy," said Foote. "Detective Langmead said that we can put them on after the chief trots out all the drugs and guns."

"Good luck with that," said Windflower. "We're still working on a lead on one of the outstanding missing girls, Mandy Pardy. I'll let you know how that goes."

"Thanks, and good luck," said Foote.

Windflower went into the emergency department and got directed to one of the rooms on the edge of the ICU.

Inside, the Hodders were sitting around the bed of their daughter, who was sleeping and hooked up to tubes and monitors.

"Sergeant Windflower, glad you're here," said Martin Hodder. "They moved Brittney out of the ICU, but they still want to keep an eye on her."

"I heard she's doing better," said Windflower. "I'm glad. How are you, Barb?"

"My nerves are shot, but I feel better just being here," said Mrs. Hodder. "Thank you for all your help. We so appreciate it."

"I'm just a small cog in the wheel," said Windflower. "The Constabulary did most of the work."

"Constable Foote was here when we got in last night," said Martin Hodder. "It's too bad about the other girl. Her parents must be devastated."

"Yes, I'm sure," said Windflower. "Do you need anything? Some food or coffee?"

"No b'y. We have everything we need right here," said Martin Hodder, pointing at his daughter. "We'll get something at the cafeteria later on."

"Okay then," said Windflower. "I have to be going. I have a meeting. But if you need anything, anything at all, just give me a shout."

Martin Hodder shook Windflower's hand. His wife came and gave him a big hug. "We will never forget what you've done for Brittney, for our family," she said.

Windflower smiled and left the room. He walked to his car and silently drove across town. Why does one child live and another die? That was the question on his mind all the way back to the office and right up to the time for his second Zoom call with Grand Bank.

He grabbed a sandwich and coffee on his way up, and once he was at his desk, he got logged on. He had a chance to eat about half his lunch before the Zoom meeting started. This time was much smoother, and he was soon in the conference with Smithson and the people from Grand Bank: Lundquist, Tizzard and Harold Bennett and his son.

Robbie Bennett was a younger version of his father with much more hair and, by the initial look of him, much more attitude too, thought Windflower.

Lundquist opened the call by introducing the Bennetts again and turning it over to Windflower.

"I guess we know why we're all here," he started. "Robbie, you're in a lot of trouble, son. And you have a choice. You can either cooperate with us, or you're going down with them. We're already picking them up all over the area and in St. John's. Most of the guys you know are going to jail for a long time."

The younger Bennett sneered back into the camera and onto Windflower's computer screen. Windflower continued. "I'm assuming that you've talked to your father, so you know how serious this is. And this is your one and only chance. If we don't have an agreement at the end of this call, we're going to charge you with human trafficking."

"You can't do that," said Robbie Bennett. "You've got nothing on me. I didn't do anything."

Harold Bennett spoke next. "Son, they're going to charge you, and when that happens, your life is going to be ruined. Think about your mother. How's she going to feel to see you dragged into court again? For human trafficking? For once in your life, listen instead of telling everybody what you know. Sergeant Windflower will help you get out of this. Won't you, Sergeant?"

"I'm going to try," said Windflower. "Here's what I can do, Robbie. If you tell us everything, right now, you'll have a good chance of having all charges against you waived."

"They'll kill me. He'll kill me," said Robbie Bennett.

"Who will?" asked Windflower.

Windflower could see that Robbie Bennett was weighing his options. His dad was trying to convince him to talk. But the boy stayed silent, frozen.

"We can provide protection," said Windflower. "You won't be the only witness against them. We've got at least five girls with us now, including Brittney Hodder."

At that name, Robbie Bennett sat straight up in his chair and stared intently into the screen.

He knows her and what happened to her, thought Windflower.

"I heard she was in a coma in St. John's," said Robbie Bennett.

"I saw her and her family this morning," said Windflower. "She's out of intensive care and is going to be fine."

The blood drained from the younger Bennett's face, and now he looked like what he was, a scared young man.

"Listen, Robbie," said Windflower. "I talked to Inspector Quigley in Marystown this morning. We'll have people watching you to give you protection until the trial. After that the bad guys will be put away for a long time, and we can all go on with our lives. So, what do you say, Robbie?"

Windflower could see Harold Bennett give his son a nudge.

"It's Marco. It was all Marco. He set this whole thing up. And he killed Freddy Hawkins," said Robbie Bennett.

60

Windflower wasn't expecting that. It took him a second to catch up.

"Okay," said Windflower. "Robbie, I want you to make a full statement with Corporal Lundquist."

The boy was crying now, and his father had his arm around him. "It's going to be okay," Windflower heard him say.

"Thank you, Sergeant," said Lundquist. "We'll take over from here. Constable Tizzard, will you take Robbie's statement? You can stay if you want, Mr. Bennett."

Windflower signed off. Well, that was interesting, he thought. Then he thought of something else. He phoned the Grand Bank RCMP office. Betsy answered.

"Hi Betsy," said Windflower.

"Good day to you, Sergeant," said Betsy. "I was just talking to Muriel this morning. She really likes you."

"I like her too," said Windflower. "Betsy, will you give Corporal Tizzard a message for me? Can you ask him if Marco Hoddinot's prints were found at the house across the brook?"

"I will," said Betsy. "How are you keeping in St. John's? I hope you think about us from time to time. We all really miss you."

"I miss you too," said Windflower.

After hanging up with Betsy, he finished his sandwich and sat quietly for the first time since early that morning. He felt things were starting to move now and not because of anything he was doing. But that was often the way with cases, especially complex ones like this one. You just had to follow one lead, take one action and see what happened. Finding the boy in Grand Bank was a great piece of police work. Getting him to talk was almost the easy part.

Now it felt like they, and he, had a handle on what was going on. Just keep moving forward, he said to himself.

He must have said it out loud because Morecombe was standing in his doorway and asked, "What are you moving?"

"I was just talking to myself," said Windflower, feeling a bit sheepish.

"I do that all the time," she said. "It's when I argue with myself that it's a problem. How's your case going? I hear good things."

"You know, it's going really well, except we lost one of the girls."

"I heard. 'All the adversity I've had in my life, all my troubles and obstacles, have strengthened me.'"

"That's very wise."

"Walt Disney said it. Do your best and learn from your mistakes. That's what I say."

"That's good too," said Windflower. "How is your husband?"

"We're at the end. I wanted to tell you that I will be going on leave. I may or may not come back. Robbins will take over as acting. He desperately wants my job anyway."

"All the best to you, and I will say a prayer for your husband," said Windflower. "But I wish you would consider staying. You have a lot of skills and experience."

"Thank you for saying that and for your kind thoughts about my husband," said Morecombe. "But I think it may be over for both of us."

Windflower looked at her and smiled. "'Death is not extinguishing the light. It is only putting out the lamp because the dawn has come.'"

"I actually know that one," said Morecombe. "Tagore, right?"

Windflower smiled again, and Morecombe waved goodbye.

Sheila called shortly afterward to remind him to pick up Amelia Louise. "How's Stella doing?" he asked.

"She's much better," said Sheila. "We were making cookies, peanut butter and oatmeal raisin."

"My favourites," said Windflower.

"She also said she wanted to go skating this weekend."

"You mean, she spoke, like a full sentence?"

"Yes, so you better deliver, mister."

Sheila was laughing and Windflower laughed too. "I guess the pressure is on," he said.

He hung up with Sheila and drove home to pick up the car. He waved to Sheila and Stella and drove back in Sheila's car to pick up Amelia Louise. She was still a bit groggy from her nap time but was happy to see him. Must have forgotten about being abandoned this morning, thought Windflower. He carried her to the car with her little knapsack on her arm and strapped her in.

He had just arrived home when his cell phone rang. He took Amelia Louise in and answered. It was Eddie Tizzard. He went back out to his van and took the call.

"Hey, Sarge. Thought you'd want to know. I've got the kid's statement and it's a doozy," said Tizzard. "I guess since he got a pass, he thought he should confess everything and get pardoned for the works."

"Surprises?" asked Windflower.

"Fingering Marco was the big one. He laid the whole thing out, how they recruited the girls. He got paid in dope and a trip to Ottawa. He said that Marco ran that house across the brook as a party palace. Free dope and booze for all the girls. And yes, Marco's prints were all over the place."

"So, what did the kid say about Freddy Hawkins?"

"He said that Marco started talking about Hawkins a few times over the last little while. How this fat little lawyer wouldn't play ball. He told the Bennett kid that Hawkins was going to get it," said Tizzard.

"That's pretty circumstantial."

"It gets better," said Tizzard. "Young Robbie said that he was with Marco on the night he shot Freddy Hawkins. He drove with him to Marystown. And he knows where Marco stashed the gun."

"I assume you're on your way to pick up Marco," said Windflower.

"Lundquist and Carrie are already there by now. He has a house in Frenchman's Cove just off the main road."

"Very good. Keep me posted."

"I will. I have a question for you though, Sarge. How did you know to check out that white house?"

"I just had a hunch. You should trust your instinct more."

"The last time I trusted my instinct I ended up in jail in Las Vegas," said Tizzard.

"Oh yeah, I forgot about that," said Windflower. "That's when you were going to leave the RCMP and become a private investigator."

"That seems like years ago, and it was only back a few months. Anyway, I'm glad you suggested taking a look at that house. It kind of opened everything up. Now it feels like we're getting ready to not only close the file on the missing girls but the one on the murder of Freddy Hawkins too."

"'Wisely and slow,' Eddie," said Windflower. "'They stumble that run fast.'"

"True enough," said Tizzard.

"Lots could go wrong yet, and we haven't found Mandy Pardy either," said Windflower. "Call me if anything else happens."

61

As good as everything was going, Windflower had more than a few nagging suspicions about where they were in the case. Yes, they were making progress. But whenever things went too smoothly, there were inevitable snags that had to be ironed out later. Luck was an unreliable tool in the criminal investigation toolbox. There was a quote about that somewhere. Finally, it came to him. 'Good luck is often with the man who doesn't include it in his plans.'

Remembering that quote made him feel good. So, too, did the idea of getting some of those homemade cookies Sheila had talked about. He went inside to check that out. They were as good as advertised. He had one of each while he chatted with Sheila about his day. Then Sheila put a casserole dish in the oven, took a frozen loaf of garlic bread out of the freezer and put the bread in alongside the casserole.

"You made lasagna?" said Windflower. "You are amazing."

"A woman of many talents," said Sheila. "Stella helped too."

Stella beamed at this acknowledgement, and not to be outdone, Amelia Louise also chimed in. "Mila help too," she said.

"I'm sure you did," said Windflower. "Hey, let's build a fort in the living room." The two girls squealed with delight at that suggestion. Sheila was pretty happy as well.

"Thank you," she said. "I just need a few moments of peace and quiet to regain my sanity. I'll be upstairs."

Windflower got the blankets and flashlights, and the girls brought their toys and dolls. It was great fun for the hour they waited for supper. By the time Sheila came back down to take the lasagna and garlic bread out of the oven, Windflower thought his knees would go weak with the aromas that were emanating from the kitchen.

Supper was as good as it smelled, and Windflower had two helpings of both the lasagna and garlic bread as well as a smaller portion of steamed broccoli. "Don't want to ruin my appetite for lasagna," he said to Sheila.

After supper and cleanup, Windflower took Lady on her nightly walk. The evening was cool and crisp. Another great night for making a skating rink, he thought. He checked the weather on his phone and smiled at the chilly forecast through the weekend. His phone rang while he was looking at the weather. Again, it was Eddie Tizzard.

"Marco's dead," said Tizzard.

"What?" asked Windflower.

"He's dead. Shot, in the back of the head. He was dead when Lundquist and Carrie got there. They found him lying on the floor of his house with the doors wide open."

"Any evidence, clues, witnesses?"

"Carrie is canvassing right now. All I know is that they found Marco and a number of guns. Lundquist is checking them now to see if there might be a match to Freddy Hawkins. Other than that, right now we have no witnesses and no suspects. The only one we know didn't do it is the kid. We kept him here while we went to pick up Marco."

"I'm sure the now-late Marco had it coming to him. But it leaves a lot hanging in our case now."

"Yeah, lots of people will be happy about this turn of events, including Robbie Bennett 'cause he won't have to testify and can now walk away unscathed," said Tizzard.

"Okay," said Windflower. "Always more questions than answers. Keep me posted."

He hung up and didn't have much time to think about Marco or anybody else as Lady pulled him along to get going on their walk.

"I'm coming, I'm coming," said Windflower. They didn't stop again until they came near Wilf Pittman's house. The spotlight was on, and Wilf was out back watering his rink. Windflower went closer to say hello.

"Hey, Winston, how are ya b'y?" asked Wilf.

"We're good, great in fact," said Windflower. "You got a nice rink going now."

"It's pretty good. It keeps me going. Maybe my grandkids will come over on the weekend to keep me company."

"It must get lonely by yourself."

Wilf Pittman looked like he was going to cry. "When I'm busy it's okay," he said. "But when I slow down, it's hard. Right now, Lucy would be making the hot chocolate and we'd go in and watch the news together. I still really miss her."

"I miss my Auntie a lot too. She was like my mother after my real mom died. It's like a hole inside of you that doesn't get filled," said Windflower.

"That's exactly what it feels like. People say it gets easier. But I think that in some ways it gets harder, deeper somehow."

"One thing that really helped me was a book by Richard Wagamese. He's an Ojibway writer who I read sometimes. He reminded me of something that my Auntie Marie used to say about missing people well."

"What's that about?" asked Wilf.

"Auntie Marie always talked of people who had passed as still being with her and of being reminded of their good qualities when good things arose in her life. Richard Wagamese has the same message. He says we should try to miss people well by seeing them, their image, or memories of them in a beautiful sunrise or a startling sunset. If we can do that, then we miss them really well," said Windflower.

"Like when I look out at this beautiful rink, I can think about Lucy and miss her really well?" asked Wilf.

"I think you got it."

"Thanks, Winston. I really appreciate it. You still putting in your rink this weekend? Want some help?"

"That would be great. I was going to do it on Saturday morning and then flood it overnight."

"I'll be over, for sure."

Windflower waved goodbye and went home to tell Sheila the good news.

She was happy, maybe too happy, thought Windflower.

"I can do this by myself," he said.

"I know," said Sheila. "But don't you know there's nothing wrong in asking for help or listening to the women in your life?"

Windflower had no response to that. Instead he picked up Amelia Louise and Stella and carried them both upstairs.

After bath time Windflower read Amelia Louise her story while Sheila looked after Stella. Tonight's book was The Watermelon Seed, about a crocodile who loves watermelon. But he's terrified of what might happen if he swallows some of the seeds. Amelia Louise loved this book, and it was one of the first in which she pointed to words and read them out loud. Of course Windflower had to read the book twice, but he and Amelia Louise still got through their story time before Sheila and Stella did theirs.

Windflower went downstairs, made the tea and put a small tray of cookies together. He went to the living room and turned on the TV. He was mindlessly watching the cartoon channel and munching on a cookie when Sheila came down.

"You have an interesting taste in television programming," she said.

"I wasn't watching," said Windflower. "I was thinking."

"What were you thinking about?" she asked as she poured herself a cup of tea.

"Wilf Pittman," he said.

62

Windflower told Sheila about his interaction with Wilf on the way home.

"That was good advice," she said. "I use that, too, when I miss my mom and my Grandmother Irene. I try to see the good in the world and thank them for it."

"I'm glad he's coming over to help," said Windflower. "It'll be good for him, and yes, I can use the help. Plus, I don't want to screw up Stella's first skating rink."

"She's pretty excited," said Sheila. "I've been thinking about her a lot lately. I mean she's around all the time, but I mean about her future."

"She's like our daughter now," said Windflower. "Our real daughter."

"That's what I mean. I know it's only been a couple of months, but I'm wondering if we should make it permanent."

"Adopt her?"

"Why not? I'm sure the paperwork takes forever, but why not start the process? If you're okay."

"I can't imagine her not being part of our family, and Amelia Louise would kill us if we allowed her big sister to live somewhere else."

"Okay," said Sheila. "I'll talk to the social worker and find out how it works."

"Perfect," said Windflower. "Can we watch some adult programming now?"

Sheila laughed and turned on the news. There was a fire downtown and some political announcement, and then the RNC Headquarters building flashed onto the screen. The announcer talked over the chief as he displayed the drugs and guns that had been seized in the raid. When the chief finally spoke, he talked about how big the raid was and that they had made a dent in organized crime in the city. He praised the work of the RNC officers behind him, including Langmead, who Windflower pointed out again to Sheila.

After the chief, Foote and Larissa Murphy's mother walked to the podium. In a calm and clear voice, the mother told the story of her daughter being found safe, and she thanked the police and the public for their help. Her last comment was to other girls who might still be out there. "I know you're scared, and you don't know where to go for help," she said. "But the help is here. You can call Constable Foote or anybody else at the Constabulary. They can get you home. Your family misses you and loves you."

When Mrs. Murphy had finished, the announcer came on again and a number flashed on the screen. "If you're in trouble or need help, please call," said the announcer.

"That was good," said Sheila. "Let's hope someone hears the message."

"Let's hope," said Windflower. He put the tea and cookie tray away and let Lady out. While she was doing her thing, he said a prayer that any girl who was out there suffering and struggling would call. He let Lady in and went up to bed. He fell asleep easily and before long found himself in a dream.

It was nighttime in this dream. That was unusual because his dreams usually unfolded in daytime. He wondered if that meant anything. He looked around and found his hands. It was a dream all right. Despite it being night and dark, somehow he could see.

There was a fire burning in the distance, and he started to walk towards it. As he neared, he could make out a shape covered in what looked like a blanket. When he got really close, the blanket moved.

"Hello, Nephew. Come sit by the fire with me," said Auntie Marie.

"How are you, Auntie?" asked Windflower.

"If I'd known how good it was over here, I'd have come long before," said his aunt, laughing so hard she nearly keeled over. "I see you are making progress."

"In my case?" asked Windflower.

"No, in your life," said Auntie Marie. "Your work is a very small part of your life. In fact, what's going on outside is really the dream. It's what's going on inside your heart that counts."

"So, what did you mean by progress?"

"You are not as reluctant to ask for help, and you are beginning to listen to the women in your life."

"Oh, Morecombe."

"And that young woman police officer whose name I forget. And even your daughter."

"You mean Foote," said Windflower. "Which daughter are you talking about?"

"You have always listened to Amelia Louise. She is your first born, and she will always own your heart. But the silent one is now speaking, and she has great lessons for you."

"Yes, Stella has started speaking a little," said Windflower.

"It's not just by words that we communicate," said his aunt. "Your new daughter is teaching you how to recover and how to love again. It is a powerful message from Creator being directly delivered to you. Listen carefully."

"I will, Auntie."

"There are more teachers coming very soon. Stay awake." With that, Auntie Marie was finished speaking and a big wind came up and blew the flames higher and higher until Windflower thought they would reach the sky. Then, just as quickly, the fire faded, and his aunt was gone. There was only darkness, and he woke back in own bed again.

He managed to get back to sleep and was awake before the alarm sounded. He went downstairs as quietly as he could, put on the coffee and let Lady out. He followed behind shortly afterwards with his pipe. It wasn't Auntie Marie's pipe anymore. It was his now, he said to himself.

He put a pinch of tobacco in and lit the pipe. He sat quietly on the deck in the cold and still-dark morning. He puffed and watched the smoke curl up into the morning air. Then it hung there, hovering over his head. He closed his eyes, and when he opened them, he could see a skating rink in front of him. Stella was skating around and around by herself. She motioned for him to join her.

He looked down and noticed that he, too, was wearing skates. He stood and walked slowly towards Stella. As he neared her, she reached out for his hand and pulled him towards her. But instead of landing on the ice, Windflower was lifted up into the sky, and he and Stella were flying over St. John's. He kept his eyes wide open and looked for landmarks. He passed Confederation Building and then the university. He kept going across town, past Bowring Park and then into what he knew was Mount Pearl. He and Stella dipped down, and he got a glimpse of a street sign—Lindburgh Crescent. Stella stopped in front of a house on that street and pointed.

Then everything faded away. Stella, the rink and everything but Lady and his backyard were gone. Lady had that he's-going-crazy-again look in her eyes. Windflower petted her on the head and went back inside. He sat and drank his coffee, trying to process all that had happened outside and in his dream. Tired and confused, he couldn't make sense of any of it. He sipped his coffee until he heard Amelia Louise crying out and he went up to get her.

63

Windflower brought Amelia Louise down with him while he made scrambled eggs for breakfast. She helped by watching the toast for him, and when it popped, she yelled that it was ready.

"Ready, Daddy. Toast," she screamed as loud as she could. "What's going on down there?" asked Sheila.

"Toast," yelled Amelia Louise.

Windflower just laughed and kept going with breakfast. He cut a melon into slices, and he and Amelia Louise set the table. He put her in her chair and gave her some toast, eggs and melon. Her face was full of all three when Sheila came down with Stella.

"Amelia Louise made breakfast this morning," said Windflower as he gave them their breakfast and sat at the table.

"Mila breckie," said Amelia Louise.

"I can see that," said Sheila. "Thank you very much."

After breakfast Windflower cleaned up and Sheila got the girls ready. When they were out the door, Windflower took Lady for a quick trip around the block. His morning tasks complete, he jumped in his van and headed to work. It was a light traffic day, being Friday, and he was there in no time.

He had just arrived at his office when his cell phone rang.

It was Anne Marie Foote.

"Good morning, Sergeant. How are you?" she asked.

"I'm good," said Windflower. "I saw you and Mary Murphy last night. She was great."

"She's a trooper," said Foote. "We started getting calls right afterward. Four or five more this morning. I'm over at the Health Sciences right now getting one of them checked out. Even better than that, Cassie left me a message last night. She said that Mandy

Pardy reached out to her after seeing the press conference. I guess they knew each other from being around the bikers."

"Wow, that's good news," said Windflower.

"Yeah, she's agreed to meet us somewhere out in Mount Pearl."

Windflower thought about telling her about his dream and the house in Mount Pearl. But he resisted. Instead, he asked about Cassie.

"She's doing well," said Foote. "I'm heading over to pick her up at the shelter, and then we're over to see the Pardy girl. And I have more good news. Brittney Hodder is awake and in a private room. I saw her parents. They're pretty happy. I thought you might like to talk to her."

"Thanks very much," said Windflower. "I'll head over this morning. Let me know how it goes with Mandy Pardy. We got the boy who was involved down in our area, but the head guy got shot last night."

"A lot happening all at once."

"Sometimes it works that way. Okay, talk soon."

Before anyone else could get him, Windflower left the office and drove to the hospital. At reception he asked for directions to Brittney Hodder's room. When he got there, Martin Hodder was coming out.

"Good morning, Sergeant," said Hodder.

"Morning," said Windflower. "I hear there's good news."

"She's going to make a full recovery," said Hodder. "She's a bit groggy but awake. Thank God."

"We need to ask her a few questions. It won't take long. But it may help other girls."

"No problem by me. If we can help another family, we'd be happy to. I was just going to get coffee, but that can wait."

"No, go ahead."

"Can I get you one?"

"That would be great, just black," said Windflower as he went into the room.

He said good morning to Barb Hodder and walked closer to Brittney's bed. The girl was heavily bandaged around the upper part of her body and had bruises on her face, but she had a healthier complexion than the pallor he had seen earlier.

"Good morning, Brittney," he said. "I'm Sergeant Windflower. You might remember me from Grand Bank. I have a few questions that I'd like to ask. Would that be okay?"

Brittney Hodder saw her mother nod, so she nodded too.

"Thank you," said Windflower. "We know a bit about the clubhouse in St. John's, and somebody will be by to talk to you about that. I'm more interested in what happened in Grand Bank."

At the mention of her hometown, Brittney Hodder's body tensed up and she looked again at her mother. Barb Hodder smiled and squeezed her hand.

"You are not in any trouble," said Windflower. "But the people who got you into this situation certainly are. We want to stop them from taking girls away from their families. Will you help us?"

Brittney Hodder nodded again. Her mother gave her a small sip of water. She cleared her throat and began speaking in a near whisper. Windflower bent down closer to hear her. "In Grand Bank it was the Bennetts," she said.

"Robbie Bennett?" asked Windflower. "We have already spoken with him. We know he was involved."

"And his father," said Brittney Hodder.

Windflower tried not to act surprised, but he was shocked. Barb Hodder sat there in stunned silence as well.

"Harold Bennett?" he asked.

"Yes," said Brittney Hodder. "He paid for the trips to Montreal and Toronto, the first few parties in St. John's. The other guys like Marco came in later on."

Martin Hodder came in with the coffees.

"What's going on?" he asked as the room was deathly quiet.

"We're just talking to Brittney," said Windflower. "She told us that Harold Bennett might be involved in all this."

"Bennett?" said Hodder. "If he had any part in hurting Brittney, I'll kill him."

"Martin and Barb, I know this is hard, but I need you to stay calm and support Brittney. She really needs you now," said Windflower. "I also need you to keep this among ourselves for now. Let us do our jobs. There are more girls that need our help out there.

If Harold Bennett was involved, we'll look after him. In fact, I'm going to call and have him picked up right now."

Martin Hodder was still pretty upset, but he heard what Windflower had to say and nodded.

"Okay then," said Windflower. "Get better Brittney. Thank you for your help. If you'll excuse me, I have to go back to the office."

Windflower left and only started breathing normally again when he got near the front door. He pulled out his phone and called Lars Lundquist in Grand Bank.

64

Lars, we need to pick up Harold Bennett," said Windflower. "I just spoke to Brittney Hodder. She says not only the boy, but the father was involved too."

"I'll go over right now myself," said Lundquist. "We've got some more information about Marco's death. It was the same calibre gun used to shoot Freddy Hawkins. I've sent it to the lab in St. John's to get a ballistics check, but it looks like the murder weapon, and it's got Marco's prints all over it."

"Okay. Get the father. Do you still have the boy?"

"No, we let him go. Nothing to hold him on, and once Marco was dead, he was in the clear."

"In more ways than one," said Windflower. "Pick him up too. They're obviously a tag team."

"Okay, I'll call you back soon," said Lundquist.

Windflower left the hospital and drove back to the office. He tried to make sense of these latest developments but only got a bit more confused. Even worse, he forgot his role as roving RCMP ambassador and almost ran over a student crossing the parkway. He waved his apologies and got a finger salute in return. Exactly the opposite response his van was seeking. But he still managed to get back to his office in one piece, even before his phone rang again.

"Mandy Pardy talked about the Bennetts," said Foote. "Not just the kid, the father too. I can't believe it."

"I know," said Windflower. "Brittney Hodder gave me the same info. We're picking both of them up right now."

"Good. We expect this behaviour from the outlaw bikers, but from a community member…"

"Looks like he and the boy were in it together. They may have even been involved in getting rid of Marco, the head biker down there."

"Let me know how it goes. The good news is that Mandy Pardy is okay. She's not going back right away, but she's got a safe place to stay, and she said she'd call her parents."

"I guess that's as much as we can do, for now anyway," said Windflower.

"Call me when you get that...," said Foote, unable to finish her thought.

"Yeah. I know what you mean," said Windflower.

He hung up the phone and sat there dazed. That didn't last long, though, as his phone rang. It was Lundquist again.

"He's gone and the boy too," said Lundquist. "No vehicle and no people."

"Check with the boy's friends," said Windflower. "Kids always tell their friends what's going on. Maybe they know something we don't."

"I'll get Tizzard on that right away. Evanchuk has something, too. Got it from her canvassing. Neighbours saw a red pickup leaving the house where Marco was shot. Guess who has a red pickup?"

"Harold Bennett. Figures. I'm going to call the inspector and get him in on this. We'll need all the help we can get."

Windflower paused for just a second to collect his thoughts and then phoned Ron Quigley in Marystown. He quickly gave him an update.

"That creep," was Quigley's first response. "In our own community too. What do we know about him?"

"Not very much," said Windflower. "Up until a few hours ago, he was a candidate for father of the year. We can check that out. In the meantime can we put a bulletin out for him, maybe driving a red pickup? Although I have to confirm that."

"I'll put a check in at the airports too," said Quigley.

"Let's hope we're in time," said Windflower. "Oh, and we found Mandy Pardy."

"That's wonderful news. You're ticking them off, one by one."

"That's kind of how it works," said Windflower. "One foot in front of the other."

That would normally have been a cue for Quigley to add a poignant quote of the day, one he'd been saving up especially for Windflower. But he didn't seem to have it in him today. He simply said goodbye and hung up.

The next couple of hours flew by, and Windflower was almost ready to go home for the day when Tizzard called.

"Hey, Sarge," said Tizzard. "Robbie Bennett's friends say he's gone to Toronto with his dad. May be gone for a few weeks."

"Thanks, Eddie," said Windflower. "Did you call the airport?"

"I got Smithson on it. I think he's monitoring all the cameras himself. But, yeah, I called it in to the inspector. And we've got plates on Bennett's pickup. Carrie is going back to talk to the neighbours to see if they can identify the truck or if they saw anybody."

"Good stuff, Eddie," said Windflower. "Keep me posted."

Windflower was closing his computer when Terry Robbins came by.

"You heading out?" asked Robbins.

"I was," said Windflower. "Unless you need me for something."

"Just a couple of minutes," he said. "I thought you'd want to know that Morecombe's husband died this afternoon."

"That's too bad."

"Yeah, even at the end, I'm sure it's hard. We'll do a collection."

"Count me in," said Windflower.

Robbins nodded his head but didn't leave. "Is there something else?" Windflower asked.

"Yeah, actually there is," said Robbins. "I could use your help."

"My help?" asked Windflower. "I don't know much. I'm the new guy around here, remember? I have a lot yet to learn about public outreach and communications."

"I don't know about that," said Robbins. "I've watched you navigate around Morecombe until she was singing your praises, work with the RNC without anyone having a major meltdown, and access the tactical unit of the RCMP. No questions asked. I'd say that's pretty good outreach. I'd say that's pretty good communications."

"What do you want me to do?" asked Windflower. "Although, whatever it is will have to wait until we finish what we started with the missing girls."

"Understood," said Robbins. "I'm taking over from Morecombe, and I don't think she's coming back. So, I need to make a good first impression so that my time here isn't just long but is smooth as well. You can coach me, give me tips."

"Like what?"

"Like all those sayings you have about asking for help and everything. I'm asking you, now. I need someone to show me how to relate to people. I know how to spin a story, but this job is bigger than that. Will you help me?"

"Let's have coffee when I'm done with this file and we'll talk," said Windflower. "You may already have the answers you're seeking from me inside of you."

"That's what I'm talking about," said Robbins. "We'll get together next week. Have a good night."

Windflower smiled to himself. His Auntie Marie had told him one time that he would know when he was growing up because someone would ask him for help. "Thank you, Auntie," he said as he closed his door and left for home.

65

Sheila called Windflower as he was leaving.

"I got home a little while ago. Let's go get groceries when you get here," she said.

"I'm leaving right now. I'll meet you there," he said.

"There's a surprise waiting for you when you get here."

"What is it?"

"See you at the supermarket."

A few minutes later all four of them were walking along the aisles in the supermarket at the old Memorial Stadium. Well, the two adults were walking. The kids were each getting a ride in a cart pushed by their parents. Everyone was in a good mood. It was Friday, and all was right with their little world. They had just loaded up at the checkout and were waiting for their order to be processed when Windflower's cell phone rang.

He ducked to one side where it was a little quieter and answered.

"Hey, Sarge, it's Smithson. We've got the Bennetts booked on the last flight out to Toronto tonight. Business class, of course."

"What time is that?" asked Windflower.

"Eight thirty," said Smithson. "Our guys are lined up, and the inspector called the RNC for backup as well."

"Okay," said Windflower. "Who's our contact at the airport? Can you get him to call me if anything happens?"

"It's Sergeant David Roche," said Smithson. "I'll pass the message along."

Windflower hung up and went back to his family. Sheila was pushing a full cart with two little girls in tow. Windflower took his girls by the hand and followed behind Sheila. More than one shopper stopped in amazement at the sight of two little girls and their large RCMP dad skipping out the door.

When they got home and had unloaded the groceries, Sheila pointed out to the backyard. Windflower turned on the spotlight. The whole backyard had been cleared with only a thin layer of snow remaining. The rest had been pushed up against the fence.

"Wilf Pittman," said Sheila. "He came by after I got home. He said it would be easier to have this out of the way tonight so that you could get started right away in the morning. He'll be over after breakfast."

"It's amazing," said Windflower. "He's amazing."

"He certainly is," said Sheila. "Now help me put all this away."

Supper was another Friday night special of fish sticks with french fries and vegetables and a cookie tray for dessert. Then it was movie time. Tonight's show was The Lion King, a favourite of the whole family. They ate popcorn. Windflower and Sheila sang along to all the songs. So did Amelia Louise, who made up the words as she went along. Stella had a good time, too, humming along. It was a lot of fun, and when it came time for their baths, Sheila took the girls upstairs and Windflower went out with Lady.

They made a large circle downtown and then back up again by the hotel and down Kings Bridge Road. They had just turned onto Forest Road when Windflower's cell phone rang.

"Windflower," he answered.

"It's Roche at the airport. We got your people," said the other officer.

"Any trouble?" asked Windflower.

"They were surprised, at least the father was. He had no idea this was coming. A bit indignant even," said Roche. "We told him we wanted to talk to him about the death of Marco Hoddinot. That's when he got really upset. Started asking for a lawyer."

"People watch too much TV. Where is he now?"

"We're putting both of them in holding cells at HQ. When do you want to see them?"

"Let them sit overnight. I'm going to ask the RNC to send someone along when we interview the father. Does Inspector Quigley know about all this?"

"Your man Smithson knows," said Roche. "Okay, we'll hold the pair overnight. Call security in the morning, and they'll arrange an interview room."

"Thanks for your help with this."

"Happy to help. The guy sounds like a real beauty. Have a good night."

When Windflower got home, he called Langmead with the good news and asked for Foote to accompany him to the interview with Harold Bennett.

"That's a nice touch," said Langmead. "She'll appreciate it, and so do we."

"No worries," said Windflower. "We've been in this together. Let's see if we can't close this off together as well."

Windflower got back home just in time for stories. Tonight Windflower and Stella read together while Sheila was with Amelia Louise. Stella picked Wolfie the Bunny, a hilarious book about a rabbit family adopting a wolf son. Dot, the Bunny daughter, is the only one who realizes that her new brother can actually eat them. Both Stella and Windflower laughed a lot as he read, and when he kissed her goodnight, she gave him an extra tight hug.

Later downstairs Windflower and Sheila finished off the popcorn and watched the news. There was nothing as spectacular as the previous night, just the usual combination of robberies and muggings that were plaguing several of the city's neighbourhoods.

"Time for more public outreach, Sergeant," said Sheila.

"Terry Robbins came to me today," said Windflower. "He's taking over for Morecombe. He asked for my help."

"I hope you said yes," said Sheila.

"Absolutely. I was just surprised that he asked me to help him with public outreach."

"You're actually pretty good at it. You kept a mayor happy for years, didn't you?"

"I thought that was just my charm. Oh, and I forgot to tell you my big news."

He ran through all of the stuff with Robbie Bennett, Marco and then Harold Bennett. "I'm going in early to interview Bennett with Foote from the Constabulary," he said. "But I'll be back in time to put in the rink with Wilf."

"That's good," said Sheila. "Somebody we know would never forgive you. And as far as Harold Bennett goes, I never liked him. I always thought there was something weird about him."

"What's his story?"

66

Harold Bennett is a bit older than I am," said Sheila. "He fancied himself a ladies' man, but all the women I know found him creepy. He's been married three times, each time to a younger woman. For the life of me I can't see what they saw in him."

"Any trouble?" asked Windflower.

"The rumour was that he beat them, but none of them ever said anything about that in public. People said he bought them off."

"Did he have money?"

"A long time ago his family had a store, but I don't think he ever even had a job. He told everybody he was in the import/export business one year and capelin roe another. He always had a story. And he travelled a lot. He was forever going to Toronto or Montreal with his latest girlfriend."

"What do you think was really going on?"

"I think he was selling drugs, not necessarily in Grand Bank, but that was the whisper on him. He was somehow connected with people who did that kind of thing."

"Should be easy enough to check his financial records. That's how Al Capone finally got caught. Tax evasion. We'll take anything we can get. Do you think he's capable of trafficking in girls?'

"A man like that has no respect for women. He's capable of anything."

"Thanks for your help. I don't know him at all. And I certainly don't trust him, especially after the stunt he pulled with his son."

Sheila came closer and gave Windflower a hug.

"What's that for?" he asked.

"For not being a creep," she said with a laugh. "For being kind and gentle but strong. Like grass."

"Have you been reading my Richard Wagamese book?"

"Let Lady out and come to bed."

Windflower did as he was told and minutes later was snuggling in beside Sheila. A few minutes after that he was solidly asleep.

Sheila was up first and had the girls helping her make a batch of muffins for breakfast. Stella seemed particularly excited and tried to follow Windflower and Lady out the back door when he got up. "Not yet," said Windflower. "Later, when Mr. Pittman comes over, honey."

He could see her little face pressed up against the window as he breathed in the cold air and surveyed his neatly groomed snow field in the backyard. Lady went off to investigate the snow bank that Wilf Pittman had made, and Windflower had a few minutes of peace to get ready for the day. There wasn't enough time to smudge, but there was lots of time to pray.

He prayed for all the people in his life and made a special point to include the girls that had been rescued and others who were at least safe today. And he also prayed for all the other girls who might be still out there suffering, maybe even dying, sometimes quickly, sometimes slowly. Finally he prayed for guidance and wisdom to do the right thing in his work today. He could feel a sense of something like evil around him, and he prayed for the goodness of creation to accompany him and Foote in their task this morning.

He called Lady and went in to have fruit and coffee with Sheila and the girls. He called over to security at the RCMP and made arrangements for the interview room and for Harold Bennett to be brought up once he and Foote arrived. He said goodbye to Sheila and kissed the girls with a promise to be back soon to start work on the skating rink. Stella was so excited she was dancing, and Amelia Louise started dancing too. Windflower was still laughing at the thought of his two girls dancing when he pulled into the RCMP parking lot.

Anne Marie Foote was waiting for him at the reception desk. He asked for their interview room and called security to have Harold Bennett brought to them.

"Ready?" he asked Foote when they found their room and got the technician to set up the recording behind the glass.

"More than ready," she said. "Thanks for bringing me into this."

"We're a team," said Windflower.

A bedraggled Harold Bennett was brought into the room, clearly having spent the night in his clothes. His mood was fouler than his look. He started yelling about rights and lawyers and how he was going to sue the RCMP and Windflower personally. Windflower let him go on for a while, and when Bennett started to peter out a little on the venom, he asked him a question.

"What do you do for a living?"

Bennett looked at him strangely, and for a second he thought he had an opportunity to start another web of intrigue with the RCMP officer.

"I'm a businessman," said Bennett.

"What kind of business?" asked Windflower.

"Listen, I don't have to talk to you, and as soon as I get my lawyer, you will have to let me and my son go. You don't have any reason to hold me or him," said Bennett.

"We'll get you a lawyer," said Windflower. "And you can answer our questions or talk to commercial crime. And while we're at it, why don't we talk about the girls and Marco Hoddinot?"

That got Bennett's attention.

"I'm sure this has all been a mistake," said Bennett. "I run an import-export business. Everybody knows that. I bring in goods and materials from all over the world, and I help the local economy by buying things nobody else wants to sell. As for the girls, Robbie told you all about Marco and those bad guys. I thought we were through with that. We're getting ready for a trip to Toronto to plan his fresh start."

Windflower looked at Foote and indicated she should go ahead.

"I talked to Mandy Pardy," said Foote. "And Sergeant Windflower talked to Brittney Hodder."

"Those girls are screwed up," said Bennett. "I gave them a helping hand when no one else would."

"How did it work?" asked Windflower. "Did Marco and the other guys pay you cash, or did you get it all in dope?"

"What are you talking about?" asked Bennett. "Cash and dope? You're going crazy now. I told you. I'm a legitimate businessperson."

"Then you won't mind if we take a look at your books?" said Windflower.

"Screw you," said Bennett. "I want my lawyer. I'll be out of here by noon and in Toronto tonight."

"I don't think so," said Windflower. "Just one more question. How could you bring your son into this?"

Bennett started to yell and stood as if to come towards Windflower. Foote deftly rose, pulled Bennett's arms behind his back and pushed him to the floor. She knelt on him and put on the handcuffs.

"Nice," said Windflower.

"I may be small, but I'm fierce," said Foote.

"Go ahead and do the honours, although commercial crime will want to talk to him for sure," said Windflower.

"Harold Bennett, I am arresting you on charges of human trafficking, profiting from the proceeds of human trafficking and for the murder of Marco Hoddinot," said Foote.

"I'll call security to have him brought downstairs until we can arrange the transfer," said Windflower.

Minutes later they were standing outside the reception area again.

"Thanks again for bringing me in," said Foote. "I thoroughly enjoyed that."

"We've done our part," said Windflower. "The Crown will have to figure out how they want to proceed, but our friend is going to do some serious time."

"Another break in the chain. Let's see how long it takes for them to set everything back up again."

"True, but for today, at least this morning, we claim victory. 'The wheel is come full circle.'"

Foote smiled and waved goodbye as she went to her car. Windflower smiled to himself too. May not be a perfect day or a perfect case against Harold Bennett, he thought, but there's enough to start justice moving in the right direction. Now, to see a man about a skating rink.

67

Wilf Pittman was just coming up the driveway as Windflower came back from the RCMP building. He invited him in, and together with Sheila and the girls, they had some of the homemade muffins and coffee.

Afterward the two men went outside where Wilf helped Windflower put up the boards. They stood back to survey their work.

"That looks good," said Windflower.

"Yes b'y," said Wilf. "You've got a good start. As soon as it gets dark, put on your first coat. Light, so it attaches to the snow. That'll give you a great base. I'll pop by later tonight to see how you're doing."

"Thanks again, Wilf," said Windflower. He looked back in, and Stella was standing in the window, staring out at him. He gave her the thumbs-up signal. She held two thumbs up in return.

After lunch Sheila had some errands, and she offered to take one of the girls with her.

"Why don't Stella and I go visit Bill Ford?" asked Windflower. Stella smiled at that idea.

"Okay," said Sheila. "I'll pop by Halliday's to get some steaks if you'll barbeque tonight. Not too cold is it?"

"No b'y," said Windflower. "I'm almost a hearty Newfoundlander now."

Bill Ford was happy to see Windflower but almost happier to see Stella. She was pretty happy too. She was even happier when Ford told her to go to his desk and she pulled out two small plastic bags of candy.

"Thank you," she gushed. She opened one and started eating and handed the other to Windflower.

"I think you got a fan," said Windflower.

"Easy to buy with a few sweets," said Ford. "I'm glad you stopped by. They're cutting my treatments. I'm going home on Monday."

"That's great news," said Windflower.

"Well, not so great," said Ford. "They're moving everybody they can out. Apparently, there's some big virus coming that they're all worried we'll catch."

"Like the flu?"

"Way bigger than that. I heard the nurses talking. They said it's in China now, but it's coming our way."

"Anyway, I'm glad you're going home. Feel any better?" asked Windflower

"Physically about the same. But it will take time and effort on my part. They've given me exercises I can do at home. That should help. But the biggest change is in my head. I think I'm coming out of my depression, if that's what it was. I want to live again and make the most of whatever time I have left. I called my daughter, and she's coming to visit, and as soon as I'm well enough, we're going to take a cruise."

"I always wanted to take a cruise. But what about if you get sick on one of them?"

"Ah, don't worry about that b'y," said Ford. "They're as safe as being on land, even have doctors."

Windflower nodded. He was so busy talking to Ford he didn't notice Stella had finished her bag of candy and now had red cherry smears all over her face.

"You had to eat it all, didn't you?" said Windflower as he took a tissue and wiped her face.

"They're only small once," said Ford.

"That's why she likes you. You understand her. We should be going. I'm glad your head and thinking are clearing up. I look forward to seeing you at the fishing hole this summer."

"I'll be there," said Ford. "And you look after this little princess and the other at home."

Stella was holding Windflower's hand, but before she left, she ran back and gave Bill Ford a huge hug.

"Thank you," said Ford. "You made my day, Stella. See ya."

Windflower and Stella took their time walking back, and when they got home, they peeked in over their own backyard to take a look at the budding rink. Windflower lifted Stella up, and she smiled broadly when she saw it again.

Inside Windflower put on a movie for Stella and lay on the couch to watch it with her. But a few minutes later he was out cold and didn't wake until he heard Sheila and Amelia Louise come back.

He went out to inspect the meat.

"These steaks are gorgeous," said Windflower.

"Halliday's is the best," said Sheila.

There were three T-bone steaks, medium-sized, perfect for the grill. He got his special steak rub out of a sealed container in the cupboard. It was his own concoction of garlic powder, paprika, onion powder, coriander and turmeric, with more than a little black pepper and sea salt. It brought out the flavours of the meat without overpowering it. He coated the steaks with the rub and put them in a plastic bag.

He cleaned and scrubbed four baking potatoes and wrapped them in tinfoil. They could go on the barbeque soon. He also peeled and sliced carrots and put them in a tinfoil packet with butter and a spoonful of maple syrup. Then he sliced a couple of onions and mixed them with a can of button mushrooms and butter in another packet. His prep all done, he went out and fired up the grill. When it was hot, he put the potatoes on.

He spent a few minutes horsing around with Amelia Louise in the living room and then went back out to put on the vegetables. After a few more minutes, he got the steaks and went out on the deck with Lady. He moved the potatoes and veggies around and put the steaks on the grill, searing the meat to seal in the juices. Then he moved the steaks to get the desired preferences. His and Sheila's were medium rare, while the kids seemed to prefer the meat a little more well done. Then, he turned off the grill and let the steaks stand for a few minutes before coming back in to declare supper ready.

He cut up one steak and added half a potato and veggies for each of the girls. He and Sheila had the others.

"Okay," said Sheila. "I'll have to keep you."

"This is so tasty," said Windflower.

"Tasty, tasty, tasty," said Amelia Louise.

"I like it," said Stella.

"That's good," said Windflower. "We'll need all our energy to get our skating rink ready."

68

After dinner Sheila cleaned up while Windflower got the girls dressed to go outside with him. He laid out the hose and turned it on so the water came out slowly, just like he'd seen Wilf Pittman do. He let the water seep into the snow until it looked to him like it had a level of ice on top. He would come out later to add another layer, but that was it for now.

Back inside, the girls got into their pajamas, and their parents let them run around and play until they got tired. After story time Windflower went outside again and put down another layer of water. It was starting to look a lot like a skating rink.

He and Sheila watched an old James Bond movie on TV until they heard a knock on their door. Windflower peeked out. "It's Wilf Pittman," he said. He grabbed his coat and went out to meet Wilf. Together, they walked to the backyard where Wilf did a full inspection.

"Great job b'y," said Wilf. "You're ready to flood her now."

Those were magical words to Windflower's ears. He turned on the hose and let the water run until Wilf signalled for him to stop.

"Let her settle now. It should be good to go in the morning," said Wilf.

"Thanks a lot," said Windflower, feeling pretty proud of himself as he went inside.

Sheila had gone up to bed and was sitting up reading when he came in.

"So?" she asked.

"I think we have a rink," said Windflower.

"Stella will be so pleased," said Sheila. "You must be cold though."

"I am a little."

"Come closer and I'll warm you up."

Windflower and Sheila fell asleep in each other's arms. She stayed sleeping. He did not. He woke sometime after in another dream.

The racoon was back, his eyes glowing in the darkness.

"Thank you," said the racoon.

"Why are you thanking me?" asked Windflower.

"Are you really that dense?" asked the racoon. "I thought you were back here to thank me. I did help you, in case you forgot."

"Oh, thank you. Thank you very much," said Windflower. "It was a great help once I figured it out."

"Geez. It's never enough for you humans, is it? We find all these girls for you, solve your murder cases and then you want more. What is wrong with you?"

Windflower figured he should thank the racoon, who seemed to feel unappreciated, again.

"Thank you," repeated Windflower. "Do you have a message for me? And I'd prefer not to have a riddle. It takes me too long to figure it out."

"Well, you're honest. "That's something, I guess. But I don't know how to tell you this without scaring you to death."

"Try me. I am a police officer."

The racoon snorted. "There is a plague coming, and few will be left untouched. You won't be able to see it or feel it until it is too late. Guard your elders and stay safe."

"That's it?" asked Windflower.

"That is more warning than millions of people will receive," said the racoon. "And don't go on that cruise."

The racoon's eyes stopped glowing, and Windflower could feel himself being pulled back into his own world. He woke holding Sheila, who was sleeping peacefully. He started thinking about his dream, but Sheila and the warmth of their bed lulled him back under, and he didn't stir again until the morning.

Windflower was up first and put the coffee on. Then he spent all the time it was brewing to admire his amazing skating rink. He was standing at the patio window looking out when Stella came downstairs. She, too, stood transfixed. Windflower opened the door to let Lady out, and Stella almost screamed when it looked like the dog was going to stain their perfect surface. But Lady went to the snowbank and did her business there.

"It's beautiful," said Stella.

"It is indeed," said Windflower.

He let Lady in and heard Amelia Louise moving around upstairs. He got her and brought her down. Stella took her little sister by the hand and led her to the window. Amelia Louise was transfixed too.

In a few minutes they returned their attention to the kitchen where Windflower had found a box of Pop Tarts in the cupboard. That wasn't there before, he thought. Where did it come from? The girls grabbed their pseudo breakfasts and went into the living room to watch cartoons with their dad. They loved Sunday mornings with Windflower.

When Sheila came down, most of the incriminating evidence was gone, and Windflower scrambled to hide the rest.

"I figured I might as well buy some," said Sheila. "Last week it was frozen pizza. What's next? Hot dogs for breakfast?"

Windflower thought about that, but he didn't have a chance to reply because his cell phone rang. "Sorry," he said. "It's Ron Quigley." He went to the kitchen to take the call.

"Good morning, Sergeant," said Quigley. "Sorry to intrude on your domestic bliss, but I have some info on Harold Bennett that I thought you'd like to have."

"Excellent," said Windflower. "What's the news?"

"Well, I talked to Langmead this morning," said Quigley. "I called him because you were right. Commercial crime does want to talk to Bennett. Apparently the national drug people and the Canada Revenue Agency are in the lineup too."

"But they're proceeding on the human trafficking case first, right?"

"They are. It'll be a federal case with the Department of Justice taking the lead, and then we'll move on the murder of Marco Hoddinot. We haven't got as much on that one, but Bennett's going to get charged anyway."

"What about the kid?"

"I guess the old man tried to make a deal to cut the kid out, but the RNC said no. We don't need his testimony to make the case. Robbie Bennett is getting charged too."

"Good."

"I still don't know how they got away with this for so long and right under our noses."

"I know," said Windflower. "Too many people turned a blind eye to the horror show being played out in our community. It'll take a while to get over this."

"True enough," said Quigley. "'The evil that men do lives after them; the good is oft interred with their bones.'"

"Anyway, I have to go, my friend. A soon-to-be-famous figure skater is waiting for me. And before you say it, I know. 'I bear a charmed life.'"

"You do indeed, Sergeant," said Quigley.

After Windflower had hung up, he looked around him and all three of Sheila, Stella and Amelia Louise were dressed and heading out the back door. Stella even had her skates on.

"Hey, wait for me," said Windflower.

THE END

ABOUT THE AUTHOR

Mike Martin was born in St. John's, NL on the east coast of Canada and now lives and works in Ottawa, Ontario. He is a long-time freelance writer and his articles and essays have appeared in newspapers, magazines and online across Canada as well as in the United States and New Zealand.

He is the author of the award-winning Sgt. Windflower Mystery series set in beautiful Grand Bank. There are now 10 books in this light mystery series with the publication of *Safe Harbour*. *A Tangled Web* was shortlisted in 2017 for the best light mystery of the year, and *Darkest Before the Dawn* won the 2019 Bony Blithe Light Mystery Award. Mike has also published *Christmas in Newfoundland: Memories and Mysteries*, a Sgt. Windflower Book of Christmas past and present.

Mike is Past Chair of the Board of Crime Writers of Canada, a national organization promoting Canadian crime and mystery writers and a member of the Newfoundland Writing Guild and Ottawa Independent Writers.

You can follow the Sgt. Windflower Mysteries on Facebook: https://www.facebook.com/TheWalkerOnTheCapeReviewsAndMore/

Manufactured by Amazon.ca
Bolton, ON